"Damn you, Celeste!"

Ethan's mouth came down hard on hers, crushing its softness. His hands swept down to her waist, and he held her close to him. She shuddered against him, but suddenly he tore his mouth from hers and shoved her away from him.

"I swore I'd not let you get to me again." He gave an angry laugh. "All it takes is a few drinks and a moonlit night and a melting look from a pair of lying eyes."

"That's not fair!" Celeste protested, an icy shiver running down her spine at the contempt in his voice.

"Okay. Let's leave it. There's no point in going over old territory. Let's say we both got a bit carried away. Come on."

She looked at his face, and as he turned his tortured eyes on her, she felt all her anger and hurt dissolve in a tug of compassion.

"Don't be so hard on yourself, Ethan," she said softly.

Dear Reader,

Welcome to the Silhouette **Special Edition** experience! With your search for consistently satisfying reading in mind, every month the authors and editors of Silhouette **Special Edition** aim to offer you a stimulating blend of deep emotions and high romance.

The name Silhouette **Special Edition** and the distinctive arch on the cover represent a commitment—a commitment to bring you six sensitive, substantial novels each month. In the pages of a Silhouette **Special Edition**, compelling true-to-life characters face riveting emotional issues—and come out winners. Both celebrated authors and newcomers to the series strive for depth and dimension, vividness and warmth, in writing these stories of living and loving in today's world.

The result, we hope, is romance you can believe in. Deeply emotional, richly romantic, infinitely rewarding—that's the Silhouette **Special Edition** experience. Come share it with us—six times a month!

From all the authors and editors of Silhouette **Special Edition**,

Best wishes,

Leslie Kazanjian,
Senior Editor

LAUREY BRIGHT
A Guilty Passion

Silhouette Special Edition

Published by Silhouette Books New York

America's Publisher of Contemporary Romance

SILHOUETTE BOOKS
300 East 42nd St., New York, N.Y. 10017

ISBN: 0-373-09586-4

First Silhouette Books printing March 1990

Printed in the U.S.A.

LAUREY BRIGHT

has held a number of different jobs but has never wanted to be anything but a writer. She lives in New Zealand, where she creates the stories of contemporary people in love that have won her a following all over the world.

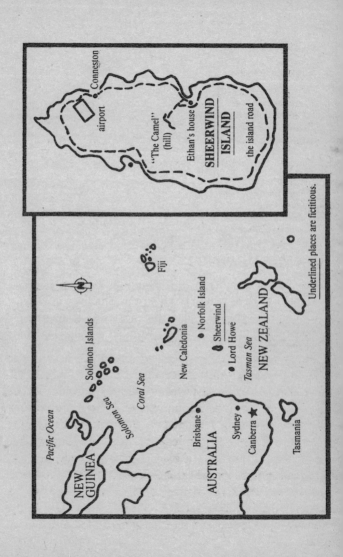

Connexion

airport

"The Camel" (hill)

Ethan's house

SHEERWIND ISLAND

the island road

Pacific Ocean

NEW GUINEA

Solomon Sea

Solomon Islands

Coral Sea

Fiji

New Caledonia

Norfolk Island

Sheerwind

Lord Howe

Tasman Sea

AUSTRALIA

Brisbane

Sydney

Canberra

Tasmania

NEW ZEALAND

Underlined places are fictitious.

Chapter One

Ethan Ryland was late for his stepbrother's funeral because he hadn't wanted to encounter the widow until the service was over. He would make some excuse later about the difficulty of transport to Sydney from the island.

He couldn't see Celeste at the front of the crowded church, but when the service was concluded and she followed the coffin out, his eyes unwillingly travelled beyond the polished casket and found the slight figure in black—slighter even than he remembered. But perhaps that was the effect of the dress; he had read that black was supposed to be slimming. She wore a black lace head covering, too, contrasting with the wheat-coloured hair that glimmered through it. The ends of the mantilla were draped at her throat, framing a face that shocked him by its pallor, by the hollows in the cheeks and the dull, sunken look of the green eyes.

He made an involuntary movement, and her gaze swivelled to his. She paused, and her pale mouth breathed his name. "Ethan!"

He had heard her say it in very much the same way in utterly different circumstances, and memory tightened his lips and brought a hardness to his almost navy blue eyes.

She said it again, murmuring a little louder, "Ethan." And she held out her hand to him. "You should be with me." He stood unmoving, and her face seemed to grow a shade paler. She whispered, "With him."

Behind her others were respectfully waiting, and as he remained where he was, a shadow crossed her features. Her outstretched hand, with its suggestion of pleading for comfort, wavered.

He stepped out of the pew and took her fingers in his, gripping them as he tucked her hand into the crook of his arm and led her from the church.

Outside it was incongruously sunny. Celeste had to introduce him to most of the people who paused at the church door to offer sympathy. But there were a few whom he recognised as colleagues of Alec's from earlier years, and there was, surprisingly, Aunt Ellie, who must have flown over from New Zealand. In his school days Aunt Ellie had always vaguely reminded him of a battleship. She presented her cheek to them both for a kiss, told him, "You were late," as though he might not know it, then subjected Celeste to a piercingly critical glance but said only, "It was a very suitable service."

Aunt Ellie was really Alec's aunt, not his. His mother had once said with a mixture of tolerance and exasperation that Ellie was "an impossible woman, but her heart's in the right place, I suppose." She was slightly deaf and given to making blunt comments in a penetrating contralto, and although Ethan couldn't have said that he knew her well, he had grown used to seeing her at every family occasion. The last time had been at Alec's wedding.

While he stood at Celeste's side accepting commiserations, and later sat with her and Aunt Ellie in the undertaker's limousine, he didn't need to look at her. After the interment, he stayed behind at the graveside for a while, and when he turned to follow the others, he found that she was waiting for him by the car.

Coming towards her, he studied her dispassionately. She was very composed. Her eyes were dry, and he doubted she had shed a tear since Alec had died. Apart from that, she was the picture of a grieving widow. Not even any makeup. She looked almost plain. Playing the part to the hilt.

"You should have gone on," he said, when he reached her.

"I wouldn't have left you," she replied as he opened the door for her. "Aunt Ellie went ahead with someone else," she told him after he had joined her. "The chancellor of the university has made a room available for the ... mourners. They've arranged some kind of refreshment, too. I'm afraid ... we'll be expected."

"Of course."

"They've been very kind," she said. "Taken over, really. The flat isn't big enough for so many people. And I don't think I could have catered. Alec had a lot of friends ... colleagues."

Ethan didn't answer, and she said, "I'm sorry I had to let you know so ... abruptly."

"It must have been a shock for you, too."

She said, after a moment's pause, "Yes, it was."

It might have been a shock, but a wholly unwelcome one? He reminded himself that this was no time to pick a fight. Oddly, he wanted to. More than anything he wanted to accuse her, yell at her, vent on her some of the accumulated rage that had been building inside him ever since she had telephoned him and said calmly, "Ethan, I have something to tell you. It's bad news. . . ."

She said now, "I asked the vicar to wait for you to arrive, but there was another service after . . . he couldn't . . ."

"It doesn't matter. My fault for being late."

"Where are you staying?"

"A hotel."

She turned to him. "Oh, but . . . you could come to the flat if you like."

She didn't sound particularly eager. Ethan was staring past the driver at the windscreen. "No, thanks. You said the flat was small."

"There is a spare bedroom."

He looked at her then. A thorough, deliberate stare. "I hadn't doubted it for a moment," he said.

She didn't even flinch. The apology that hovered on his tongue died an instant death. If she could take that with such composure, she didn't need any apologies.

"I suppose I'll have to move out," she said. "The flat goes with the fellowship, and now that Alec's . . . gone, I won't be entitled to . . ."

Her voice trailed off, and he said, "You have the house in Wellington. Alec said in one of his letters that you didn't want to leave it when he got the fellowship in Sydney."

"Did he?" she said with faint surprise. "Yes, I'm fond of it. But it was leased for the two years of the fellowship, and that's not up yet. And anyway, I'm not sure that I . . ."

"That you want to return to it without him?" Not seeming to notice the scepticism in his voice, she bowed her head briefly, and then turned to gaze out of the window.

When they arrived at the place he took her elbow and escorted her like a considerate brother-in-law, then stood by with a glass of whisky while she sipped sherry and fielded more condolences with languid grace. The room was large and tastefully decorated and impersonal, and he wondered if Celeste had purposely stationed herself in front of the wine-red velvet drapes that made her appear frail and fairer than ever in her narrow black dress. She had let the lace mantilla fall on her shoulders, and her hair, which he remembered as fine and soft like spun silk, was pulled back and pinned at her nape. Her profile, he thought angrily, was surely perfect. No lack of makeup could detract from that bone structure.

He turned away to find somewhere to deposit his empty glass, and was waylaid by Aunt Ellie, shaking her jowls at him and saying tartly, "Now don't you go drowning your sorrows, young Ethan. Your brother was too young to die, but he did a lot of things in his life, more than most people do in twice the time God gave him. Maybe it was enough."

Ethan smiled slightly. "Maybe. I'll try to remember that, Aunt Ellie. And I've no intention of drinking any more. I've just realised how little I've had to eat today."

Food had been the last thing on his mind, and he wasn't sure how long ago he had eaten a hasty and meagre breakfast, but come to think of it, he'd had no lunch, and it was now past three.

"Well, at least someone's given that girl a sandwich," Aunt Ellie said approvingly, nodding over his shoulder at Celeste. "And I hope she eats it. I've no patience with all this dieting that young women go in for. Told her last time I saw her, before they came over to Australia, eat up and get some meat on those bones of yours, girl. Picking here, picking there. Not enough to keep a bird alive. 'Celeste likes to be slim,' Alec said. 'She wouldn't look so good in her nice clothes if she was fat. Don't nag her, Aunt Ellie.' Well, I think it's unhealthy!"

A couple of people cast amused glances in their direction, and Ethan said, "I could use a sandwich myself. What about you?" Gently he steered her in the direction of the discreetly laid out buffet table.

As he handed Aunt Ellie a plate of asparagus rolls, he saw that Celeste was talking to a young man who leaned towards her with a protective air—almost an air of intimacy, Ethan thought, his eyes narrowing as he watched. The man had fair hair highlighting a golden tan, and a cleft chin. He put a hand on Celeste's arm, stroking it briefly. Celeste gave him a tiny smile and lifted the dainty sandwich she held, biting into it. The man's hand lifted to her shoulder and squeezed, his head bent toward her. Ethan's jaw clenched. Someone else came up to them, and the man kissed Celeste's cheek and moved away.

Ethan left as soon as he decently could, but was waylaid at the door by a rather good-looking man with well-combed brown hair greying at the temples. Ethan vaguely recalled being introduced to him.

"Grant Morrison," the man obligingly refreshed his memory. "I'm an old friend of your brother's, and I'm also his solicitor. I wonder if I might see you with Celeste later? I'm sorry, but I've got to fly back to Wellington early tomorrow. It's about the will."

"Where?" Ethan didn't care about the will, but he supposed it was one of the things that must be attended to. When, he wondered, would he get some quiet, alone time to grieve?

"I've suggested to Celeste that I come to the flat this evening, about seven. Is that okay with you?"

Ethan shrugged. "Okay."

"You know where it is?"

"I know the address. I'll get a taxi."

"Fine. What about now? Can I give you a lift?"

"Thanks, but I'd like to walk."

The solicitor nodded sympathetically. "He was a great man, your brother. One of the best in his field, I'm told. See you tonight, then."

Aunt Ellie opened the door to him that evening.

"Are you staying here?" he asked her, slightly surprised.

"No, with a friend I went to school with. Haven't seen her in years. Christmas and birthday cards. Pity it takes a funeral to bring us together."

"Yes," Ethan agreed as she led him into a small but elegantly furnished sitting room.

Celeste turned slowly from a corner table where she had been arranging several glasses and a decanter. She still wore the black dress but had taken off the mantilla. "Hello, Ethan," she said quietly.

He nodded, unsmiling. Her face, like her voice, was almost expressionless, and he couldn't help examining her curiously. When they had first met he had thought that he had never known anyone so alive, her every mood and emotion reflected in her face and especially in her clear green eyes. Alec, he remembered, had said, "She's like a butterfly, a gorgeous tropical butterfly, and I wanted to catch her and keep her for my own."

Celeste's eyes flickered away from his. "Please sit down. Would you like a drink?"

He fancied a strong whisky, but as he took a seat on the long couch, Aunt Ellie said, "It's a good dry sherry."

"Thank you," he said. At least it would give them something to do while they waited for the solicitor.

Celeste poured the amber liquid into three glasses, and he went over to take two of them. As she picked up the third he saw that her hand was not quite steady. He glanced at her sharply, but she turned away and went to sit in one of the armchairs facing the sofa, leaving him to pass Aunt Ellie her drink and reseat himself.

No one proposed any toast, and they sipped at their drinks in silence, until Aunt Ellie boomed, "You're looking peaky, girl! Have you eaten since this afternoon?"

Celeste said, "I had some coffee and leftovers. I'm not very hungry."

Aunt Ellie clicked her tongue. "Starving yourself won't do any good. You should have let me come back with you after the funeral."

"It was kind of you to offer, but...I wanted to be alone."

"Hmmph!" Aunt Ellie finished her sherry. "The thing is, are you fit to be alone? If you're not going to eat—"

The doorbell rang, and Celeste put down her glass with an air of suppressed relief. "I'll let Grant in."

She ushered the lawyer into the room, and he sat in the chair next to hers and declined the offer of sherry. He seemed to hesitate over the papers he slid from the pigskin briefcase he carried. Then he looked up at Ethan, glanced at Celeste and said, "Well, I suppose we should get on with it. Do you want me to read it aloud?"

Aunt Ellie said decisively, "Just tell us what it says, young man. No need for any legal palaver—we don't want a scene from an Agatha Christie novel. And speak up."

Grant Morrison gave a faintly embarrassed smile. "Well..." He paused and, looking down at the sheets of paper in his hands, said, "What it boils down to is, the house in Wellington was in joint ownership and it passes to Celeste, with its contents, except for Alec's research library and his original research notes. Those are to go to the university there. Some of the books, I understand, are quite rare. The bulk of his estate—investments, royalties from his books and so on—is bequeathed to Ethan Ryland, his stepbrother. Ethan is named trustee under the will, too."

"Can a trustee be a beneficiary?" Aunt Ellie asked.

"There's no legal bar against it," the lawyer said. "Of course, if a beneficiary is a minor an older trustee is usually appointed." He glanced again at the document. "Celeste is to have the interest from a couple of trust accounts, which is paid twice a year, these payments to cease when she, hmm, remarries. It's only a couple of thousand per annum," he added. "There is provision for any children, but . . . I guess that's theoretical."

Celeste sat with her hands loosely clasped in her lap, her head bowed. Ethan said, "May I see?" and held out his hand for the paper.

The lawyer handed it over. He cleared his throat and asked Celeste, "Do you have a solicitor of your own?"

She looked up rather blankly and shook her head. "Would you . . . Can't you act for me? If I need anyone . . ."

Ethan skimmed the document in front of him. It was dated about a year ago. Alec, he saw, had been surprisingly well-off, quite apart from his salary. All his books were concerned with his subject of Pacific archaeology, and several had become textbooks for universities. A series of television documentaries on his work had led to more popular books aimed at the interested layperson, and it appeared that he or his advisers had displayed a flair for investment.

Grant Morrison was saying to Celeste, "I'd be glad to act for you, if that's what you want."

Ethan looked up to see her turn on the lawyer what seemed to be a gaze of helpless appeal. "Please," she said.

Morrison's sympathetic answering look was laced with admiration. Ethan said, his voice overloud in the small room, "Could Celeste challenge this? Contest it?"

Celeste slowly shifted her gaze to him. "Contest?"

Morrison said cautiously, "Possibly."

Celeste said, "But if Alec—"

"As your legal adviser," Morrison interrupted her, "I think it would be best to say nothing at the moment." His eyes briefly met Ethan's, then moved back to her.

"But . . ." she started. Then obediently she lapsed into silence.

"Will you be returning to New Zealand?" Morrison asked her.

"I . . . I haven't thought about it. The house is leased, so I can't go back there. But I can't stay in this flat. The university will want the place."

"The lease—it's all paid up?"

"I believe so. I think it was paid six-monthly in advance. Alec handled all that sort of thing."

"So the money will be . . . ?"

"I suppose . . . in one of his investment accounts."

Morrison frowned. "Have you any money of your own?"

Celeste shook her head.

"You do have a joint account of some sort?" the lawyer asked.

"Just for day-to-day expenses. Alec put some money in it each month for me to draw on."

"What about insurance policies? Did he have any that I don't know about?"

"I don't think he believed in them."

"In other words," Aunt Ellie said loudly, "he's left you with no home and practically no income."

Morrison cleared his throat. "She does own the house. I persuaded him to put it in joint ownership at the time of purchase, when they were married. If we could prove where the lease money is . . ."

"You don't need proof," Ethan said flatly. "I'll make over the amount to Celeste straight away. There's no doubt she's entitled to that."

"It's not so simple," the lawyer objected. "Probate will take about three months and," he lowered his voice and said to Celeste, "if there's a question of the will being contested, the process could take longer."

"What's that?" Aunt Ellie demanded. She turned to Ethan. "What's he saying?"

"I should really discuss things with my client in private." Morrison was beginning to look flustered.

"I don't mind," Celeste said listlessly. "Ethan is involved, too, and Aunt Ellie is a relation...well, of Alec's." She turned her head away a little, almost as if removing herself from the conversation and leaving it for them to sort out.

Aunt Ellie said, "The girl's exhausted. She needs a good night's sleep. Why don't you come back tomorrow?"

"I have to go back to New Zealand," Morrison explained patiently. He glanced at Celeste's admittedly pale face and fished a card from his pocket. "Look, here is the address of our Sydney associates. When you feel up to it, contact them, and they can get hold of me then, okay?"

She took the card and said without reading it, "Thank you."

"And if you need money in the meantime, get in touch. We'll work something out." He glanced at Ethan, who looked back at him with a hint of grim amusement. He concluded that the lawyer thought Celeste had a case for argument over her share of what Alec had left, and that he didn't want her to accept money from Ethan in case it could be construed legally as some kind of settlement.

Morrison left the copy of the will and took his leave. Ethan followed suit, scribbling the address of his hotel on a piece of notepaper and leaving it on the table. Aunt Ellie declined the offer of a shared taxi, declaring her intention of making sure Celeste went to bed early with a hot drink and a decent supper inside her.

At his hotel Ethan headed for the bar, where he downed a much needed whisky and ordered another, which he sipped with deliberation. He both wanted to be alone and dreaded it. Sitting in the busy bar, he let the noise wash over him, and tried not to think. A woman came in and sat at a table not far from him, looking about her with a coolly speculative air. He felt her gaze light on him, assessing his crisp dark hair that he hadn't had cut in a while, the deep blue eyes under the stark line of his brows, the jut of a straight nose and stubborn chin. Her interested eyes slid over his broad shoulders and taut torso to the long legs stretched out before him, then returned to his face. She smiled.

It was an invitation, and for just a moment he was tempted. She was blonde, more than pretty, and made up discreetly rather than obviously. She looked as though she might have some intelligence, and the prospect of a pleasant hour or two of forgetfulness was definitely an attractive one.

She slipped off the jacket she wore, and shook back her hair, a dangling earring catching the light. It stirred a memory, and Ethan shut off his mind, placed his empty glass on the counter and got up, striding past her without a glance. He had been putting it off, keeping it at bay, for long enough, he told himself as he pressed the button for the elevator. Now was his time for grief.

Chapter Two

After a sleepless night, Ethan breakfasted early and went for a walk. Sometimes the noise and bustle of cities stimulated and even refreshed him, but today he found himself longing for the tranquility and slower pace of life on the island where he had made his home for several years. Even in the tourist season, when thousands of visitors spent their days lazing on palm-fringed beaches and their nights dancing to disco music or "authentic" island bands using electric guitars, Sheerwind, several hundred miles off the east coast of Australia, to the northwest of New Zealand, was still close to being a subtropical paradise. It had most of the amenities of civilized life, with few of the drawbacks. There was even a daily air service to Brisbane and Sydney.

Usually when he visited the mainland, he would nose around computer shops and software outlets to see what was new in the business, and take home magazines and books on the subject. But today he headed for the oasis of Hyde Park. Maybe later he would feel like picking up the threads.

Even as he walked under the green trees, with the rumble of traffic a little abated by distance, he knew that again he was putting off something that had to be done, and was annoyed with himself for his procrastination. It wasn't like him to dither around. He had always faced up to whatever life dealt him. Before he returned home he had to see Celeste again and find out just what had happened to his stepbrother. He owed Alec that much.

He decided against phoning first, although it might have been more considerate. He wasn't sure just how much consideration his brother's widow deserved. And he had a sneaking though admittedly unsubstantiated suspicion that she might make some excuse to avoid him. He didn't want to take that chance.

So he gave her until ten o'clock, then pressed the bell outside the flat.

It was several minutes before she came to the door, tying the belt of a white satin robe as she wordlessly let him in. She flung back a long hank of hair that hung across her shoulder. The gesture reminded him of the girl in the hotel bar, and he felt a renewed surge of the anger that he thought he had exorcised last night.

He said, "Did I get you out of bed?" He meant to sound merely polite, but was unable to keep an edge of sarcasm from intruding.

Her flush was noticeable because she still had that pale, washed-out look that had shocked him yesterday. She turned away from him. "Aunt Ellie insisted on giving me a sleeping pill. I'm sorry." Her voice sounded tired.

Stiffly, he said, "I should have phoned first."

"It's all right. If you'll excuse me, I'll have a shower and get dressed. Or... are you in a hurry?"

"No hurry." His voice was clipped. He went over to a window, saying distantly, "Take your time." He studied the view, because he didn't want to look at her. She unsettled him, with her narrow bare feet peeking from under the robe that was now belted tightly about an unbelievably slim waist. Her pale, unpainted face, her enormous green eyes and lank, sleep-tangled hair that had lost the silky sheen he remembered, gave her a deceptive air of vulnerability.

When she came back the hair had been combed back and bundled into a knot. Her feet were shod in plain flat-heeled black shoes, and her dress was a rather shapeless affair in a colour that was neither brown nor cream. He wondered briefly where she had found it. It wasn't the sort of thing he would have imagined she would give room to in her wardrobe.

"You take this widowhood business seriously, don't you?" he remarked, slightly appalled at himself but unable to resist a desire to needle her.

She blinked and said, "What?"

It was an effective tactic, he thought. Whatever Celeste was, she had never been stupid, but if she preferred to pretend she didn't understand him, he'd let it pass. This time. Because he needed to keep at least on civil terms in order to find out what he had to know.

"Don't you want to sit down?" she asked.

He didn't, particularly. He would rather have paced about the room, but it wasn't really big enough anyway. He said, "Aren't you hungry?"

She shook her head. "I'll have something later. Unless you...?" She had seated herself on the couch, but made to get up again.

"No," he said. "Don't bother."

She sank back, leaning into the corner of the couch as though she needed its support. He finally took the other end, half facing her, noting the faint flicker of apprehension in her eyes as he did so.

"I want to know what happened," he said.

She was staring down at her hands now. For a moment she neither moved nor spoke. Then her eyes reluctantly rose to his. "I told you—"

"The bare facts," he said harshly. "There's got to be more to it than that!"

Her head moved slowly in negation. "I'm sorry, Ethan. I told you all I know. I...don't understand it, either. But there isn't any more."

Ethan said, watching her with narrowed eyes, "Oh, there's more, all right!"

She stared at him, but he couldn't read the expression in her eyes. The pupils were enlarged, and she looked almost blind. "No," she murmured.

Ethan leaned towards her, stretching out a hand, and with the first clumsy movement he had ever seen her make, she got up and said, "I'm going to brew some coffee. Would you like some?"

She said it with her back to him, her head down, shoulders hunched. Ethan stood, too, swinging her to face him more roughly than he had intended, and holding both her arms.

She stood passively between his hands, her gaze on the buttons of his shirt. "I don't want coffee," he told her. "I want answers!"

Almost whispering, she said, "I don't have any answers for you. I don't have any for myself."

He said, his voice low and hard, "Look at me."

Her head came up slowly. Her eyes were dull, with a strange, unfocused blankness in them. She began to droop again, turning aside.

He said fiercely, "Look at me!" And he put a hand under her chin, his fingers and thumb biting into her skin.

It was a mistake. He knew it as he felt the texture of her skin, smooth and cool against his fingers. Her eyes widened, and there was a little kick of satisfaction in his stomach as he saw that for an instant he had her entire attention. He removed his hand from her face and stepped back, even as her lids drooped and he felt the sudden unexpected weight of her against the loosened grasp of his other hand before she slid from his hold and fell soundlessly at his feet.

He was down on one knee beside her in an instant. He had little doubt that it was a genuine faint, even before he gave her cheek a small, sharp slap and produced no reaction at all.

Picking her up, he realised how very light she was. He shouldered open a door that he guessed—rightly—must lead to a bedroom, and laid her down on the bed. She had taken the time to straighten it and pull up the quilted burgundy cover.

A bathroom opened off the bedroom. He found a facecloth, wrung it out in cold water and pressed it onto her forehead.

It seemed a long time before the closed eyelids flickered, and as she turned her head fretfully, he said quietly, "It's all right. You fainted. Just lie still."

He freshened the cloth, and after a while her cheeks were less than paper white. She looked at him and said, "Thank you."

He returned the cloth to the bathroom, came back and said, "I'll make you something to eat. I suggest you don't move until you've had it."

"It's all right," she said. "I can—"

"You can't," he argued. "Stay where you are."

He found the makings of an omelette in the kitchen, and some bread and butter.

"It's not much," he said, when he carried it into the bedroom. "But it's nourishment. Which appears to be what you need. How long is it since you had a decent meal?"

"You sound like Aunt Ellie," she said weakly, sitting up carefully. "It looks very nice."

He adjusted a couple of pillows behind her. "How long?" he repeated.

She shrugged. "I eat all right. Really. I just...haven't been very hungry."

"Get that down you, and I'll make the coffee."

When he brought it, she had finished the omelette but left the bread. He didn't comment on that, but gave her a mug of coffee. "Milk, no sugar, right?"

"Yes. Thank you."

He sat on the side of the bed, another mug held in his hands. "You're not pregnant, are you?" he asked. He supposed it was possible, even after eight childless years of marriage.

"No." She was looking down at her coffee. She didn't add anything to the bald denial, just lifted the mug and took a sip. "This is good. I'm...grateful."

"Maybe we should get a doctor."

"I'm sure there's no need. I told Aunt Ellie that last night."

"Had the same idea, did she?"

"You know Aunt Ellie."

"Yes, I do." He paused. "What's been going on, Celeste?"

She said, her voice very husky, "Nothing's been going on, except that Alec's dead, and...and..." Her hands began to shake, and she tried to clasp them about the cup, her head bent.

Ethan took the cup from her, placing it with his own on the bedside table.

She put her hands to her face and took a deep, shuddering breath. Ethan reached for her and made to pull her into his arms.

She stiffened and pushed him away. "No, don't!" she said. "Leave me alone. I'll be all right."

He stood, shoving his hands in his pockets. After a minute she passed a hand over her eyes and turned to face him, not quite meeting his hard, reluctantly compassionate gaze. "I'm sorry," she said. "You've been very kind, but would you mind going, now? I'd rather like to be alone."

"There are things we must discuss."

"Yes, I suppose so. But not now, please. When are you going back to the island?"

"I'll stay until after the inquest. I have business I can do while I'm here. They still think a couple of weeks?"

"Yes, but they said it's just a formality. Do you want to come here again tomorrow?"

"Any particular time?"

"In the morning, if you like. I won't take a sleeping pill."

He said, "Are you sure you're all right?"

"Perfectly, thank you." She sounded cool and distant now, as though he were a stranger who had done her a passing service.

He said, keeping his own voice polite and level, "Ten o'clock?"

She nodded. "That would be fine."

Aunt Ellie came to see him later that day, after phoning and declaring her intention. He met her in the lobby and took her up to his room. It was a long way down the corridor, and she stopped halfway and said, "Hold on there a minute, young Ethan. My legs aren't as long as yours."

Surprised and contrite, he said, "I'm sorry, Aunt Ellie." Preoccupied with his thoughts, he had been walking too fast for her.

She stood holding her hand to her heart, and he noticed she was panting. "Are you all right?" he asked, taking her arm. Cursing his own thoughtlessness, he said again, "I'm sorry, I didn't realise..."

She wheezed, grimacing. "Damned doctor was right, I suppose. I ought to slow down at my age."

When she had recovered and he had walked her much more slowly the rest of the way, he put her into a chair in his room and said, "Can I get you anything?"

"Glass of water."

When he brought it, she had a small white pill in her hand.

"Your heart?" he asked quietly, taking the glass from her to place it on the table.

"Among other things. Don't worry, I'll be all right when I've rested a bit. Now, about Celeste..."

Ethan said, "I'm more concerned about you."

"I have a very good doctor," she said. "My health is his job, nothing to do with you." She glared at him, and he gave in to her obvious wish to keep her problems to herself.

"All right," he said. "But please promise me that you'll go to see him the minute you get back to New Zealand."

"Oh, I promise," she conceded grumpily. "Now, will you listen to me about Celeste?"

He shoved his hands into his pockets and stood near the window, half turned from her. "What about Celeste?" he said stiffly.

"That extraordinary will," she said, "for a start. What was Alec thinking of?"

He contemplated telling her as gently as possible to mind her own business, but was well aware that he might as well tell a steamroller to be careful of the roadside flowers. "What's your guess?" he asked her.

"He didn't trust her with his money," Aunt Ellie said bluntly.

Ethan said nothing, and she sighed gustily. "Alec was very clever in some things, but as far as women were concerned, he was a fool!"

Alec, Ethan thought, had come to the same conclusion, too late for the insight to be of any use.

Aunt Ellie said, "What will you do if Celeste contests the will?"

Ethan turned. "Fight it."

She was mildly surprised. But all she said was, "Hmmph. Of course, she has nothing now. He's left her a pittance, and the first payment won't be for months."

"I know."

She peered at him, but against the light from the window she couldn't see his expression. "It looks...odd, you know. Leaving her virtually nothing. He would have expected you to take his place, I suppose. Financially, I mean. Thought you'd manage the money better. All I can say is—"

He interrupted quite gently. "Aunt Ellie, leave it."

"Well," she said, "I suppose it's none of my business." Disappointed that he didn't contradict her, she went on. "She said something about getting a job."

Ethan gave a disbelieving little laugh. At Aunt Ellie's questioning glare, he said, "Celeste has never had a job in her life. She didn't even finish her degree."

"Yes, well, your brother was responsible for that!"

"I don't think Celeste was that keen to complete it," he said cynically.

"Certainly not once she'd met Alec," Aunt Ellie agreed.

No, his brother had been a much better meal ticket than any degree, Ethan thought. And at that particular period of his life, Alec had been easy game for a pert beauty with an eye on the main chance.

Aunt Ellie said, "I don't think she's fit to work at the moment. I offered to take her home with me, but she said no. I have to go back, the neighbours can't feed the cats forever, only I don't like leaving Celeste."

Ethan said, "She'll survive."

"In her state?" Aunt Ellie said sceptically.

"What state?"

"The girl's almost catatonic. You must have noticed!" As he just stared back at her, frowning, she said in exasperation, "No, you men never notice what's under your noses."

Ethan said, "She's not the only one who's depressed! There'd be cause for surprise if she wasn't, wouldn't there?"

"I'm not talking about the sadness and grief of bereavement. I've seen grief before. This is different. Reminds me of a niece who spent some time in psychiatric care."

"Whatever else she is, I don't think Celeste is crazy!"

Aunt Ellie said tartly, "You're an intelligent man, Ethan. You know very well there are degrees of mental illness. And no one is immune."

Of course he did. He bowed his head in acknowledgement of the reproof.

"I think Celeste should see a doctor," Aunt Ellie said.

"I did offer to get her a doctor yesterday," he said.

"Why?"

"She fainted," he told her reluctantly.

Aunt Ellie clicked her tongue. "Someone ought to look after her. She's got no family left. And she won't let me...."

Ethan said, "I'll make sure she sees a doctor. I'm meeting her tomorrow, anyway." He still had doubts about her condition, but a medical opinion might clear them from his mind.

Evidently, that was what Aunt Ellie had come for. Refusing a cup of tea or coffee and a snack, she took her leave, apparently relieved that the responsibility had been lifted from her shoulders.

When Celeste opened the door to him the following day, he inspected her closely. She had dressed in a pair of dark trousers and a white shirt, with the same flat shoes as yesterday. Her hair was pulled back again, and she still wore no makeup. Was it possible that her pallor was natural and her dejected manner assumed? Uneasily, he thought not.

She let him in and asked him to sit down, offering a drink, which he refused. Sinking into a chair opposite, she looked down at her clasped hands. Then apparently fixing her eyes on the right shoulder of his jacket, she said, "What did you want to talk about?"

"Never mind that now," he said. "Aunt Ellie thinks you should see a doctor."

"Aunt Ellie is a dear, but she fusses."

"I think you should, too," he told her.

Her eyes met his in slight surprise, then slid away. "I'm all right," she muttered.

"Are you?" He stood up. "You weren't yesterday."

"Reaction. Lack of food. Don't worry about me, Ethan."

"Why do you think Alec didn't leave you his money?" he shot at her.

He saw the way her hands suddenly tightened on each other. "I...imagine because he wanted you to have it," she said, almost inaudibly.

"He knew I'd always had enough of my own. My work brings me more than I need." Creating custom-designed computer software programmes paid very well indeed.

"Then perhaps," she said, without any particular inflection, "he just didn't want me to have it."

Ethan said, "He wasn't that vindictive."

She flashed him a glance then, and he saw briefly a bitterness that seared him, before the shutters came down and her face resumed its cold indifference.

"Has it occurred to you," he asked, "that it was because he expected me to look after you?"

"No," she said baldly.

"That's what Aunt Ellie thinks."

She cast him another glance, and he waited for her to ask if it was what he thought, but she said instead, looking down at her hands again, "You don't have to provide for me. I'll manage."

"I'm sure you would. It shouldn't take too long to find another husband who can keep you in the style Alec accustomed you to."

For an incredulous moment or two he thought she wasn't going to react. Then she lifted her eyes and with the puzzled expression of a hurt child said, "Why don't you like me anymore, Ethan?"

"Because," he said deliberately, refusing to remove his gaze from those amazingly innocent eyes, "I know all about you, Celeste."

He watched the slow, delicate colour reach her cheeks. Consummate actress that she was, she couldn't control that betraying blush, and his eyes hardened as they watched until the colour receded, leaving her deathly pale. He was afraid she was going to faint again, and a niggling suspicion entered his mind. He had heard of people who could faint at will, just as some women could turn on tears whenever they wanted.

He said, harshly, "Don't pass out on me again!"

"No. No. I w-won't!" Her breasts rose and fell quickly beneath the white shirt, and she closed her eyes, drawing in another breath, her hands still tightly clasped.

"Stop it!" Ethan said. He leaned over her and gripped her shoulders, giving her a little shake. "Stop it, Celeste!"

She said, "I'm...s-sorry." She was gasping, her eyes now wide and frightened. "I feel very...strange."

He hauled her to her feet and pushed her down on the couch. She was taking deep, shuddering breaths.

"Better?" he asked curtly.

She made a small, moaning sound. "It's like...high tension wires right through my body, my arms, legs...tingling." She put a shaking hand to her forehead, then lifted both hands in front of her, saying, "I can't move my fingers."

The fingers were rigid, he could see.

Ethan said, "I'll get a doctor."

She didn't argue, telling him where to find the number. Following the doctor's instructions he found a paper bag in the kitchen and told her to breathe into it. She obeyed without question.

As the attack subsided, he removed the bag and told her, "The doctor said it sounded like hyperventilation. He'll drop in later to see you."

"Thank you," she whispered. Her eyelids drooped, and he said, "Go to sleep if you want." He fetched a blanket from the bedroom, tucked it about her and waited for the doctor.

"What she probably needs is a good long holiday," the man said later, as Ethan ushered him out. "There's no physical ailment. She's underweight and in a state of nervous depression. I could prescribe antidepressants, but if she's able to relax properly for a while, she'll most likely recover perfectly well without any medication. Of course, losing her husband...but it's usually better to let grief take its course, rather than mask it artificially. Some things pills can't cure."

Ethan thanked him and closed the door, then went to the bedroom where Celeste was lying on top of the burgundy cover.

"You're looking better," he said, studying the faint colour in her cheeks.

"I feel a fool. I thought...for a few minutes...that I had some kind of paralysis. It was horrible."

"I could see you were scared." And it had, he realised bleakly, brought him no satisfaction.

"You've been very kind," she said. "Although as it turns out, calling the doctor was quite unnecessary."

"Not quite." He came over to the bed and stood gazing down at her. "He said you need a holiday. I'm taking you back to Sheerwind with me."

She stared up at him, then said, "No. I can't."

"You can't stay here," he said. "You told me so. And you won't go with Aunt Ellie back to New Zealand. Anyway, she couldn't look after you."

"I don't need looking after."

"You do. At least for a while. And I'm the only one there is to do it."

"No, Ethan. I—" She started up, and he pressed her back on the bed.

"Rest," he said. "Doctor's orders. What would you like for lunch?"

"I can fix it." She made a feeble movement, then gave up at the firm persuasion of his hand on her shoulder. "I don't know," she said tiredly. "I don't care."

He fetched her sandwiches, made with tinned salmon he had found, and ate some himself in the kitchen. She brought her plate in, and when he frowned at her she said, "I wasn't told to stay in bed all day. He just said to take things easy."

"How do you feel?"

"Fine. Really."

"Good. We could leave for Sheerwind straight after the inquest."

"Ethan, I told you—"

"You'll need clothes for at least a month. Might as well bring the lot. I'll help you pack the rest of the stuff into boxes and we'll have it stored. Is any of the furniture yours?"

"No, the place was furnished, but—"

"That makes it simpler. I'll notify the university for you. Leave the arrangements to me."

In the end she gave up arguing, and just sat on the couch and bowed her head as though the effort was too much. Ethan thought he should feel some kind of triumph in the small victory. Instead he was vaguely ashamed of himself, and because he felt that was unfair, the shame turned to anger with her. When he said he was leaving she stirred herself and listlessly accompanied him to the door. He said, "I'll see you tomorrow."

One shoulder lifted in a tiny shrug. "All right." She had that unseeing look again, and for a second he had a crazy desire to shake her into awareness, or— His mind clamped down on the thought that followed as his eyes involuntarily traced the shape of her pale mouth.

No, he told himself firmly. That was a sure way to disaster.

Chapter Three

On the day of the inquest, Celeste was conscious of a faint gratitude for the fog of indifference that seemed to have surrounded her since her husband's death. Ethan picked her up from the flat and ushered her into a hired car with the impersonal consideration that had become the hallmark of his behaviour towards her. He had been as good as his word, organizing everything with calm efficiency, leaving her nothing to do except make an occasional decision, such as to give away Alec's clothes to the Salvation Army. When she tried to thank him he said, "Aunt Ellie wouldn't have gone home unless she knew someone was taking care of you." Which was probably true, but it chilled her a little. In spite of his determined courtesy and apparent concern for her, even through the lethargy and indifference that affected her she sensed something in him that gave her a feeling of unease. Something hidden and dangerous.

Which must be nonsense, she told herself, as he seated her in the courtroom and took his place beside her. Ethan had never done anything to make her afraid of him. In spite of his size and his strong build, he was one of the least violent men of her acquaintance.

She scarcely heard the official evidence, the police and the doctor giving their dry, unemotional accounts. Then it was her turn, and she left Ethan's side and was given a Bible. When she had repeated the words she was asked to say, she was allowed to sit down, and the coroner expressed his regret at her loss before she was questioned. Everyone was really very kind, she thought distantly, as she tried to concentrate on the questions, answering mechanically.

"Was there anything unusual in his behaviour that evening?"

"No. He seemed tired."

"Only tired?"

She said, "A bit tense. That wasn't unusual. He worked in his study for about an hour, before he went out. I suppose to unwind."

"And was that usual?"

"He did sometimes go driving at night, alone," she said. No, it wasn't a regular occurrence, but an occasional one. He might be gone for a couple of hours or more. No, she didn't know where he went, he had never told her. She thought he just drove around. No, he had not mentioned where he intended to go the night that he died. She was in bed, reading, and had heard him leave.

"And he left no message for you, no note?"

"There was no note." The police had asked her that at the time.

"You know the place?" she was asked. "The place he went to?"

"Yes. I know it. We had been there together when we first came to Sydney. Someone told us about the view."

"The view of the sea, from the top of the cliff?"

"Yes." She swallowed, her hands tensing in her lap. It had been a perfect day, the sea glittering in sunshine, and Alec had seemed relaxed and affectionate and looking forward to his work at the university. She had been hoping that in a fresh environment, and with the stimulation of the fellowship and the obvious esteem in which he was held by his colleagues, Alec would be happier and their marriage might have a chance for a new beginning. They had left the car and peered over the safety rail at the rocks below with the water roaring over them. When she shivered Alec had put an arm about her waist and said, "You wouldn't have a chance if you went over, here. It would be instant death."

"Did your husband mention suicide, Mrs. Ryland?"

She hesitated. "No. Not really."

"Not really?"

She became aware of Ethan's eyes fixed on her with sharp intensity, and for a moment the blessed fog wavered and lifted. "I mean, not specifically." She wrenched her eyes away from Ethan. "He...talked about it sometimes in general terms. When there was something in the paper or on television about...about people who had killed themselves."

"And you had not had any argument the night that Mr. Ryland died?"

"We never argued," she said simply, and her gaze returned to Ethan, a shiver running down her spine as she met his eyes. He didn't believe her.

After she resumed her seat, Alec's doctor gave evidence that Alec had been in good heath, except for some mild discomfort from old injuries, for which he had adequate medication. That would account for the traces of painkiller found at the autopsy. The packet it came in carried a warning about not driving after taking the drug, but he would not have expected any serious impairment of function unless other factors were present—alcohol or, yes, possibly fatigue.

The head of the Department of Pacific Studies at the university said Professor Ryland had been progressing well with the study he had commenced under the terms of the fellowship. He had expressed appreciation of the calibre of the assistance he had received from the university, and certainly had no reason to be depressed about his work. The day of his death had been a particularly busy one, with a graduate class in the morning and a field trip in the afternoon with first-year anthropological students. Only the previous day he had completed a week-long trip to an ancient aboriginal site with a group of students and lecturers. The fellowship did not oblige him to take part in these activities, but Professor Ryland had always been extremely generous with his time and expertise. He had seemed rather tired on his return.

The coroner nodded. There was no reason, he said when all the evidence had been given, to suppose that Professor Ryland's death had been anything but a tragic accident. After a strenuous week or so, and being on medication that might have the effect of making the patient drowsy, he should not have undertaken a lengthy drive at that hour of the night. He had probably fallen asleep at the wheel or, in the dark and in his weary state, simply misjudged the distance to the edge of the cliff. There was indeed no sign that he had braked before the car hit the safety rail and smashed right through it. The authorities should perhaps consider improving the standard of the railing, but on the other hand, such structures could hardly be expected to withstand the impact of a vehicle driven at speed.

Outside the courtroom, someone stepped toward Celeste, saying her name, but Ethan's hand was on her arm, and he brushed the man aside and hurried her to the car, gunning away from the curb with a forbidding frown on his face.

"Who was that?" she asked, wondering if she should have been polite and stayed to accept more condolences.

"A reporter," he said shortly.

There had been some mild interest from the press. Alec was a minor celebrity, and the nature of his death had of course engendered curiosity.

"Well, I hope they're satisfied now," she murmured.

"Satisfied?"

"That it was an accident. A ghastly accident."

He glanced at her and said, "*Was* there a note?"

She turned to stare at him. "You heard me tell the coroner—"

"I know what I heard," he said harshly. "Now *I'm* asking. Was there a note?"

"No! Why should I lie?"

He shrugged. "To avoid fuss and publicity. Or for more personal reasons."

She shook her head. "I don't understand you. There was no note," she added flatly.

She made coffee for them both on their return, and Ethan was standing by the window of the sitting room while he drank his, when the doorbell rang.

She brought the visitor into the room and introduced him. "This is Steven Craig. He's a postgraduate student who was assisting Alec in his work. Steven, this is Alec's brother, Ethan Ryland."

Ethan recognised the fair young man who had been standing with Celeste after the funeral, while he and Aunt Ellie were at the buffet. The one who could hardly wait un-

til her husband was cold in his grave before he started paw-
ing the widow, he thought, and gave the man a nod, not
offering to shake his hand.

Steven Craig was a little older than he had first appeared, probably in his mid-twenties. The blond hair and
boyish good looks were deceptive.

Celeste said, "Please sit down, Steven. Will you have a
cup of coffee? It's made."

While she fetched it, he sat in one of the armchairs, and
looked up at Ethan, still standing by the window. "I'm sorry
about your brother," he said. "It's a great loss to us all."

Ethan nodded again.

"I counted it a privilege to be working with him," Steven added.

Ethan said politely, "I'm sure."

"He was one of the most respected men in the field. In his
time, of course, he'd been quite a pioneer. I mean, those
studies he did in the New Guinea highlands on one of the
last of a truly Stoneage people. And the work he carried out
there, before his accident . . ."

Celeste came back into the room with a steaming cup,
which she handed to Steven. Ethan noted that she hadn't
asked how he liked his coffee.

She sat opposite Steven, and he said, "I'm sorry to barge
in like this just after the inquest, but someone said you're
going away."

"She'll be staying with me," Ethan said.

Steven shot him a look, then nodded. "I see." To Celeste, he said, "I guess you'll be relieved that it—the inquest—is over."

"Yes," she said. "Were you there?"

"At the back," he answered. "You left too fast for me to
speak to you."

"There was a reporter," she explained.

"Oh. Well, the verdict should put paid to any gossip. I mean..." He paused, embarrassed.

"It's all right. I know there was some...speculation that Alec might have committed suicide."

Steven looked down at his coffee, frowning. "You never had reason to think so, did you?"

Ethan's glance sharpened, flicking from the young man to Celeste as Steven raised his head and looked full at her.

"No," she said. "Of course not."

Steven nodded, and Ethan said, "What are you getting at, exactly?"

Steven turned to him. "Nothing," he said—a shade too quickly, Ethan thought. "There've been rumours, and it must be a relief to Celeste to have them laid to rest. I'd have said Alec would be the last person..." He paused. "Anyway, I'm sure you both would rather drop the subject. I just wanted to say that I'm glad about the coroner's decision. I know it must have been an ordeal for Celeste."

He sipped his coffee, and Ethan banged his empty cup into a saucer and said, "Was there anything else?"

"Well, yes, as a matter of fact." He spoke to Celeste. "I'm sorry to bring this up now, but I wondered if you'd found some of Alec's notes about the project we were working on. And...I wanted to ask you if you'd mind if I finished it on my own. It would be a sort of memorial to him, and...well, frankly, I've put so much work into it myself that I'd hate to see it all wasted."

"You're welcome to anything you can use," she said immediately. "I'm afraid I don't recall...Ethan?"

He had helped her clear the small study; in fact he'd done most of the packing of Alec's books and papers. "I figured it was probably all at the university," he said.

Steven said disappointedly, "There's very little there. He used to bring a lot of work home. I thought..."

"Sorry," Ethan said curtly.

"It could be on computer disks, not paper. He had a computer here. It's still in his study?" he asked Celeste.

"Yes," Celeste said. "It was on loan from the university. There was a box of disks, wasn't there, Ethan?"

"Blank," Ethan said.

"Blank?" Steven was dismayed.

"Unused," Ethan told him. "I checked them all."

"Are you sure? I mean, if you're not accustomed—"

"I do know about computers. I design software for a living," Ethan told him. "There was nothing on any of the data disks."

"Sorry. It's just that I don't understand. He must have left some notes somewhere!"

"The car," Celeste said.

Both men looked at her, and she said, "The police found...there were some disks among the things in the car. I'd forgotten. The police still have them, I think."

Steven groaned. "Immersed in sea water. They'll be ruined, won't they?"

"Very likely," Ethan said unemotionally. After a moment, he added, "I could try to recover the data from them."

"I'd be awfully grateful!" Steven said, his face lighting up.

"For my brother's sake," Ethan said crushingly. "It would be a pity to see the last year of his life go for nothing."

Steven flushed. "Yes, of course. We'd all like to see his study published."

"And yours," Ethan said dryly.

"Look," Steven said. "I did do a lot of work on it. It's important to me. I'm sorry if I seem selfish—"

"I understand," Ethan said. "Leave it with me. I'll get in touch. Through the university?"

"Yes, or at home. Celeste knows the number, don't you?"

"I have it," she said as he turned to her.

"Right," Ethan said crisply. "If that's all . . . ?"

Steven put down his half-finished coffee and said, "Will you give me an address? I may need to contact you, if anything turns up at the university after all, for instance."

"'Ethan Ryland, Sheerwind' will find me. The post office at Conneston, which is the only real town on the island, keeps my mail for me to pick up. There is a phone, too." He gave Steven a card.

When Steven had gone, Celeste said, "You didn't need to hurry him off like that."

"Did you want him to stay? Hold your hand, perhaps, like he did at the funeral?"

She stared at him, and then said quietly, "That's offensive, Ethan. He did nothing of the kind."

"I apologise. Although I take issue with your definition of 'nothing of the kind.'"

A faint frown appeared between her perfect brows. "Perhaps you could explain that."

"Stroking your arm, kissing you . . ."

She blinked. "It didn't mean anything." With a slight flaring of anger, she said, "Lots of people kissed me at the funeral. Some of them I barely knew."

"How well do you know Steven Craig?" he rapped out.

She opened her mouth, then closed it again, swallowing. "I refuse to answer that," she said, her voice unsteady. "I can only guess that grief is affecting your judgement—and your manners. Perhaps you'd like to go now."

"If that's what you want."

"I think it is. And I'm not sure that going to Sheerwind with you is such a good idea after all."

"Don't be stupid. The tickets are bought. You've got to be out of this flat by tomorrow anyway. Where else could you go?"

"A hotel, until—"

"Until what? Don't cut off your nose to spite your face because of a moment's anger with me, Celeste. I'll see you tomorrow."

He should have been more careful, he told himself as he reached the street outside. Antagonising her at this stage would do him no good. He didn't want her backing out of the arrangement before they got to the island. He had been reluctant at first to suggest she should stay with him, but on second thought the idea had several very cogent merits. He wanted her where he could watch her and analyse her reactions, and eventually, he hoped, remove the huge question in his mind over his stepbrother's death.

Ethan had booked them on the evening flight. When he arrived at her flat in plenty of time to pick her up, Celeste looked at him warily and made a halfhearted attempt to cry off the idea of going with him.

He ignored her muted demur and simply marched into her bedroom, closing the last of her cases himself. And almost before she knew it she was whisked off to the airport. There, too, Ethan took charge. Celeste couldn't help feeling numbly grateful for that. Her pitiful attempt to assert herself having failed, she was dimly thankful that she didn't have to be responsible for presenting tickets and checking baggage and finding the correct departure gate and searching for seat numbers.

She spent most of the flight gazing unseeingly out of the window while the water below them turned from green to blue to inky, reminding her of Ethan's eyes, dark and fathomless. And cold. When he touched her arm, she shivered, and he said, "Do you want a blanket?"

He was handing her a glass, and she took it from his hand and said, "No, I'm fine."

"Drink up," he said. "It'll do you good."

"Alcohol?"

"Drink it."

Once she would have challenged an order as peremptory as that. She tried to muster a spark of annoyance, but it was too much trouble to argue. Instead, she simply obeyed, and when a warm, fuzzy sensation spread through her, she handed the glass back and closed her eyes with a sigh.

Minutes later, it seemed, he was urging her to eat the light meal provided by the airline, and then coffee with a sweet biscuit. He was, she told herself, being nothing but kind and thoughtful, and the flutter of panic she felt as they circled the island, lying like a tear-shaped emerald in a darkening sea, was nothing to do with the fact that she was probably going to be virtually alone with him for an indefinite length of time.

With a feeling of unreality, she sat beside him in the car he had collected at the airport. They passed through Conneston, a pretty town with unpretentious buildings softened by palms and rubber trees and hibiscus. Then the lights that were beginning to wink on were left behind and the car took a narrow road uphill, later descending to skim by the sea, before climbing again.

"How far is it?" Celeste asked when Ethan had been driving for twenty minutes.

"Nearly there," he replied. A few minutes later he turned into a steep driveway winding downhill among the trees, to draw up before a house that seemed built into the hillside.

"I'll let you in, and then fetch the bags," Ethan said.

He opened the door with a key, fumbling inside for the light switch. She blinked as the light met her eyes, and he said, "Go straight ahead, there's another switch on your left inside the room at the end of the passage."

She went down the passageway and stopped in the doorway. Facing her was a wall of glass, giving a breathtaking view of a starry sky and moonlit ocean. She turned on the light and walked across the room on thick natural wool rugs to the spectacular windows, gazing out. She saw Ethan's reflection as he paused in the doorway behind her.

"It's beautiful," she said, turning to face him.

"Great in daylight, too," he said. "Follow me and I'll show you your room."

The main room occupied the whole side of the house facing the sea. At one end was a staircase of natural timber, and he led her up it, turning at the top to shoulder open the door to a bedroom that, like the big room downstairs, looked out on the sea. There was a double bed covered with an apricot-coloured spread, matched by the cushion on a peacock chair standing in one corner. The rest of the furniture and a pair of louvred wardrobe doors were painted white. On the polished wood floor lay an Indian rug, and the whole effect was one of lightness, coolness and comfort.

"I'm next door." Ethan deposited her bags on the floor. "And the bathroom is just across the way. Do you want one of these cases lifted onto the bed?"

Celeste shook her head. "No, thank you. It's very nice. Do you . . . live alone?"

He looked at her with a faint quirk of his lips. "Is that a problem?"

"I just wondered if there was a housekeeper or . . ."

"Or a live-in lover?" he queried. "No, to both. There is a lady who comes twice a week to clean the house and do the laundry and ironing. She lives not far from here, and the arrangement suits us both. I can cook—and do the rest, for that matter, but I prefer to pay someone else to do the boring bits." He paused. "Are you concerned about the proprieties? I can assure you no one on the island will be bothered."

She said, "Neither am I. It isn't important."

"But then you're not bothered by much these days, are you?" he said. "I wonder what it would take to get a real reaction from you."

She blinked. A flicker of apprehension shadowed her eyes. "I'm not sure I know what you mean."

"Never mind," he said abruptly. "The bed will be made up. I phoned and asked Mrs. Jackson to prepare the room. And you'll no doubt find she's put clean towels in the bathroom for you. She'll have left milk for us, too. Would you like a drink of something?"

"I know it's early, but I'd rather like to have a bath and go to bed," Celeste said. "If that's all right." The bed looked very comfortable and inviting, and it held no bitter memories.

"Fine." Ethan shrugged. "If you need anything, just yell down the stairs."

"Thank you. You're very kind, Ethan."

He turned on his way out, his eyes slightly narrowed. "Don't count on it," he said briefly.

She refused to examine the implications of that, as she unpacked a nightdress and light cotton wrap. In the bathroom, attractive and functional in pale green and apricot, she found fluffy apricot-pink towels folded over a rail with a discreet bronze plaque above it inscribed, "Guests." The green ones on another rail were for Ethan, she supposed.

A small basket on the counter held sachets of shampoo and conditioner, some bath salts and a shower cap. It seemed that Ethan was prepared for female guests. She wondered how often he entertained a woman, and quelled the thought as she ran hot water into the pale green bath.

After a luxurious soak in the tub, she returned to the other room feeling pleasantly relaxed. The bed was as comfortable as she had expected, and it faced the windows. Outside the room a wide balcony ran the length of the house. She had left the curtains undrawn, so that the last thing she saw before she closed her eyes was the starry sky outside. The sound of the waves washing an unseen beach lulled her to sleep.

When she woke the sun was streaming in on the bed. Except for the night that Aunt Ellie had pressed a sleeping pill on her, she hadn't slept so well for ages.

She lay for a few minutes just watching the restless blue water outside and the tips of the trees that she could see. Then she threw aside the covers and went barefoot to push open the sliding glass door and step out onto the balcony.

The house was about halfway up a steep slope that was covered in a thick press of green trees and bushes broken by splashes of colour—purple bougainvillea, scarlet hibiscus, and yellow ginger plants with red stamens and large, floppy green leaves. There was oleander and sweet-scented frangipani, too. Leaning over the railing, she could see that outside the living area was a large terrace, on which stood a wrought iron table and chairs and a sun lounger. Steps led from the terrace to a path that disappeared into the trees. The beach was not visible from here, but no doubt the path would end there. There must be a beach. She could hear the murmur and swish of water, but the waves didn't thunder as they had at the spot where Alec...

Shutting out the thought, she stepped back into the bedroom. There was no sign of Ethan as she used the bathroom, although the door of the room next to hers was ajar.

At the end of a short passageway, another door was firmly closed. Perhaps he was working. A glance at her watch had showed her that it was near ten o'clock.

She dressed in a white shirt, blue denim skirt and sandals, and tied back her hair with an elastic band. The air was warm and very pleasant. She went down the stairs and found a covered tray and a note placed in a prominent position on the long, low table in the living room.

Help yourself, said the note. *And make yourself at home. Coffee in the kitchen. I've gone to get supplies and collect mail. Back before twelve.*

Under the cover was a glass of fresh orange juice, a bowl of wheat flake cereal, with a small jug of milk, some sugar in a matching bowl, and a dish on which reposed a fresh yellow papaya and a lemon.

She took the tray outside to the little table, and sliced open the papaya, eating it sprinkled with lemon juice. She made a halfhearted effort at the cereal, but in the end most of it went into a garbage pail she found in the kitchen that opened off the main room, toward the back of the house. After washing up her dishes, she strolled outside again. When Ethan returned she was sitting on the lounger, her legs stretched out, eyes closed, her hair loose because when she leaned back it had been uncomfortable, so she had pulled off the elastic and pushed it into her pocket.

She heard him say, "Hello," and she opened her eyes and made to get up.

"Stay there," he ordered. "I see you found your breakfast."

"Yes, thank you. It was very thoughtful of you."

"No problem." He shrugged. "Sleep okay?"

"Fine, thank you."

He had a bundle of letters in his hand, confined by a rubber band. "Mind if I open my mail?"

"Of course not. Please go ahead."

He slipped off the rubber band and began riffling through the envelopes. When he stopped with a smothered exclamation, Celeste said, "Something wrong?"

He looked at her strangely, as though he could see right through her, and drew one envelope out of the stack, tossing the rest onto the nearby table. "It's from Alec," he said tightly. "Postmarked the day after he died."

Celeste gasped. "That's impossible!"

"Not impossible," Ethan answered curtly. "He must have posted it just before . . ."

"Oh. Yes, of course." She swallowed. She had phoned Ethan almost as soon as she herself had been told of Alec's death. The letter might have been posted that night, before he drove the car off the cliff. It would have taken a couple of days to arrive at the island, and Ethan had probably left for the funeral without picking up his mail. She felt sick, her temples cold.

Ethan turned away from her and paced to the edge of the terrace. He stood there with his back to her for several seconds, before bending his head and ripping open the envelope. She watched him put it into his pocket before unfolding the sheets of paper he had taken from it. Celeste closed her eyes.

A few minutes later she opened them again as Ethan bent over the chair, his hands on the armrests.

He said roughly, "Are you all right?"

"Yes," she murmured, her cheeks warming as she saw the hard, glittery look in the eyes that suddenly swept over her.

Her own eyes widened, and her heart pounded uncomfortably. "What is it?" she asked. "Ethan, what are you doing?"

"Doing?" he repeated, holding her eyes with an implacable gaze. "Just looking, Celeste, taking a long, hard look at the woman who caused my brother to commit suicide."

Chapter Four

"Suicide?" Celeste whispered. Her gaze locked with his. "It was an accident! The coroner said—"

"The coroner was willing to give it the benefit of the doubt to spare Alec's family and friends. But *you* know what was going on in his mind before he drove off that cliff, don't you, Celeste? You know he did it deliberately."

"No," she said, her voice shaking. "Oh, no!"

Ethan's mouth was an ugly line. He straightened, as though he couldn't bear to be close to her. "Oh, yes!" he said. "And you're responsible . . . you little tramp!"

Celeste gasped. *"Ethan!"*

"Have I shocked you? My, what delicate sensibilities we have all of a sudden. Can't you stand a spade being called a spade?"

She swung her legs off the lounger and stood. "It isn't fair to blame me," she said unsteadily. "I didn't do anything. . . ."

"Didn't you? This," he said, looking down at the letter clutched in his hand, "is as near to being a suicide note as you're ever likely to see."

"Suicide note?"

"Chapter and verse. He knew that you'd soon be leaving him—for someone younger, someone he had trusted." He held the letter out to her. "Read it."

Recoiling from it, Celeste cried, "It isn't true! He couldn't have thought..."

"Alec was a scientist. He didn't jump to conclusions easily. He'd have looked at the evidence, weighed it carefully."

Celeste said, trying to be reasonable, "But in his private life he was different. You hardly saw him for years at a time. Do you really know what he was like? If I even spoke pleasantly to a man, he thought I was flirting.... It was all in his imagination."

"*All* of it?" Ethan sneered.

"Ethan, you have to realise... he was abnormally sensitive about some things, and getting more so.... I wondered sometimes if he was mentally unbalanced."

Ethan gave a short, harsh laugh. "You expect me to believe that? About *Alec*?"

Celeste gave a hopeless little shrug. Of course she shouldn't have expected it. Ethan worshipped his older brother; it was the habit of a lifetime. Nothing she could say was going to alter his opinion. Bewildered, she stood with her hands clenched at her sides, staring at him.

He said, "You can cut out the innocent act. I told you, I know all about you. I didn't see much of Alec over the past few years, thanks to you and...certain related factors which we needn't go into just now. But we were always close. He wrote to me often. Long letters, Celeste, very private letters in which he told me a lot of things that he would never have discussed with anyone face-to-face. It was a safety valve for him, to be able to pour out his heart over a marriage that had gone sour, over a wife who was . . . faithless.''

Celeste cried, her cheeks losing all colour, ''That's not true! Ethan, you *can't* believe that's true.''

''Why not?'' he said, unemotionally. ''You might say I've had a sample of the evidence—at first hand.''

Wordlessly, Celeste shook her head. ''No,'' she murmured. This couldn't be real, she told herself. It didn't feel as though it was real. It felt like a dream, a nightmare from which she must surely wake.

She turned and headed for the house, wanting to get away from him, to be alone behind a closed door.

Hard hands grasped her and swung her around. Ethan said, ''Celeste!'' and the hands on her shoulders tightened, gave her a little shake. She knew she was going to faint, and she thought, *Not again.*

Vaguely she was aware that he had hoisted her into his arms and was carrying her. She felt cold and floaty, and very dizzy, quite unable to help herself.

After what seemed a long while, she began to feel less sick and the blood seeped back into her veins. She opened her eyes and found that Ethan had placed her on the bed where she had slept last night, and dropped a light duvet over her. A folded facecloth lay over her forehead.

Ethan frowned down at her. ''Better?'' he inquired curtly.

She murmured, ''This is becoming a habit. I'm sorry.''

''Maybe that's my line,'' he said. ''Lie still.''

She did, closing her eyes, but said, ''Are you apologising?''

''If I caused this, yes. I'm not a sadist.''

''But you're not sorry for . . . what you think,'' she said tiredly. ''Are you?''

For a moment he didn't reply. Then he said evenly, "Don't worry about it just now. The letter was a bit of a shock. Maybe I overreacted."

"But if you really believe..." She moved her head, and her eyes fluttered open, finding his.

"I said don't worry about it," he repeated, reaching down to adjust the cloth, which had slipped. "You're obviously not up to discussing it. Just stay there for a while. I'll get you a cup of coffee."

Too weak to do otherwise, she obeyed him. When he had brought the coffee, Ethan stood by the window, his hands thrust into his pockets. Celeste sat up on the bed, against the pillows he had adjusted for her, and sipped at the cup, then suddenly put it down and rushed out of the room and across the passage to the bathroom.

When she had finished being sick and rinsed her mouth with water from the basin, she found Ethan beside her, holding her arm as she straightened. Fleetingly glancing at his face, she saw that he was pale and tight-lipped.

"I'm all right," she said, making a halfhearted attempt to evade his hold, but she swayed in the doorway. He picked her up, carried her to the other room and deposited her on the bed again.

Celeste raised a hand to a clammy forehead. The room was whirling, but it gradually steadied, and she could see Ethan frowning down at her. "Lie still," he commanded. "You'd better stay in bed for the day. Where's your nightgown? You do wear one?"

"Under the pillow."

He found it and turned down the bed, moving her gently over to do so. Then he slipped the canvas shoes off her feet, and sat on the bed and began unbuttoning her blouse.

"I'll do that," she said.

"Sure you can manage?"

"Yes."

He stood. "You don't want any more of this?" He picked up the coffee cup.

"No, thank you." She shuddered.

"I'll come back in ten minutes," he promised.

When he returned she was lying in the bed with her nightgown on and the sheet up under her arms. She felt frail and exhausted but mercifully uncaring. She knew what Ethan thought of her, and it didn't seem to matter.

He left the room, and she lay quiet, and even dozed, waking up to realise it was late afternoon.

She went to the bathroom, and Ethan must have heard her moving about, because when she returned, with her wrap loosely over the nightgown, he was in her room. Automatically, she drew the edges of the wrap together.

"How do you feel?" he asked.

"A little dizzy, still." She sat down thankfully on the bed, and he helped her off with the wrap and pulled the blankets over her.

"Could you eat something?"

She shook her head.

"Fruit juice, then. Diluted, perhaps. You musn't get dehydrated."

"All right."

She drank the juice but refused anything else. Later he brought an omelette, and she managed a few mouthfuls, followed by weak tea, and afterwards cleaned her teeth in the bathroom. By the time Ethan looked in on her again, she was fast asleep.

When she woke it was full daylight, and she knew she had slept for hours. She lay there for a time, reluctant to leave the bed, even though her watch told her it was after eleven o'clock. Then, with a sigh, she got up slowly and, finding that she could stand without dizziness, had a shower, dressed in a blouse and skirt and made her way carefully down the stairs.

Ethan came out of the kitchen, his face quite expressionless. "Feeling better?" he queried.

"Yes, thank you," she answered stiffly. "Ethan, I think it would be better if I left."

"You only just got here," he reminded her. "And anyway where would you go? You're obviously in a poor state of health. This is the only place you can rest and recover, which is what you badly need."

She moistened her lips. "How can I do that, if you ... if you're going to be accusing me of..." A hand wavered to her temples. She felt perilously close to tears.

Ethan came swiftly forward, taking her arms and shoving her gently into a chair. "Listen," he said. "You don't have a choice. I'm the only one around to care for you."

"Care for me!" A flash of sarcasm lit her eyes.

"Look on that episode yesterday as an aberration. It won't happen again."

"But you think that I—"

"Forget it," he said shortly. "I lashed out without taking time to consider what I was saying. I want you fit, before I ... before we talk about it again. I owe it to Alec to look after you. Just stay until you're back to normal, okay?"

The familiar lethargy was creeping over her again. She didn't want to think about the terrible things he had suggested. It was tempting to relegate the whole episode to the back of her mind and pretend it had never happened. Especially when Ethan was being so persuasive, his voice quiet and reasonable. Her brain felt muzzy, and she wasn't up to arguing, let alone making arrangements for the flight back and someplace to live and the myriad other decisions that would be needed if she left. She knew it was weak and spineless, but the very prospect of having to do all that both frightened and exhausted her. "All right," she agreed, stifling the warning voice at the back of her mind. "I'll stay."

He said, "Good." Then he left her, to return later with two plates of salad. "Think you can get this down?" he asked.

"It looks delicious." She wasn't hungry but, somewhat to her shame, she was grateful for his determination to take care of her.

"Outside?" he suggested. "I've got a sun umbrella up now."

She had not noticed, even though she had spent the last five minutes staring out at the patio and beyond it to the sea.

While they ate they spoke little, but gradually Celeste was aware of the slackening tension, and as they sipped coffee afterwards, Ethan said, "Did you go down to the beach yesterday morning?"

Celeste shook her head. "I saw the path. Is it safe?"

"Perfectly." He cast her a sharp glance, and she knew that he was thinking of how Alec had died, smashing onto the wave-swept rocks at the bottom of a cliff. He said, almost too casually, "If you're nervous I'll take you down the first time."

Celeste said, "No, I'll be all right on my own. I'm sure you have things to do."

"Some. Work has a habit of piling up when I'm away. If you're thinking of going there now, perhaps you shouldn't be alone, though."

"I feel fine," she lied. "And I'd like to see the beach." She didn't feel fine, but she wasn't dizzy or sick anymore. She was quite capable of walking a few hundred yards.

"Don't be surprised if you see a naked body or two. Only locals use the beach, and it's accepted that nude swimming and sunbathing are okay."

"Thanks for warning me. It's safe for swimming, then?"

"Unless a storm blows up. But I think you should wait until you feel stronger before swimming on your own."

"I don't really feel like swimming today, anyway." They were talking like strangers, politely but with no warmth. "I'll do the dishes before I go," she offered.

"Don't bother. It'll only take a minute. You're the invalid." He gathered up the plates and got to his feet.

"I'm not," she said. "I mean, it's just..." Her voice trailed off. She didn't know what it was, but it seemed an age since she had felt truly alive.

"Depression, the doctor said," Ethan told her.

"Yes, but he thought..."

"Thought what?" His gaze had sharpened.

"It doesn't matter," she said listlessly. The doctor had obviously assumed that Alec's death was the cause, and she had not told him that this lack of energy and even of interest had begun long before that, only intensifying to unmanageable proportions in the days after Alec died. She shook her head and stood up. "I'll go down to the beach."

"Sure you're all right?"

"Yes. I'm sure."

He watched until she entered the trees, then turned and went inside.

The path was steep, Celeste found, but quite easy to negotiate. In some places steps had been cut and a wooden railing provided. She emerged from the trees onto soft white sand and looked about her. The cove was an almost perfect crescent, with headlands enclosing it. About a hundred yards from the shore, the sea cut off one of the headlands from a flat-topped rocky islet, bare of vegetation and ideal for sunbathing, if one wanted to swim that far. Looking back to the shore, among the trees on the surrounding slopes she could see a couple of roofs. So there were other houses about. But the beach was deserted. No bodies, naked or otherwise. She took off her shoes and slowly walked along the water's edge until she reached the rock shelf, grey and worn smooth by the water. Climbing up easily, she wandered along beside a series of pools filled with anemones and tiny crabs and little black fish, and sat down in the shadow of a tree growing low on the cliff. She leaned back against the smooth sandstone and watched the sun's restless glitter on the water.

Someone called her name, and her eyes flew open. For a moment she was disoriented, the hushed sound of the sea in her ears, the dazzle of shimmering water in her eyes. The sun had slipped low, and the sea had a brilliant orange sheen. Her arms were cold, and she shivered and rubbed them as a shadow against the light resolved itself into the figure of a man. Ethan, his eyes dark and angry. She realised that he was barefoot and had rolled up the legs of his jeans to the knees, but even so they were wet.

"What on earth do you think you're doing?" he demanded. "Did you faint again?"

Celeste blinked. "No, I...I must have fallen asleep," she said feebly, starting to get up.

Reaching down, he curled a hand about her arm, almost yanking her to her feet. He examined her closely, and said, "Are you all right?"

"Yes."

"You chose a hell of a place to sleep. Didn't it occur to you the tide might cut you off?"

"I didn't intend to sleep at all. It just happened. I'm sorry if I've worried you."

"Never mind," he said briefly. "Let's get you back."

They picked their way around the rocks, but in the end the water was between them and the sand, and Ethan splashed into it up to his thighs.

Celeste paused to hitch her skirt, but Ethan had turned and before she knew what he was going to do he had her in his arms and was wading to the shore.

He let her down on the dry sand, and she said, "That wasn't necessary."

"No sense in both of us getting wet clothes. Come on."

He led the way up the path. Following him, Celeste found herself panting when they got to the top. He turned and frowned at her. "Why didn't you say that I was going too fast for you?"

She stopped, catching her breath. "I seem to have put you to a lot of trouble already."

His frown deepened. "No trouble," he said curtly. "Take it easy. I'll go and change."

Watching him disappear into the house, she wondered why tears were prickling at her eyelids. Blinking them away, she trailed after him as far as the lounger on the terrace. She settled herself on it and laid her head against the cushion. If only she didn't feel so lifeless. No wonder he was irritated with her. Having to be rescued from her own foolishness like some brainless damsel in distress. Fainting at his feet, not once but twice. She would be disgusted with herself if she could only muster up enough energy to feel such an emotion. To feel any emotion at all.

You did feel something, an inner voice whispered. *Down there on the beach, when Ethan held you in his arms.*

Yes, for a few seconds she had been wholly alive again, feeling the beating of his heart against her breast, the warmth of his skin through the shirt he wore, the strength and sureness of his hold on her.

Firmly she shut that out of her mind. A momentary awareness, like the sudden awareness in the coroner's court when she had looked up and found his eyes on her with hard disbelief. And like the rush of relief and gladness that she had felt when at the funeral she had seen him waiting for her at the rear of the church. When she had thought, *He's here. Ethan's here. Everything will be all right now.*

Only, of course, he hadn't been waiting for her. He had come to see his brother buried, and everything was not all right. Everything was wrong, horribly wrong. Ethan didn't trust her, he didn't like her at all, and he blamed her for causing Alec's death.

"Nothing will ever be right again," she whispered to herself, shivering. "Never."

The stark truth hit her, and she raised her hands, rubbing at the sudden gooseflesh on her arms. She got up and went inside, running up the stairs to her room, arriving there breathless and with tears on her cheeks. She wiped at them impatiently. She had never been the weepy, swooning type. *Pull yourself together,* she admonished sternly, *for heaven's sake!*

Her feet and her hair felt gritty with sand, and she decided to shower and change. Her sandals had been left lying on the beach, she realised, wondering if they would be there tomorrow or if the tide would have washed them away. She couldn't be bothered going down there again to find out, and she daren't mention it to Ethan. Already he thought her several kinds of idiot. She didn't want to give him reason to add to the list.

She washed her hair in the shower, and after towelling it half-dry, she pinned it back in a knot. She put on the dress she had donned when Ethan called the day after the funeral, and slipped her feet into a pair of fawn-coloured medium-heeled shoes. When she went downstairs it was to find

Ethan in clean dark blue slacks and a lighter blue shirt, standing with his hands thrust into his pockets, and looking out at the rapidly fading sunset.

He must have heard her, and it seemed to her that he turned reluctantly as she reached the bottom of the stairs. His gaze swept over her and she thought he looked rather disparaging. But all he said was, "Are you ready to eat?"

"Have I kept you waiting? I—"

"Don't start apologising again," he said curtly. "We'll have it in the kitchen if that's okay with you."

"Perfectly." The kitchen was large and well-appointed; a table was tucked into one corner by the window, with a banquette to sit on.

Ethan had already set two places, and he gestured for her to sit down while he brought a casserole from the microwave oven and set it on the table. Several slices of buttered French bread nestled in a napkin-lined basket, and a plate of sliced cucumbers and tomatoes were already on the table.

The casserole contained rice and fish with a spicy flavour, and when she had eaten a modest plateful, she said, "You're a good cook."

Ethan shrugged. "I can do a few simple dishes. It's all I need when I'm on my own. If you want variety, you may have to take a hand yourself."

"I'd be glad to do my share," she said politely. "There's no reason for you to wait on me all the time."

"When you feel up to it."

"I told you, I'm not an invalid."

"Maybe not," he conceded. "Have some more."

Celeste shook her head. "No thanks, I couldn't."

"That wasn't much of a meal. My talents don't run to sweets, but there is some cheesecake in the freezer."

"No, really. I don't eat sweets often."

"You're much too thin," he told her.

She had lost weight in the last few years. But then she had grown older—much older. Trying to lighten the subject, she said, "It's fashionable to be thin. Do you prefer plump women?"

"Fashion," he said caustically, "has a lot to answer for." He recalled Aunt Ellie's remarks at the funeral. "You were never plump," he told Celeste. "But I remember—"

When he stopped abruptly, she looked up and then away, her pulse quickening.

Ethan got up and took her plate, clattering it against his. "If you don't want a sweet," he said, "how about some fruit and cheese, and then coffee? We'll have it in the living room."

"That sounds very nice," she said huskily. "Can I help?"

"I'll manage. Go and sit down in the other room."

He brought a couple of cheeses, and a bowl of bananas, melons and papayas on a tray. "Help yourself while I bring the coffee," he invited.

Afterwards, Celeste said, "Please let me do the dishes. I feel useless."

He nodded, and she spent the next ten minutes in the kitchen, coming back to find him standing in front of the window as he had before, only now it was dark outside. He had switched on some side lights that cast a soft glow but hid his expression from her as he turned. "I'm going for a walk," he said. "If you want something to read, there are books over there." He nodded to a bookcase that occupied almost the whole of one wall.

So he wanted to be alone. "Thank you," Celeste said. "I think I'll go to bed early." In spite of her long sleep, she felt very tired.

He nodded. "Fine. Good night, then."

He went out, taking a torch from a drawer in a dresser near the door. Perhaps he made a habit of having an evening stroll.

Celeste ran her eyes over the bookcase. Ethan seemed to have a very catholic taste, she thought. There were a few classics, a shelf of Australian and New Zealand fiction, and several recent bestsellers. All of his brother's books were there, and she hastily skimmed over those to a solid row of books on oceanography, marine animals and natural history, giving way to a mixture of topics including a history of Australia, an ecological handbook and a book on prison reform, as well as two thick volumes on the workings of the human mind, and a guide to Western philosophy.

Tonight she wanted something light and easily digested, so she bent hopefully to the shelf of paperbacks near the floor, going down on her knees to examine the titles.

Most of them were thrillers, with one or two westerns and some paperback editions of popular novels. At the end of the shelf were thin volumes of pamphlet size, one of them a short history of Sheerwind Island. She took that and a couple of thrillers and went up to bed.

She had read just five pages before her eyelids drooped, and she switched off the bedside lamp, only to spend the next hour or so waiting for sleep to come.

It was some time before Ethan quietly climbed the stairs and went into the bathroom. She heard the water running as he showered, and the soft closing of his bedroom door later, then muted sounds and finally silence.

At last she went to sleep, but woke again in the early hours. Prey to disconnected thoughts and disturbing emotions, she tossed restlessly and tried to shut off her mind. When dawn streaked the sky she slept again, and the next time she opened her eyes it was full daylight, her watch showing her the time was almost ten.

Going down to the living room, she found a woman with her back to the stairs, running a cloth over the low table.

"Good morning," Celeste said.

The woman straightened. "Oh, good morning." She had a pleasant, middle-aged face under pepper-and-salt curls. "You must be Mrs. Ryland."

"Yes, Mrs...Jackson, isn't it?"

The woman smiled. "That's right. Mr. Ryland's told you about me, then. I'm sorry about your husband."

"Thank you."

"Mr. Ryland said to tell you there's breakfast in the kitchen, and if there's anything else you want, to ask me. I hope you found all you needed in your room and the bathroom. I expect you've got your own shampoo and stuff, but I bought a few things in case you'd forgotten. A lot of men just use soap for their hair, and I know I can't do without a good shampoo myself."

"Everything was perfect. It was very thoughtful of you. Where is Mr. Ryland?"

"He's in his workroom, upstairs. He doesn't like to be disturbed once he's started work."

"I won't disturb him. And I don't think I'll need to disturb your work, either, Mrs. Jackson."

"That's all right, dear. Anything I can do..."

Celeste thanked her again and made for the kitchen. She washed up the dishes afterwards and made her way down to the beach. Her sandals were not on the sand, and she clambered onto the rocks, searching along where she had been yesterday.

There was no sign of them. The tide was coming in, and she didn't want to have the same experience as the previous day, so she scrambled back to the sand, to find a man coming out of the trees.

"Hi!" he hailed her. He was tall and brown-haired, dressed in a pair of cutoff jeans and a white T-shirt. As he came closer she saw that he had brown eyes and a pleasant grin.

A little cautiously, Celeste smiled back. "Hello."

"Lost something?" he asked her.

"Yes. I left my shoes on the beach yesterday, but I guess they got washed away by the tide."

"I saw you wandering about as though you were looking for something, when I was on my way down from my place. I'll help you, if you like."

"Thank you very much, but I don't think it's much use. You live up there?" She could see faint signs of another path and the gleam of window glass among the trees on the slope.

He nodded. "I'm Jeff Saunders, by the way. You're staying with Ethan?"

She saw the slight hint of speculation in his eyes, and said, "I'm his sister-in-law. Celeste Ryland."

"Very glad to meet you, Celeste." He paused, obviously putting two and two together. "Then it was your husband who...died recently? Ethan's brother?"

"Yes."

"I'm really sorry. Ethan was cut up about it, I know."

"Yes. He and Alec were very close."

"How long are you staying?"

"I don't know yet. It depends on...a number of things."

Jeff nodded sympathetically. "Look, if there's anything I can do..."

"Thank you. Everyone's very kind, but there isn't much anyone can do."

"I guess not. Did you come down here to be alone? If you want me to—"

"No, it's all right. Ethan's working, and Mrs. Jackson is cleaning the house. I just thought I'd find my sandals and keep out of their way for a while."

"How would you like to come up to my place for a cup of coffee or a fruit juice? I could do with some company. Haven't seen a soul since Ethan left for the mainland. Most of the houses nearby are holiday homes, you know. Except for the Palmers—they live over there, just about dead opposite my place—Ethan and I are the only permanent residents. And both of us spend weeks at a time away from home."

"What about Mrs. Jackson?"

"Oh, she comes from around the point. There's a community in that bay, bigger than ours. About a dozen residents, and more holiday places. In the season it's pretty lively there. Here it just stays nice and quiet, except for the odd picnic party."

"What do you do?" Celeste asked as they climbed the steep path through the trees.

"For a living? I'm a writer."

"What do you write?"

"A bit of everything. I'm trying to make a living at it, which isn't easy. I've had a couple of thrillers published, which have done quite nicely but not set the world on fire, and a lot of travel writing and other journalism. And a short history of Sheerwind."

"Oh, I thought your name was familiar. I was reading it last night."

"Hope you enjoyed it."

"I went to sleep," she confessed. Well, she hadn't really, but she had felt sleepy. She caught the grin he gave her over his shoulder as he led the way up the path, and said, "Sorry! But I was very tired."

"It's okay. Perhaps I'll give you a copy of one of my thrillers, and see if it will keep you awake."

"I promise I'll finish the history," she said. "What I did read looked interesting. I hadn't known the island was named after a ship that was wrecked here."

"Well, it was a long time ago. Last century. Wait till you get to the bit about how the survivors reacted to their situation, and the struggles for leadership. Jealousies, sexual rivalry, intrigues, murder, the lot. I defy you to fall asleep over that!"

"I'll look forward to it."

"The research was fascinating," Jeff said, as they reached the house, which was set into the hillside, with plenty of glass in front to make use of the view. "Come in."

Chapter Five

To her surprise, Celeste enjoyed herself, sipping coffee and talking with Jeff Saunders. When she said she ought to go, he took her cup and got up. "I'll walk you back. If Ethan stops for lunch today, there's something I want to see him about, anyway."

"He doesn't always?" she queried.

"We both have rather erratic working habits. We've been known to take a boat out and go fishing when the weather and water look promising, and have to stay up half the night afterwards to meet our deadlines."

"You're good friends, then."

"I guess. Ethan's very helpful when I strike trouble with my computer, and I've sometimes helped him write instruction manuals for his programmes. He says it's useful having my input because I'm practically illiterate in computer language, even though I use a word processor for my work, and some of his programmes will be used by people like me.''

''I can understand a writer living in a place like this,'' Celeste said. ''But I would have thought Ethan would need to be nearer to a city.''

''Designing software is not just technical, you know. It involves imaginative thinking. We creative types need to be able to get away from the madding crowd and let our thoughts flow. At least, that's the theory. Actually, of course, we just like an excuse to live in a place as beautiful as this. Ethan spends a fair amount of his time away from the island, though, just as I do. He has to contact clients, and keep up with what's happening in his field. There was that conference in Sydney last month, for instance.''

''Conference?''

''Big computer buffs' convention that he went to. Didn't he see you, then?''

''No,'' Celeste said baldly. She knew nothing about that.

''Oh.'' Jeff seemed surprised. ''Well, I guess the conference schedule was pretty heavy.''

When they reached the top of the path to Ethan's house he was standing on the terrace, and watched them coming towards him. Jeff had not taken the path at the same pace that Ethan had the day before, but the climb was quite steep, and Celeste's cheeks were flushed when she emerged from the trees at Jeff's side.

Jeff lifted a hand in casual greeting. ''Hi. I found your sister-in-law wandering all alone on the beach.''

Ethan gave him a nod and transferred his gaze to Celeste. ''You look better,'' he said.

Jeff turned to her. ''Have you been unwell?''

Suddenly impatient, she said, ''I'm perfectly all right. I'll just go and wash my hands.''

"Lunch is ready," Ethan called after her as she made for the stairs.

She hadn't realised it was so late. Mrs. Jackson must have left. When Celeste came downstairs again, Ethan was alone at the table on the terrace, but another plate was set opposite his, and he was helping himself to salad and French bread and sliced ham.

As she paused in the doorway he said, "Come and eat."

"Thank you. Jeff didn't stay long, did he?"

"Disappointed?"

Suspecting a sneer in his voice, she looked up quickly as she took her chair, but he was spreading butter on a thick piece of bread. "He seemed nice," she said. "You didn't invite him for lunch?" There was plenty of food on the table, more than she and Ethan could possibly eat on their own.

"I did," Ethan said shortly. "He declined."

"I'm not surprised."

It was Ethan's turn to look up, his brows sardonically raised.

"You seem to be in a bad mood," Celeste said. "If it's because you felt obliged to make lunch for me, you really needn't have, you know."

"I'm not in a bad mood."

"All right, you're not. You're just naturally surly."

He put down his fork and sat back. His mouth was grim, but a gleam of reluctant humour lit the dark eyes. "Okay," he said. "I admit it. But it has nothing to do with making lunch for you."

"Work not going well?" she guessed.

He paused, then picked up his fork again. "Not particularly. I take it *you* had an enjoyable morning."

That sarcasm was there again, but she decided to ignore it. "Yes, thank you. Jeff says you often skip lunch."

"I forget it sometimes. I eat when I'm hungry."

"I could make lunch for you," she said, "and bring it to your workroom if you don't want to stop."

"Thanks, but you needn't wait on me."

"By the same token," she argued, "*you* don't need to wait on *me*. I can make my own lunch if I'm hungry. And I can cook dinner, if you like. I feel I should do something to earn my keep."

He shrugged. "If you insist. Sure you feel up to it?"

"There's nothing wrong with me."

"So you keep saying." He regarded her thoughtfully.

Celeste said, "Jeff says you attended a conference in Sydney."

"I attend quite a number of conferences."

"Last month. He seemed surprised that Alec and I hadn't seen you then."

"I saw Alec. We had lunch together on the second day. He didn't mention it?"

"No." She didn't look at him, concentrating on her salad. "He didn't say anything about it."

A constrained silence fell, and Celeste pushed away her plate.

"You haven't finished."

"I've had enough." She stood. "Do you want a cup of coffee?"

"No, I'll take one up to the workroom with me. What do you plan to do this afternoon?"

"I have no particular plans. But I might swim. I haven't been in the water yet."

"I'll come with you."

"There's no need—"

"I'm not sure I ought to allow you to go in alone."

"You said it was safe."

"For a normally healthy person and a strong swimmer, yes. Don't argue, Celeste. Give me half an hour and we'll go together."

After dealing with the dishes, Celeste pinned her hair up, covered most of her body with sunscreen and donned a one-piece black swimsuit. Then tucking a towel about her like a sarong, she went to wait for Ethan on the terrace.

When he joined her he was wearing dark blue trunks and had a towel slung around his shoulders. His skin was well tanned, and she guessed he must spend quite a lot of his time in the sun.

He let her lead the way, and when they came to the beach he said, "Straight in, or do you like to soak up the sun first?"

"For a little while," she answered politely. "But don't let me stop you if you want to go in."

He nodded, threw the towel on the sand and strode to the water, flinging himself in and powering away from the shore in a fast crawl. Celeste lay down on her towel and closed her eyes.

The world gradually floated away, and it wasn't until she felt a light showering of cold droplets on her skin that she opened her eyes. Ethan was standing over her, his hair sleek with water and his body gleaming.

"I hope you put on some sun lotion," he said. "Going to sleep was not the idea."

"I wasn't!" she protested, sitting up.

"Looked like it to me." He dropped down beside her and subjected her to a piercing scrutiny. "What *is* all this falling asleep at the drop of a hat?"

"I didn't sleep well last night," she admitted, "that's all."

"Did I disturb you?"

She shook her head. "No, not at all. I quite often have trouble sleeping."

"And then make up for it in the daytime?"

"Sometimes."

"I think I'll get Henry Palmer to check you over. He's one of the neighbours, and a doctor."

"I already saw a doctor," she reminded him. "If I want to see another one, *I'll* make the decision."

She got up and walked to the water, allowing it to reach her thighs before she dived into its silken caress. In a few minutes she knew that Ethan had joined her and was swimming not far away, keeping an eye on her, no doubt. She ignored him, and floated, dived, swam gently for twenty minutes or so, before making her way to the shore. She felt as though it had been hours.

Ethan splashed out beside her. As she reached the dry sand, he suddenly trailed a finger over her shoulder blades. "You're much too thin," he said. "These bones didn't used to be so visible."

She flinched away from him, half turning. "Don't!"

He stopped short, standing in her way. "Don't touch, or don't criticise?"

"Both."

"Things change, don't they, Celeste? And people. For the record, you're the last woman in the world I'd be tempted to ravish."

He went past her and picked up his towel. As she came slowly after him, he said, "I'll see you later. Don't go out of your depth if you want to swim again." And he walked away from her to the path up the cliff.

She stayed on the beach all afternoon, moving into the shade for a doze when the sun had dried her body, later wandering along the water's edge, then having another quick dip.

When she was dry again, she went back to the house and showered off the sand. She changed into the same dress she had worn the night before, then investigated the refrigerator and the well-stocked freezer and walk-in pantry.

When Ethan came down, she had a couple of pork chops almost ready, with vegetables and a crisp salad.

"Smells good," he commented as he looked into the kitchen. "Like a drink before we eat?"

"A small sherry, thank you," she answered, "if you have it."

"Coming up." He brought it in for her and leaned on the counter, watching as she put the finishing touches to the meal. "I think this rates opening a bottle of wine," he said when she had placed the dishes on the table. "White?"

"Yes."

He seemed to be going out of his way to be nice, she thought, and tried to match him. When he had poured the wine into two glasses and begun helping himself to the meat, she said, "I hope the work went better this afternoon."

"A bit." He commented, "You've caught some sun. It suits you, but don't overdo it, will you?"

Tempted to tell him to mind his own business, she said instead, quite meekly, "I won't."

Ethan looked up. "So I'm a bully. Put it down to a feeling of responsibility."

"You're not a bully," she admitted. "And I don't see that you need to feel that way at all."

"Don't you?" he said. "Alec appears to have left you in my care."

"How do you make that out?"

"It's the only sense I can make of his will. And if that's not what he had in mind—"

"I'm sure it wasn't!"

"—then I still feel morally responsible."

"I'm twenty-eight years old," Celeste said distinctly. "No one needs to be responsible for me!"

"That," Ethan said softly, "sounds almost like your old self."

Celeste took a sip of wine. She wasn't sure what her old self was, but certainly she felt rather less jaded in Ethan's company, aware that under the surface of his apparent urbanity some powerful emotion was simmering forceful enough to penetrate the indifference that held her in thrall. She shivered, gulping down more wine.

Ethan refilled her glass, and she recklessly drank that, too, before they had finished the first course. Standing up to bring cheese and biscuits from the counter where she had set them out on an oiled board, she had to pause a moment because her head was swimming slightly. When Ethan offered to make the coffee, she accepted gratefully.

"In the other room?" he suggested, and she followed him, sinking down on one of the chairs. He put on a recording of easy-listening music, and when it was finished he took the coffee cups out to the kitchen, saying, "Play something else if you like. I'm going to do a bit more work before I go to bed."

She found some other records that appealed to her and played them, not too loudly in case she disturbed him. When she went up to bed, there was a thin line of light under the door to his workroom.

For the rest of the week, Ethan breakfasted early, and Celeste came down later and spent the morning on the beach, taking a book with her. She would return for a snack sometime after midday, and in the afternoon read or rest, then cook dinner. After the shared meal Ethan went back to work, and she listened to music or read some more. Once she met Jeff again on the beach and had coffee with him, and another day she washed out some of her clothes and ironed them. Ethan asked her if she was getting bored, and she shook her head. Temporarily at least, she had no desire to lead a more active life.

"I have to go into town and get some supplies and mail," he told her. "You can come along, if you'd like."

"I need a pair of sandals. I suppose I could buy some."

"Sure. I'll be about an hour or more. We can stay longer if you want to shop."

"That should be plenty of time."

They were on their way in his car when Ethan asked, "Are you okay for money?"

"Yes, thank you." She didn't have a lot, but since coming to the island she had not had any expenses.

She found a pair of Brazilian leather sandals in a shop that sold everything from clothing to hardware and even had a counter devoted to makeup. On impulse she bought a bright red cotton dress printed with white hibiscus flowers. The dress, she knew, would highlight the lack of colour in her face, so she invested in a lipstick and blusher and eye shadow.

The shops were modest but bright and well-stocked. Trade was quiet, but in the season no doubt the wide streets, lined with tall palms and flame trees, would be thronged with tourists. The population was a mixture of races. Tall, brown-skinned Polynesians and darker, woolly-haired Melanesians mingled with a few Chinese, some Indian women wearing graceful saris, and Europeans sporting tans of varying shades. Hardly anyone would have met the description "white."

"It's a fair old potpourri here," Ethan agreed when she mentioned it, meeting him in the brick-paved square where they had left his car. "The island was apparently unpopulated until the mid-nineteenth century, when a ship was driven ashore in a storm. There was a Chinese, a Portuguese and a black American among the survivors of the *Sheerwind*, for a start. And later, of course, people of all races ended up here, for one reason or another.''

"I know. I've been reading Jeff's book. It's good, isn't it?''

"Some people think he romanticised the story. It was written for the tourist rather than the serious historian. But the facts are as he put them. A dozen men and two women and a child survived the wreck. And it wasn't long before the men came to fighting over who was to be kingpin, and which of them were going to have the women.''

"The women had no choice, I suppose.''

Ethan shrugged. "Who's to say, after all this time? Maybe they enjoyed being sought after.''

"That's a conclusion only a man would jump to.''

His look held surprised scepticism. "Wouldn't you have enjoyed it?''

"Being fought over by a lot of thugs and knowing I was the prize for the winner? No, I wouldn't. And if you think that's what any woman would like, you're more of a male chauvinist than I ever thought.''

He raised his brows at that, but only said mildly, "Before you start trying to reform me, how about some lunch? There's quite a good restaurant near the post office, and I haven't collected the mail yet.''

He fetched it on the way, and as they sat waiting for their order, he riffled through a small pile of letters. "One for you.'' He tossed it on the table, and she picked it up and fingered it. It had been posted at the university in Sydney, she saw, but the address was handwritten.

"Aren't you going to open it?'' Ethan asked her, stuffing his own letters into a pocket.

"You haven't opened yours,'' she pointed out.

"All business," he said. "Yours looks more interesting."

"Personal, you mean."

"Sorry. I wasn't intending to be nosy." He leaned back in his chair rather ostentatiously and gazed out the open window at the pleasure boats riding at anchor on the water.

She took a knife and slit the envelope open. Glancing at the signature, she said, "It's from Steven. Steven Craig."

"Ah."

His face was perfectly bland, so why did she feel that stirring of interest and disapproval? She skimmed the contents and was about to hand the letter over to him, when she changed her mind. Folding the paper, she carefully replaced it in the envelope and slid it into her handbag. "He would like to know if you've recovered anything from the disks Alec... left. I'm afraid I'd forgotten about them. Should I write and find out what happened to them?"

"I have them."

"You do?"

"I collected Alec's briefcase and the other things the police found in the car, the morning before we left."

"Oh, you didn't tell me."

"There was nothing personal. Nothing I needed to bother you with, I thought. You can have them if you like."

Celeste shook her head. "Have you looked at the disks?"

"When I find out what's on them, I'll let your friend know. Just now I have to finish a project that's already overdue. The people paying me for it have been very patient as it is. I can't keep them waiting longer than necessary."

"I'll write to Steven and tell him that you'll get onto it as soon as possible, then."

Their food was served, and he politely asked if her shopping had been successful, and whether she had all she

wanted or wished to spend more time in town, but there was
a tension in the air. He seemed preoccupied, and she was
glad when he had paid the bill and they returned to the car.

He drove fast and in silence and on arriving at the house,
said he had to work. After putting away the supplies with
her help, he disappeared up the stairs.

Trying to shake off an acute feeling of depression, Celeste went for a swim. After that first time Ethan had apparently decided she could cope on her own and had not
insisted on accompanying her. The water was warm and
clear, and she felt slightly better and fresher, but she stayed
in longer than usual, and after returning to the house and
showering she lay on her bed clad only in her wrap, and
drifted into sleep.

She woke to the sound of tapping on her door. Sitting up,
she pushed tousled hair out of her eyes and, pulling the wrap
about her, went to open the door.

Ethan's eyes swept over her. "Did I wake you? Are you
okay?"

"Yes, and yes. But don't worry about waking me. I didn't
mean to sleep at all." Dusk was falling, and she said, "I'm
sorry, is it dinner time?"

"No need to apologise. But it is. I've made a meal. You'd
better come and have some." His eyes dropped again to
where the edges of the robe met between her breasts. "Get
dressed," he said. "I'll see you in ten minutes."

She closed the door after him, and grabbed clean undies,
then stood indecisively wondering what to put on. All the
clothes hanging in the wardrobe looked drab and uninter-
esting. On impulse she opened the big bag containing the
new flower-printed dress and shook it out. She slipped it on,
brushed her hair, and snatched up the lipstick she had
bought, swiftly applying it. It was ages since she had worn
makeup, but she had not lost her touch. She smoothed on

blusher very lightly, and the merest hint of eye shadow. The new sandals slid easily onto her slim feet.

Ethan was coming out of the kitchen as she descended the stairs.

"I was just going to call you," he told her.

Slightly breathless with hurrying, she said, "Sorry to keep you waiting."

He stood watching as she came down the last few steps. She thought his mouth hardened, and was sure that his eyes had narrowed. In fact there was something about the way he was staring that made her uncomfortable. "Looks like it was worth waiting for," he drawled.

"I . . . bought a new dress today."

"So I see. It's very . . . eye-catching."

She wondered if he thought she should be in mourning. "I felt I needed cheering up," she said.

"I'm not objecting." But his comprehensive glance, ending at her face and not missing the lipstick and eye shadow, seemed to her distinctly censorious. He stepped back for her to precede him into the kitchen.

He had opened a bottle of red wine, and after the meal he didn't disappear into his workroom, but lounged in one of the cane chairs facing the windows while they finished off the wine. He put on a tape of soft, romantic ballads, and came back to his chair without switching on the lights. Outside the darkness was deepening.

Celeste cradled her glass in her hands and rested her head against the high back of the chair. Ethan turned to look at her, leaning over with the wine bottle in his hand. "More?"

She shook her head, and he poured the remainder into his glass, raising it to his lips. She felt his eyes on her, and her breathing quickened. She put down her own glass abruptly on a nearby table and got up.

He stood up, too, and she turned swiftly, the full skirt of her dress catching the glass and toppling it, sending it rolling to the edge of the table. She bent to rescue it, and Ethan stepped forward to do the same. His shoulder collided with hers, and as one of his hands righted the glass, the other closed over her arm, steadying her.

When they straightened, they were very close. She could feel his warm breath on her temple, his fingers firm on her skin.

"Celeste . . ." he said.

"Ethan . . ." Willing herself to move out of his grasp, she murmured, "I want to go to bed."

His grip tightened on her arm. His head bent a little. "Are you inviting me to join you?" he asked.

Shocked, Celeste pulled out of his hold. *"No!"*

"Forgive me," he said, not as though he meant it. "It did sound rather like it."

"You know it wasn't meant to!" she said, backing away from him. "You can't honestly think that!"

He said, "I don't know what to think about you, Celeste. I spend half my time wondering what's going on inside that beautiful head of yours."

"Nothing sinister!" she protested.

Ignoring that, he said, "Alec was obsessed with you, right to the end. And you managed to emasculate him. Why could he never satisfy you? What was it you wanted of him?"

Horrified, she stared at him in the gathering dark. The shadows made him look menacing as he loomed over her.

"You don't understand!" she said in despair.

"Damn right I don't," Ethan said quite softly. "But I'm going to, one day. Because you're going to tell me—you're going to make me understand, Celeste. I want to know exactly why my brother died."

"I can't tell you that!" she cried. "I don't *know*!"

He gave a short disbelieving laugh. Almost inaudibly, his lips scarcely moving, he said, "The hell you don't!"

"Anyway," she said, "I thought you'd decided . . . that you knew."

"But there's more to it," he said. "For instance, who was the man? The one that finally sent him over the edge of that cliff?"

"Ethan . . ." A shiver ran through her, and she brought her arms across herself, trying to stop it. "Please," she said. "Please stop it. I can't . . . I can't deal with this now."

He audibly drew in a long breath. After a long time he said, his voice clipped, "All right, let's leave it for the moment. You'd better go to bed."

Chapter Six

Celeste woke with a feeling of dread, tempted to pull the pillow over her head and pretend the world didn't exist. Remembering the events of the night before, she felt her mouth go dry, and flung a hand over her eyes, blotting out the sun. She could hear the distant hum of a vacuum cleaner and realised this was one of Mrs. Jackson's cleaning days. She should get up and strip her bed because the sheets ought to be washed.

She took them down in her arms and said, "I've made the bed up again."

"I could have done it," the woman said, as she switched off the cleaner.

Celeste shook her head. "I have little enough to do. I'll put these in the machine. Would you like a cup of tea? I'm going to boil the kettle."

"Well, thank you very much. It's just about time for one."

They sat at the kitchen table, Mrs. Jackson with tea and a sweet biscuit, Celeste with coffee and toast after eating half of a sliced melon.

"You won't put on much weight like that," Mrs. Jackson said disapprovingly.

Celeste smiled faintly. "Everyone keeps telling me I'm too thin."

"Well, you are, dear. You're a very nice-looking girl. It's a shame not to make the best of yourself."

"At the moment I don't care."

Mrs. Jackson's face softened. She put out a hand and briefly patted Celeste's. "I know, but . . . life goes on, you know. I'm sure everyone says it, and it's hard to believe, but it is true. I lost a daughter about ten years ago. You don't forget, but it will get easier. You've just got to keep yourself going."

"I'm terribly sorry," Celeste said. "And I'm sure you're right. I am trying, believe me."

She went down to the beach, and saw that Jeff was in the water. When he waded out she could see he had been swimming nude, and looked away while he drew a towel about his waist, picked up his jeans he had left lying on the sand, and walked over to her where she sat in the shade of the trees.

"Hope you're not shocked," he said.

"Not at all," she assured him. "Ethan warned me when I first came that people didn't always bother with swimsuits on this beach."

"Tried it yourself yet?" He grinned down at her.

"I'm not quite game," she confessed. "One day, maybe."

"Mind if I sit down?"

"Of course not. I could do with someone to talk to."

"Getting lonely, are you?" he asked. "I gather Ethan's very tied up with work at the moment. He gave me pretty short shrift the other day, in the pleasantest possible way."

"He said he invited you to lunch."

Jeff laughed. "I could see he didn't have his heart in the idea."

"He is busy," she said. "I gather he's fallen behind in some project, and there's a deadline on it."

Jeff nodded as he settled himself beside her. "Anything in particular you'd like to talk about?"

Celeste shook her head, then said hesitantly, "How well do you know Ethan? Has he talked to you about...about Alec and...me?"

"Hardly ever mentioned you," Jeff said frankly. "But he's talked of his brother all right. Thought the world of him."

"Yes, he did."

"Alec was a lot older, wasn't he? I met him once. I remember I was surprised."

"They weren't really brothers," Celeste explained. "Not by blood. Alec's mother left his father when Alec was just a little boy. His father adopted Ethan legally and gave him the name of Ryland when he married Ethan's mother."

"But Ethan wasn't his child?"

"Oh, no. Ethan's mother had been widowed soon after he was born. He didn't remember his own father at all. He would have been only six at the time his mother married Alec's father. Alec was already at university then."

"Alec must have been a lot older than you, too."

"Yes. I was a student when I met him. And he had already become well-known around the Pacific as an anthropological archaeologist and explorer."

"Was that before or after the New Guinea accident?"

"After. Not very long after. He was still using crutches, but he'd taken on a lectureship at the university where I was studying anthropology. I picked him up after he lost one of his crutches on the stairs."

"This was in New Zealand?"

"Yes, in Auckland. He was furious, and swearing like a trooper. I couldn't help laughing, and then he swore at me, too. Afterwards he apologised, and..." She shrugged.

"Love at first swear word?" Jeff suggested lightly.

Celeste shook her head. "It wasn't my first sight of him. I'd admired him from afar. Well, most of the girls did. He was good-looking and intelligent and physically courageous. And famous, of course. He was a very glamorous figure."

"Even after he was disabled?"

"He refused to let that ruin his life. It was one of the things that I liked about him. And of course, we'd all read about how he'd nearly died in the jungles of New Guinea after he fell, up in the mountains, and his struggle to get out and find medical help."

"Yeah, I remember. Quite a heroic story. He seems to have been some guy. For a man who'd been so active, it must have been a shock to realise he'd need help just to walk, for the rest of his life."

"Yes, it was. And to realise that field work, which he had made his speciality, was closed to him. And the kind of TV documentary he used to do, with the film crew following him into some remote location, wasn't possible any more."

"He did appear on TV a few times quite recently, though, didn't he? I'm sure I've seen him."

"Oh, yes. But even when he was able to use a cane, he wouldn't let them film him moving about. It was strictly armchair shots or behind a desk. After the accident, he changed to writing and lecturing on his subject and doing research analysis.''

''Ethan was very proud of him. He said Alec had made a success of his second career, just as he had with the first. With your help, I guess?''

Celeste said, ''When we were first married . . . he did like to give me some of the credit.''

Jeff cast her a thoughtful glance, and she wondered if she had said a little too much. Changing the subject, she asked, ''How is the writing going?''

''At the moment it isn't.'' He grimaced. ''I had this idea for a great new thriller, and the first two chapters flowed like water, but now I'm stuck. Sometimes a bit of physical activity helps.''

''And has it helped?''

''Don't know yet. The trick is to think of something totally different for a couple of hours, then go and stare at the screen and see what happens. At least, that's my method.'' He raised a hand in greeting to someone behind her, making her look around. ''Have you met the Palmers?'' he asked her.

Celeste shook her head, and he said, ''Well, I'll introduce you, then.''

The couple were in their sixties, Henry Palmer erect and white-haired, his wife Janice a head shorter than her husband, with greying curls and an aristocratic nose.

''We retired here,'' she told Celeste. ''But Henry never retired really. He's still available to people by appointment or in an emergency, although he has no regular clinic. We set up a small surgery at the house, and he has just enough business to keep him from subsiding into senility.'' She threw a teasing glance at her husband.

"Well, I had to have something to do while you mucked about with your paints and stuff," he grumbled affectionately.

"You're an artist?" Celeste asked.

"Only an amateur one," Janice said. "But I have sold a few paintings to the tourists."

"She's a very good amateur," her husband said loyally. "I prefer her landscapes and seascapes to some of those outlandish daubings you see in art galleries, with outrageous prices on them."

"That's because you know nothing about art, darling," his wife told him. "But I'm very glad there are people like you who are willing to take my work off my hands and pay me for it into the bargain."

"I'm surprised you haven't met Celeste before," Jeff told them. "She's on the beach almost every day."

"We've been away visiting friends on the mainland," Henry told him. "We read about your husband's death," he added to Celeste. "Tragic business. Very sorry to hear about it."

Janice added her condolences, and then said, "You must all come over for dinner one evening. You and Ethan and Jeff. It's a while since we've got together. I'll phone Ethan about it tonight."

Celeste half expected that Ethan would plead pressure of work and turn down the invitation, but instead he told her they were invited for Saturday night, and to wear something pretty. Over the next few days he reverted to his usual cool courtesy, and she took her cue from him, with a cowardly reluctance to stir up the emotions that had surfaced the other night.

She met the Palmers again on the beach, and asked Janice what sort of thing she should wear.

"Whatever you're comfortable in," the older woman replied. "We don't dress up much here."

She decided to wear the red dress again. She was heartily sick of everything else in her wardrobe, and it was about the only thing she had that would meet Ethan's requirement of "something pretty." Once she had owned a couple of dozen pretty dresses, but that was before Alec had started making pointed remarks about her clothes and her love of fashion. Before he had begun to tell everyone how his wife liked to look beautiful and sexy, and how much time and money she spent on her appearance. It was all done with a wry, indulgent smile, and at first she had tried not to mind, putting it down to male tactlessness. He would end by hooking an arm about her and declaring it was well worth it, inviting all and sundry to agree with him. And when she did protest in private, later, that he was embarrassing her and sometimes other people as well, he laughed and told her not to be a silly, oversensitive child.

Her clothes had not been particularly expensive, because she had a flair for fashion and an ability to pick out inexpensive garments that could be dressed up and combined to give the casual but trendy look that she liked. Over time, she had replaced them with others that were less noticeable, more conservative—and more suitable, she supposed, for the wife of a respected academic. That was another thing. She was so much younger than most of the people her husband mingled with, and it had seemed a good idea to try to minimise the age gap somehow. She did it partly by dressing older than her years, but the change in image had been so gradual that Alec apparently never noticed. He had been convinced to the end that she had a consuming and youthful frivolous interest in fashion and glamour. The red dress was, of course, the one thing that she had never worn in his company. Somehow she felt lighter when she put it on, as though a host of oppressive memories remained with the other clothing but could not cling to this new garment.

She hesitated with the lipstick in her hand, shrugged, and applied it with a steady hand. Why not? Ethan, she felt, reacted negatively to her donning makeup, but the dress definitely needed it, and anyway, she had not been freed of eight years of trying in vain to please Alec, only to start on the same self-defeating cycle with his brother.

The thought was barely formulated in her mind before she slammed a mental door on it, appalled. But one word echoed in her mind and wouldn't go away. She was free. Free. Try as she would to deny it, she couldn't help a faint lifting of the heart. In spite of the guilt that came crashing over her, so that she bowed her head on her hands and moaned aloud, that tiny spark of defiance would not be quite crushed out of existence.

"We could go by road, if you like," Ethan said, looking at her sandalled feet.

"What do you usually do?"

"Walk across the beach, and come home by the road. It'll be dark by then, but I've got a good torch."

"Let's do it that way," she said. "I can shake the sand out when we get there. I don't suppose Janice and Henry will mind."

"I'm sure they won't."

Dusk was falling as they gained the beach, and Celeste removed her sandals and went barefoot. Ethan was wearing an open-necked blue shirt and fawn slacks with matching slip-on shoes and no socks.

The sand was still warm and the water lapped quietly into foam-edged curves along the beach. Celeste stopped to admire the last of the fading sunset on the water, and Ethan, with his hands in his pockets, waited for her.

"Sorry," she said, as she went to his side. "It's so lovely here. This is very peaceful, isn't it?"

"Don't you miss the social life of Sydney?"

"We didn't have a very active social life, as a matter of fact. About the only times we went out were to university functions, and other things that Alec had to attend because of his work."

"Over here," he said, touching her arm and indicating the path to the Palmers' house.

He allowed her to go ahead of him when the path narrowed, and she climbed quickly, very conscious of him just behind her, now and then reaching across her shoulder to lift a wayward, trailing spray of purple bougainvillea or a curling tendril of trumpet vine out of her way.

When he caught her arm, she stiffened, holding her breath.

Ethan said, "Don't go so fast, there's plenty of time. You're panting."

She hadn't realised it. She nodded without looking at him and, when he released her, proceeded more slowly.

She was glad when they reached the house, a natural wood structure with a broad balcony around three sides. Henry leaned over the railing and called, "Come on up. Jeff's arrived and we're having drinks out here. Janice is doing things in the kitchen."

There was an outside staircase, and at the top, of course, a view of the bay. Henry poured drinks, and shortly afterwards Janice joined them. Celeste gradually relaxed. The Palmers went out of their way to make their guests feel comfortable, and she wished she could be a little more animated, but she had to mentally shake herself awake a couple of times. Still, she smiled and nodded in the right places, managed to carry on a conversation, and even laughed once or twice. She was, in a mild sort of way, enjoying herself.

The men volunteered to wash up after dinner, and at Ethan's urging, Janice took Celeste into her small studio to show her some of her paintings.

There were a few oils and bold acrylics, but most were watercolours. "I have one theme." Janice laughed. "This island. I love painting it."

Leaving the studio, they sat out on the balcony again, and the men joined them, Jeff drawing up a chair close to Celeste's. "What do you think of Janice's paintings?" he asked her.

"I like them. They're restful and yet interesting."

"Mm-hm. She's quite talented."

Henry called his attention with a question about some mutual acquaintance, and Celeste leaned her head against the chair back.

"Tired?" Jeff asked, turning to her again.

"Not really," she said guiltily, and made an effort to stir herself. She smiled at him and asked, "Do you know a lot of people on the island?"

"Most of the prominent ones and the old identities. I got to know them when I was researching for the book."

"Tell me about them," she invited, and managed to concentrate long enough to be genuinely entertained by some anecdotes that for one reason or another had not been included in his history of the island. "Some were too raunchy for general consumption," he said, grinning. "And some that dealt with people still living or who had a close living relative were plain slanderous. I had no wish to be involved in a libel suit. Besides, I wanted to live here, and if I'd printed everything the locals would probably have tarred and feathered me and thrown me into the sea."

"Surely not!" Celeste laughed.

"Oh, I don't know. It has happened here, you know. Though not too recently," he admitted. "There was a time when the respectable settlers were trying to get the upper hand over the beachcombers who populated the island in the earlier days, and they formed a sort of vigilante committee. One of my informants was a descendant of a bloke who allegedly 'stole the affections' of another man's wife. Which was regarded as a criminal offense, then. The committee tried him in a kangaroo court, tarred and feathered him and rolled him down the beach to the sea. It's all in the town records.''

''What happened to the wife?''

''I never discovered that. Her name wasn't mentioned, and now no one seems to know who she was. I guess her husband was responsible for seeing to her punishment.''

Celeste shivered. ''I wonder what he did to her.''

''It would depend on how much he loved her, wouldn't it? Of course, some men find unfaithfulness impossible to forgive.''

Celeste felt Ethan's eyes on her, and knew he had heard part of the conversation, even though he was talking with Janice and Henry. There was a hardness in the glance that flickered from her to Jeff and back again. She wrenched her gaze away from his as Henry stood and said, ''Anyone for another drink? I'm going to have a snifter of brandy.''

The two men accepted, but Celeste shook her head. She did feel tired now, and brandy would make her sleepier. Ethan went to help pour it, and when they returned he leaned on the rail with his, facing her and Jeff, and carried on a casual conversation until he said, ''Time we went home, I think. Are you ready, Celeste?''

''I should leave, too,'' Jeff said. ''I'll come with you.''

''We're planning to go along the road.''

''Why not take the beach route?'' Henry suggested. ''The moon's bright enough.''

"The beach is lovely in moonlight," Janice said to Celeste. She turned to her husband. "We could walk down with them and go for a swim."

"Fine," Henry agreed. "It's a warm night."

"I'll get some towels," Janice offered.

She came back with an armful of them, saying, "I've brought extras in case the rest of you would like to have a dip on the way home."

The beach was a canvas of milky white light and blue shadows. The water hissed and whispered along the sand, and the moon silvered its surface.

"Are you all coming in?" Henry asked as he slipped out of his loose shirt.

"I'm a starter," Jeff volunteered, and began stripping.

"Celeste is tired," Ethan said decisively. "I'm taking her home. Have a good time, you lot. Thanks for a very pleasant evening."

His hand fastened about her wrist as the others said good night, and he made for the cliff face and the path to his house, taking Celeste inexorably along.

He switched on the torch when they began the climb, releasing her as he let her go in front. Celeste was aware of a sluggish stirring of anger. He had been decidedly highhanded, dragging her away without giving her a chance to say what she wanted to do.

"Why didn't you want to swim?" she asked, over her shoulder.

"I didn't say *I* didn't want to."

"No, you implied that *I* didn't. Without consulting me."

"So," he said softly, "were you dying to take off your clothes in front of Jeff?"

She swung round, finding him looming close behind her. The light dazzled her, as he turned the torch upwards, and she blinked. He moved the beam to the ground, and she said, "That's a hateful thing to suggest! You know it's untrue!"

"Do I? How? After all, you've been throwing out lures to the poor guy all evening."

Shocked, she said, "You're crazy! I was being normally nice to him. And I've never thrown out lures to anyone!"

He made a small sound of disbelief. "Well, you've hooked Jeff. He can't take his eyes off you. Going nude swimming with you would have made his evening."

"You are being ridiculous," she said coldly. "It was hardly going to be a tête-à-tête, with Henry and Janice, and *you* along as well."

"Still, I'm sure Jeff would have enjoyed it. But maybe it wouldn't be a new experience. Have the two of you already been skinny-dipping on your own?"

"No, we have not! Jeff swims nude, as you very well know—you warned me yourself to expect it. I daresay you do, too. But I haven't . . . haven't tried it yet."

"Be my guest," he said, stepping aside on the narrow path. "Do you want to go back?"

"No, I don't." She wasn't going to tell him that she had been relieved at his taking the decision from her, until indignation got the upper hand. Not because she had qualms about undressing in front of Jeff and the Palmers, but because the idea of Ethan seeing her without her clothes had aroused a flood of confusing emotions. "I just think you might have asked me how I felt, that's all," she finished, and turned to go uphill again.

"Don't go too fast," Ethan's voice said behind her. "Take your time."

She didn't answer, but slowed her pace slightly. Something—a large moth, perhaps—flew out of the trees and brushed her hair. She lifted a hand to flick it away, backing instinctively, and coming up hard against the firm bulk of Ethan's body. They were both off balance, and she felt him clamp a hand on her shoulder. The torch fell to the ground and went out as it rolled away into the bushes.

"I'm sorry!" she gasped, and heard him swear in her ear.

Then he said, "Are you all right?"

"Yes, I was just startled. Is the torch broken?"

"I don't know," he said, releasing her and groping around. "I can't find the damned thing." She tried to help, but the trees were thick here and the bright moon could barely penetrate the darkness.

He said, "It's no use, we'll go on without it. Give me your hand, I'll guide you."

He knew the path well, of course, and she obeyed, placing her fingers in his while he led her the rest of the way. Near the top, she stumbled over a protruding root, and he turned, catching her with one arm about her waist, her hand still held in his. For a moment she allowed herself to rest against him, experiencing such a feeling of warmth and safety that she was loth to leave the haven of his arms. She felt the swift rise and fall of his chest as he took a deep, unsteady breath, and she made to move away. But his arm had tightened, and she raised her head to try and read his face, finding it shadowed, although the moon was bright again behind him. Her lips parted, and she whispered his name. He muttered something that sounded like, "Damn you, Celeste!" And then his mouth was on hers, crushing its softness.

Her heart gave one hard thump, and then she felt as though all feeling was suspended, except the pure physical shock of pleasure that Ethan's kiss produced in her. Her mouth opened involuntarily under his demands, and he raised both hands to her head, tipping it backwards and holding it there while he explored and tasted and probed

until she was dizzy, clinging to him as though her life de-
pended on his touch.

His hands swept down again to her waist and he held her
to him, still with his mouth on hers, her body arching within
his arms and her thighs enclosed by his. She shuddered
against him and made a little moaning sound, and he suddenly tore his mouth from hers, then grasped her shoulders
and shoved her away from him.

They were both breathing fast, and Celeste raised a shaking hand to her mouth, which felt hot and bruised.

Ethan said, ''Well, we've found a way of waking you up,
haven't we?''

''What?'' She felt confused, disoriented, and an icy shiver
ran down her spine, because his voice was hostile, cold and
contemptuous. ''What do you mean?'' she whispered.

He lifted his hand, too, deliberately wiping the back of it
across his lips as though to erase the taste of hers. ''You've
been some kind of zombie ever since you arrived here,'' he
said. ''But there was nothing zombie-like about your reaction just now. I must say, Celeste, you've lost none of your
skill. That was quite something, for such a recent widow.''

''Ethan, don't!''

''Don't what? Remind you? Perhaps I'm reminding myself. Alec was my brother, after all. If you make me sick to
my stomach, it's only half of what I feel for myself, believe
me. I swore I'd not let you get to me again.'' He gave an
angry laugh. ''All it takes is a few drinks and a moonlit
night, and a melting look from a pair of lying eyes.''

''That's not fair!''

He made an impatient, chopping motion in the air.
''Okay! Leave it. There's no point in going over old territory. Let's say we both got a bit carried away. Come on.'' He
moved forward and caught her arm, pushing her the few

steps to the top, then let her go immediately, pacing silently at her side until they reached the house.

Celeste looked at his face as he switched on the light, and found it a dark, closed mask, but as he turned his eyes on her, she felt her anger and hurt dissolve in a tug of compassion. "Don't be so hard on yourself, Ethan," she said softly. "You've nothing to be ashamed of."

His eyes narrowed on her. "Unfortunately, I don't share your hedonistic view of life," he said.

With a flash of spirit, she said, "That's a poisonous accusation! You're wilfully misunderstanding me."

"Am I? Do me a favour and get out of my sight, Celeste, before I do something that one of us, at least, may live to regret."

Chapter Seven

Surprisingly, Celeste slept well, and woke late. When she walked into the living room Ethan was sitting at the table outside with Henry Palmer. Stepping onto the terrace, she was glad that after last night she did not have to face Ethan alone.

Both men turned at her approach, breaking off their low-voiced conversation, and she had the distinct impression that she had been the subject of their discussion.

Ethan got up. "Good morning. I was just going to make a cup of coffee. Want some?"

"Thank you." She didn't quite look at him as she took the chair that Henry pulled out for her.

"I'll bring you some fruit and toast, too," Ethan offered.

She said "Don't bother," to his retreating back, but Henry smiled at her and said, "You could probably do with it. How are you this morning?"

A little defensively she answered, "Fine, thank you. How was your swim?"

"You should have joined us," he told her. "Or are you shy?"

"Ethan thought I was tired."

He was still smiling, but rather pensively. "Ethan's anxious about you. You're finding that rather smothering, perhaps."

"He's not my keeper," Celeste said shortly. "Has he been asking you for advice?"

Henry looked rueful. "Do you resent the idea?"

"I don't think I'm in need of medical attention."

"I won't force it on you."

"Does that mean you do think so?"

"Not necessarily. But you did seem somewhat removed from things last night. It was an effort for you to relate to what was going on about you, wasn't it?"

Celeste bit her lip. "I'm sorry if I was rude."

"You weren't in the least rude. And the effort was largely successful. I was probably the only one who noticed. Ethan said you were more lively than usual."

She glanced up at him, wondering if Ethan had suggested to Henry that she had been flirting with Jeff last night. There was nothing in the older man's face but a kind of detached concern that she supposed was part of his professional bedside manner.

Henry said, "Sleep all right?"

"Like a log," she replied. It was true of last night, anyway, and with luck that heralded a new trend. "I've only just got up," she pointed out.

"Ethan says you're a late riser these days. Some people lie awake half the night and then sleep in. It often doesn't help much."

Celeste looked away from him, down towards the sea, and he said easily, "Well, if you have any problems, or want to talk, you know where to find me."

He was being nice, and it was unfair to be annoyed about it simply because she was sure Ethan had put him up to this. "Thank you," she said. "I'll remember."

Ethan came back with coffee and a breakfast for Celeste on a tray. While she ate it, the two men talked on general subjects, and she took scant part. When Henry left, she gathered up the plates and said, "I'll take care of these. I expect you want to work."

"It's Sunday. And I've finished the project I was on. I thought I'd have a day off."

He hadn't had a day off since they arrived. "I'm sure you're entitled," she said.

"Like to drive around the island?" he asked her. "If we go really slowly and have lunch along the way, we could make it last all day."

So they were to pretend last night had never happened, she thought. She stood with her head bowed. "All right," she said.

"Bring your swimsuit. There are beaches everywhere."

She put on a pale green cotton blouse and khaki shorts, and rolled her swimsuit into a towel, which she pushed into a canvas hold-all with a comb and a sweatshirt.

When she joined Ethan, he said, "Do you have a hat?"

Celeste shook her head.

He disappeared into the passage between the kitchen and laundry, and came back with a soft-brimmed, army-style khaki hat in his hand. "Try this. It shrank when I washed it, so it might fit."

It did, reasonably well, and he said, "It may not be glamorous, but it'll keep the sun off. Have you been wandering around the beach all this time without one?"

"I keep in the shade a lot," she said. "I don't lie about in the sun for hours. My skin won't stand it." She had a slight tan, but it was acquired very carefully, for her skin was naturally fair.

He drove first to the highest point on the island, a two-humped hill. "Known locally as The Camel," Ethan told her. From a viewing place at the top, they could see almost the whole circumference of the island, with the capital sprawling up a gentle slope from the sea, and several smaller villages along the coast. Tourists and local families on day trips stood pointing out landmarks to one another and taking photographs.

Winding down to the coast on a road lined with lush trees and waving grasses, Ethan slowly followed the highway until it passed near a sandy beach. A few shops huddled at the other side of the road, and there were perhaps fifty people lying on the sand or swimming in the breakers.

"Want to stop?" Ethan asked.

"Not especially." The beach was evidently a popular one, but there were no trees here, just an expanse of sand and sea, and it was getting close to midday.

"There's a prettier beach farther on," he told her. "But we'd have to park the car and walk to it."

"Sounds good," she said.

"We could buy something to eat, and picnic there, or eat later when we get to the capital."

"Whatever you like."

He glanced at her sharply and drew up by one of the shops. "Are you hungry?"

Celeste shook her head. "I had a late breakfast," she reminded him. "But I'll go along with whatever you want."

His mouth curved sardonically, but he said only, "I can wait. The food will be better in Conneston."

He drove on and eventually parked at the roadside in the shade of some trees.

"From here we go on foot," he said. "Bring your hat and your swimsuit."

He carried the hold-all, although she insisted it wasn't heavy, and led her to a narrow path through the trees that soon went downhill, passing a pretty waterfall overhung with ferns. The beach was invisible until they reached the white, glistening sand, and Celeste gave an exclamation of pleasure. The little cove was surrounded by thickly growing ferns, paper mulberries and banana palms, and other trees that she didn't know the names of, all mingled in unlikely harmony. Not far out from the shore lay a conical islet crowned with low-growing trees and bushes.

"Pretty, isn't it?" Ethan said casually.

"It's lovely." The water was crystal clear, and tiny coloured pebbles and shells were visible on the gently sloping sea floor. At the end of a rock shelf extending into the sea a couple of people stood with fishing rods, but there seemed to be no one else about.

"The locals keep fairly quiet about this," Ethan said. "It's a place to get away from the tourists when the season's at its height. They say there's good fishing off the rocks there, but I've never tried it."

"Jeff said you and he go fishing in a boat."

"Sometimes."

Mentioning Jeff had apparently been a mistake. Ethan's face assumed a remote, rigid look. She looked at the rocks again and saw a gleaming, twisting object being hauled from the water on one of the lines. "I think they've caught something," she said.

"Shall we go and see?" he suggested. "Put the hat on." He hauled it out of the bag and she adjusted it on her head.

She had braided her hair in a single plait, and Ethan suddenly grinned and said, "You look about fourteen."

Without thinking, she grimaced at him. Turning her back, she stalked along the sand, taking an oblique path to the water.

Ethan laughed, and she felt a sharp little slap on her bottom as he caught up. Celeste jumped, cast him an indignant glare and ran to the water, stopping to scoop up a handful accurately in his direction, splattering his jeans. He came after her, but she was racing along the sand, laughing. When her hat flew off, she didn't pause but just kept running. Ethan stopped to retrieve it and she was almost at the rocks when he grabbed at her flying plait to bring her to a halt.

"Ouch!" she cried, although he wasn't really hurting.

"Okay, Atalanta," he said. "This is where you get your comeuppance."

Panting, she looked up into his laughing eyes, and saw the laughter change to something else. Her lips parted, and she heard him suck in his breath before he abruptly released her. The next moment he had clamped the hat down on her head, pulling it forward over her eyes. When she lifted it, he had moved back two paces. She felt a pang of regret, mingled with relief. "Anyway," she said quickly, "you've got the story wrong. Atalanta was the one who stepped aside from the race to pick up the golden apples that Milanion dropped for her, so she had to marry him, as she'd promised to marry the first man to beat her in a race."

"So Milanion won by appealing to Atalanta's acquisitiveness," Ethan said, beginning to climb the rocks.

"By cheating. He knew he couldn't beat her fair and square."

"I'd say by strategy. He must have studied her character and guessed what it would take to outwit her. You're well up in your classical mythology,'' he said, watching her as she picked her way between the little clear pools crowded with tiny starfish, waving anemones and slow-moving hermit crabs.

"I used to have a book of Greek and Roman mythology that I read over and over. It was my favourite.''

He held out a hand as her foot slipped and she faltered, but she ignored it, regaining her balance unaided.

The two who were fishing were a man and a woman in their thirties. They had a basket with half a dozen good-sized fish, and as they exchanged a friendly hello with Ethan and Celeste, the woman got another bite and was soon reeling in a large, fighting fish.

Watching it gasp for breath, bleeding from the hook, Celeste turned away. When she looked back again the fish was dead, and the lovely pale rainbow colours of its scales had become dull and lifeless. Going back to the beach, with the sea just as blue and the sun just as warm, she was silent, and the grey blanket of depression that had lifted for a time muffled her again with its deadening weight.

"Want to swim?'' Ethan asked her as they regained the soft sand.

Celeste shrugged, wondering if the effort of getting into her swimsuit was worth it. "I don't know. You go in if you like.''

He frowned. "What's the matter?''

"Nothing.'' She looked down at the sand. It was stupid to be upset by the death of a fish. She wasn't going to admit that it had made her feel squeamish.

"I don't want to go swimming alone,'' Ethan said. "If you don't feel like it, we'll skip the idea.''

"No. I'll . . . I'll come.'' She tried to shake off the sudden gloom. If she didn't give in to it, perhaps it would go away.

She changed behind some trees, and when she emerged he was waiting for her. In the distance the fishing couple appeared to be packing up their gear. Evidently they had caught enough for one day. She dropped her towel on the sand and walked towards the waves. Ethan fell into step beside her. There was the first shock of cold, but after a minute or so the water felt deliciously warm. Swimming away from Ethan, she took a course parallel with the shore, while he went on into deeper water.

The other couple gave a friendly wave as they came down from the rocks and made for the path, each with an arm about the other's waist. Celeste waved back, then turned over and floated, staring up at the intense blue of the sky.

Ethan's voice startled her, sounding close by. "Feel like swimming to the island?"

She studied it, thinking. It wasn't far, and it appeared both friendly and mysterious. "Okay," she said, and turned over, keeping pace with him.

There was no sand, but a handy rock shelf allowed them to clamber ashore, Ethan hauling her after him with strong hands. Others had been here before them, making a faint path through the low-growing bushes and small trees that grew on what she would have thought was bare rock.

"Game?" Ethan asked her, indicating the path, and she nodded. It seemed like a long way up, but she was not going to give in. Once she would have revelled in the idea. If she just made the effort, surely she would be able to enjoy life as she used to.

At the top, she ignored a slight dizziness that seized her, and sank down on her haunches, as though merely wanting to contemplate the view. After a few minutes her breathing steadied and she felt a lot better. From here they could see speckled shells on the seabed below, red seaweed and some darting fish.

Ethan sat nearby, his forearm resting on a raised knee, his tanned skin gleaming with saltwater. After a while he said, "Ready to go back?"

He was already on his feet, and she said "Sure," and followed him down the path again.

He dived, and she followed, but before they were halfway to the shore she was tired, and when he looked round he must have seen the strain on her face. He trod water, waiting for her to catch up, and then said, "Turn on your back and I'll tow you in."

"No." She kept swimming. "I can make it."

She did, but felt wrung out as she walked slowly out of the water. The trees seemed to sway, and the sun's heat made wavery lines along the sand. She gritted her teeth and was glad when Ethan's hand clamped on her arm, holding her until she reached her towel and slumped down on it, making an effort to breathe normally.

Ethan knelt beside her. "You little fool!" he said roughly. "Why didn't you say it was too much for you?"

"It shouldn't have been," she said. "I used to be able to swim that distance easily."

"I know," he said.

"I'm out of practice, I guess." That was true. Alec had been a strong swimmer before his accident; afterwards he was self-conscious about being seen at the beach, and his damaged legs had tired quickly. They had not swum often.

Ethan said, "You could have let me help you over the last part."

"I wanted . . . to do it on my own."

"What are you trying to prove, Celeste?"

"I'm not trying to prove anything. I don't need your help."

He turned away and picked up his own towel, standing to rub himself dry.

"I suppose that seems ungracious," Celeste said.

His eyes looked as hard as glass. "It just doesn't seem very sensible," he said. "Nothing is more obvious at the moment than the fact that you do need help from someone. Why not me?"

She sat up. "You're not qualified."

He stopped what he was doing, holding the towel in his hands. "Henry is."

"I'm not ill."

Ethan came down beside her again and grasped her shoulders. "You're certainly not up to par. When I first met you, that swim would have been a pushover for you. You could have done it twice over and then raced me to the end of the beach and back."

"I told you, I'm out of practice."

"I'll buy you a decent lunch," he said. As she made to get up, he added, "No hurry."

"I'm all right now." She was always saying that to him. She went to get her clothes on, and combed out her damp hair after removing it from its plait.

He made her go slowly on the walk back, and insisted on a five-minute rest halfway to the road. When they got into the car he seemed rather preoccupied, and they didn't talk much until he drew up into a parking bay on a low promontory overlooking the sea. "See those rocks out there?" He pointed to a series of dark shadows in the water. "That's where the *Sheerwind* ran aground. The plaque set into the stone on the shore here commemorates the wreck."

They got out and read the words on the plaque starkly telling the tale of the ship on its way to Botany Bay with a cargo of stores and a detachment of soldiers for the New South Wales Corps, with some of their families. The ship had been caught in a storm and thrown ashore with the loss of over a hundred lives. There was a picture etched in the

bronze showing the storm-tossed vessel with sailors clinging to the rigging, and women and children being helped
into a lifeboat.

"Down there—" Ethan pointed to a patch of ground near
the beach on which stood a small monument "—is where
some of those washed ashore were buried by the survivors.
The individual graves can't be identified anymore, but the
names of those known to have been drowned or who were
never found after the wreck have been recorded on the
monument."

Celeste shivered, and he said, "It's a local landmark, and
an obligatory stop for visitors. But perhaps I shouldn't have
brought you here. Had enough?"

"Yes." She turned with alacrity back to the car.

When they reached the outskirts of the capital they had
lunch at a restaurant decorated with fishing nets and glass
floats and seashells. Casual dress was accepted but the food
was superb.

"Their seafood is particularly good," Ethan promised
her. "I recommend the shrimp salad."

Salad sounded fine, she thought, but she was unable to
finish the generous helping presented by the chef. Ethan
frowned at her half-empty plate and offered her dessert,
which she declined, shaking her head.

"A cheeseboard," he instructed the waiter, and with his
eyes on her she helped herself to a cracker and a slice of
Gruyère, but refused any more.

"Feel up to a stroll on the waterfront?" Ethan asked her
after they had drunk their coffee.

Celeste nodded. A stone wall had been built along the
waterline, and fishing boats and pleasure craft were tied to
it. A man was selling fresh-caught fish from one of the
boats, and Ethan looked at Celeste inquiringly.

"Not for me, please," she said hastily, and he laughed. "You had shrimps for lunch," he said. "What's the difference?"

None, of course, but she said, "I don't feel like fish. You have some if you like."

"Will you cook it for me?" he asked.

Celeste paled a little. "You're a good cook. You could fix it yourself."

He shook his head. "I'll pass, today," he said kindly.

He was being so nice she couldn't help wondering if he was lulling her into a false sense of security. He drove home, taking the time to point out other landmarks, such as the overgrown ruined stone walls of a small cottage on a hillside sloping up from the road.

"That belonged to Tattie Connors, the third mate who set himself up as 'king of the island' after the wreck, but was deposed and murdered by a cabal of soldiers and sailors—though not before he'd fathered a child on one of of the women. Connors is still a name to be reckoned with on Sheerwind. The present chairman of the island council is a direct descendant."

"It's a pity the cottage hasn't been preserved," Celeste said.

"You've read Jeff's book," he said. "Tattie haunts the place. No islander would touch the stones."

According to local legend, Jeff had written, people who had dared at various times to cart off stones for building other dwellings had died shortly afterwards, one by drowning, one in a drunken fight, and two more from apparently natural causes. And one man had been found mysteriously dead among the ruins after apparently deciding to sleep off the results of an alcoholic binge within its decaying walls. The prosaic explanation was that he died of excessive drink combined with exposure, but the legend had obviously gained strength from the incident.

"Do you believe in ghosts?" Celeste asked.

"I believe the influence people have over others lives after them," Ethan said. "And by all accounts Tattie was a fairly baneful character."

A car swept past them going in the opposite direction, and as Ethan waved, he said, "There's Henry and Janice. He told me Janice likes you, by the way." He cast her a sideways glance.

She said, trying to sound light, "Do I detect a note of surprise?"

After a moment he said, "Perhaps. I wouldn't have thought you two had much in common."

"People don't always have to have much in common to establish a relationship."

"The attraction of opposites?" he said, and added softly, "Is that what it was between you and Alec?"

Her palms went instantly damp. Here was the suddenly unsheathed rapier, the unexpected thrust at the heart. She touched her tongue to her lips.

It was a perfectly innocent question, she told herself, the kind of casual remark anyone might make who knew both her and Alec. Treat it as such. "I don't think we were so opposite in our interests," she said. "I was an anthropology student, remember."

"You were supposed to major in history, weren't you?"

"Yes," she agreed cautiously, "but I was interested in anthropology."

"You told Alec once that you took the courses with the best-looking professors."

Celeste turned her head to stare. "It was a joke!" she said. She vaguely remembered making the remark. It was soon after they became engaged, and for some reason that day Alec had been feeling particularly depressed about his disability. "You're not only the best teacher of your subject," she had assured him, "as the university very well knows, but you're the most handsome professor as well." And when he said rather sourly, "Is that why you signed on for my course?" she had laughed and answered, hoping to cheer him up by some gentle teasing, "Of course! I always took the courses with the best-looking professors!"

Ethan said, "He was seventeen years older than you."

"Yes." The significance of the age gap should have diminished with the years, but she had never felt it was happening. Despite her best efforts. Alec had often reminded her of it. He had, for a couple of years, seemed to take a delight in introducing her as "my child-bride." She had eventually figured out that he felt defensive about the difference in their ages, as he did about so many things, and it was his way of defying the criticism that he imagined might be directed at them. When she had said that it was nobody's business but theirs, and anyway at twenty, an age she had achieved just days before their wedding, she was hardly a child, he had replied, "You are to me. And most of my colleagues think I'm a cradle-snatcher. Don't worry, my dear. They're all green with envy."

In a moment of insight she had realised then that having his colleagues "green with envy" was exactly what he hoped to achieve one way or another. It revealed the first crack in the pedestal on which she had put him. But she had told herself that he was entitled to have human failings like everyone else. If he'd become oversensitive since losing so much of what was important to him in life, and was not above taking a petty satisfaction in scoring points off others, it didn't make him less of a man.

It was a long time before she recognised that, although he possessed all the determination and physical courage of the genuine hero, the man she had married was using her to boost his own ego, yet at the same time subtly but surely eroding her own sense of self. Increasingly she found herself trapped in an uncomfortable double bind from which there seemed to be no escape.

Alec, she was sure, had never been fully conscious of what he was doing, or how destructive to her personality and their marriage his behaviour was. He had never lost his temper, never said an ostensibly cross word. The progress of his undermining of her confidence and her happiness was so insidious that she couldn't put a finger on when it began, or how. At first she had been ecstatically happy. She had never made love with anyone but Alec, and she found in him a perfectly satisfactory lover. He had taken care to bring her pleasure, and would repeatedly ask her to tell him how much she enjoyed their lovemaking. It was only later that she came to suspect that his anxiety was because he wanted to be assured that his wounded legs had not affected his virility, rather than a concern for her well-being.

And at first he had seemed to like her preference for eye-catching clothes. She had dressed for him, but naturally enough she received compliments from others. Accepting them innocently, as they were meant, she was sure, she had been disturbed when she noticed that Alec had ceased enjoying the gaiety and adventurousness of her style of dress, and instead regarded it as a form of showing off. He didn't criticise openly, but his comments, delivered in a tone of amused tolerance, were humiliating. That was when she had deliberately started toning down the colours, the styles, until in the end she had a wardrobe full of unexciting, neutral-coloured clothes that did nothing for her naturally pale complexion, nor for her mood, and that would not draw a second glance from anyone.

Yet still she continued to attract second glances. She didn't think that as a child she had been particularly pretty, and when she had shot up in height at the age of eleven, towering over most of her classmates including the boys, she had thought she was going to turn into some kind of freak. At thirteen she had seriously decided that she would dye her hair black, and had a passionate wish to be dark and petite with flashing brown eyes. But at sixteen she had looked in the mirror one day and realised that she was lucky in her appearance. She wasn't the most beautiful girl in the world, but neither did she have anything to worry about in that department. Her figure lent itself to dressing up, and she had a clear complexion, nice eyes, a brilliant smile. She made friends easily, and in high school she was popular and had a good time. Mostly she went out with a crowd rather than on one-to-one dates. Intending to go to university, she didn't want emotional ties and had never thought of contracting an early marriage. So she steered clear of serious relationships. Vaguely she envisaged a career in some form of research, perhaps for television. She pursued her own interests at university, working towards a history degree. Until the day she found Alec Ryland swearing on the stairs, and persuaded herself that what she felt for this man whom for months she had admired from afar was love—love everlasting.

Chapter Eight

Love everlasting. Now she doubted if there was such a thing. Certainly at nineteen she had not had any doubts on the subject. When she had found herself pursued by the famous, clever and handsome Alec Ryland, it had been easy to convince herself that this was the real thing.

She wondered if her mother had been similarly dazzled by Alec's charisma. He had a forceful personality, only enhanced by the accident and by the drive he had exerted to overcome its results. At first Mrs. Gray had expressed doubt, but on meeting Alec for herself, her objections seemed to melt away. He did look younger than thirty-seven, it spite of the pain he had mastered, and he had persuaded the older woman that her daughter was in safe hands.

Anyway, opposition would not have made any real difference. Celeste had been dazzled by Alec—his name, his fame, his interest in a pretty but unremarkable student—and nothing would have stopped her from marrying him. Unless, a voice whispered—unless, perhaps, she had met Ethan before the wedding . . .

Stifling that thought, she sighed.

Ethan said, "Tired? We're nearly home."

Home. Only, of course it wasn't home for her. And never would be. She was a visitor, someone Ethan had taken in because he felt a responsibility for her, and perhaps compassion, and because, he had hinted, he wanted something from her. He wasn't satisfied with the facts of his stepbrother's death. He wanted answers, answers that he believed Celeste could provide.

Drawing up in the garage, he leaned over and opened her door for her.

"Thank you," she said. "It's been a very pleasant day."

"For me, too," he said formally. "Celeste . . ." As she moved back, he caught her chin in his hand, scrutinising her face. She tried to look back at him calmly, tried to ignore the quickening of her pulse. "Yes?" she said.

"Never mind." He let her go abruptly and opened his door.

They made sandwiches together in the kitchen and sat outside to eat them in the gathering dusk. Celeste felt pleasantly tired and rather tousled, and when she yawned behind her hand, Ethan said, "Have I worn you out?"

"I don't mind. But I think I'll have an early night."

He didn't say that she seldom did otherwise. Last night they had been late, and that was sufficient excuse.

"Are you going into town today?" she asked him the next morning.

"Not unless you want to. Something you need?"

"Nothing urgent." She wanted shampoo and hand cream, but it could wait. "I thought you'd need to post your finished programme."

"I've installed a modem for that."

"A what?"

"I send it through the computer via a telephone link. Much faster than mailing it."

"I see."

"You've never been in my workroom," he said. "Want to have a look?"

"I'd like that." She had tapped on the door once or twice, telling him there was a meal ready if he wanted it, but had not dared to open it. Even Mrs. Jackson was only allowed in to clean the room and had strict instructions, she had told Celeste, that nothing was to be moved.

"Be my guest," Ethan invited, and led her up the stairs.

It was a large room, and there were two desks in it, each holding a computer.

"If one breaks down," he explained, "it could be days before I can get it fixed, even weeks. That's a drawback of being so far from the mainland."

"It looks very efficient." She surveyed the banks of file drawers and shelves of computer manuals and other technical books. But there was a couch with its back to the room in front of the big window, old and comfortable and sagging.

Ethan explained with a slight grin, "When I'm stuck for inspiration I stretch out and admire the view until my brain gets back into working order."

"Jeff said that what you do is creative."

"I like to think so."

"Have you . . . have you looked at the disks that were in Alec's car?"

"Started to. I think I can recover most of what's on them. I'd say they weren't quite as badly damaged as they might have been. The briefcase kept out most of the water."

"Steven will be pleased."

"I hope he'll do justice to Alec's work."

"I'm sure he will. Steven had a great deal of respect for Alec."

"He's also a very ambitious young man. I'll be printing out all those notes before I give the disks to him."

"I don't understand."

"I want to be sure that my brother gets all the credit that's due him."

Celeste said, "I don't think that Steven would steal any credit. You don't know him."

"I asked you once before," Ethan said softly, "how well you know him."

Her head came up, and she looked fully and unwaveringly into his eyes for once. Steadily, she said, "I think I told you it was none of your business."

"Something like that," he agreed.

"Nothing's changed," she said, and walked out of the room.

A few days later, on the beach, Celeste met Henry Palmer mooching about with a stick. His face brightened when he saw her, and he came towards her. "Janice is in the throes of creation," he said. "I'm at a bit of a loose end. How about coming into town with me? It's her birthday next week, and I'd value your advice on a present."

"I'd like that," she said. "I haven't seen much of the shops in Conneston."

"Ethan too busy to take you to town?"

"I've been with him a couple of times to buy supplies and collect the mail, but I haven't really needed to shop much, and he's been working on a project that has a deadline."

"Do you drive, yourself?"

"I have a licence, but I wouldn't care to drive Ethan's car." She was a good driver, but it was one of the things that Alec had wanted to do for himself. As soon as he could he had purchased a specially adapted car, and when they were together he would always drive.

She left a note for Ethan and sat beside Henry in the car, enjoying the view while he drove quite slowly into the town. There were a number of gift shops selling souvenirs and local crafts of varying quality, and after a pleasant hour's browsing and discussion, they settled on a plain wooden bowl fashioned of polished island mangrove with a lovely grain.

In the same shop were hand-painted and tie-dyed silk blouses and scarves and even a few dresses made by a local woman. Attracted by a scoop-necked, sleeveless dress with a swirling pattern in greens and blues with a hint of lavender, Celeste picked up the full skirt and spread it to examine the colours that flowed into one another like the changing colours of the sea.

"Very nice," Henry commented. "Try it on."

Celeste smiled, shaking her head.

"Why not? It would suit you," he told her.

"Oh, I just bought a dress."

"So buy another. I'd like to see you in it. Try it on. To humour an old man."

Celeste laughed. "Is this how you go on when you're shopping with Janice?"

"Depends," he said. "I'm afraid I couldn't persuade her to get into that. This, now—" he picked up a long scarf with colours ranging from strong pink through deep red and purple to black "—I can see her wearing it."

"So can I," Celeste agreed. "Yes, it would suit her."

"I'll have it," Henry decided grandly. "If you try on the dress."

Celeste gave in and the proprietor ushered her into a curtained alcove. The dress was a perfect fit, and she had to admit it did things for her. The silk was light and soft against her skin, and the full circular skirt floated deliciously about her knees.

"Don't forget I want to see," Henry called to her, and she pulled aside the curtain and stepped out in front of him.

"You remind me of a mermaid," he said simply. "Straight out of a fairy tale."

Celeste laughed, shaking her head.

"I want to buy it for you," he said. "A thank you for helping to choose Janice's presents."

"Certainly not!"

He chuckled. "I'm old enough for it not to be compromising, wouldn't you say?"

"I wouldn't dream of accepting it," she said. "I can buy it for myself, if I want it." She turned to the mirror again. It did look beautiful on her. She couldn't help coveting it.

"Go on," Henry urged. "It might be made for you, and you know it."

In the end, she succumbed, telling the salesperson she would wear the dress and asking for her skirt and blouse to be wrapped for her. And in a fit of recklessness, encouraged by Henry, she bought a pair of high-heeled pale green leather sandals to go with it, and a coral pink lipstick.

As they were returning to the car, Henry spied a wide-brimmed finely woven bleached palm-leaf hat, with a gauzy scarf tied around the base of the crown, and said, "Now, that's just the thing to finish off that dress."

"Oh, no!" she said firmly.

"I insist," he told her, and marched her into the shop. She was still protesting when he paid for the hat after she had laughingly tried it on, and marched her out again. "I want to show my appreciation somehow," he said.

"I don't think you needed my help at all," she said, as he opened the car door for her. "You seem to be one of those rare males who actually enjoy shopping."

"Guilty." He smiled at her. "But it's more fun with company."

He left her at the end of the driveway, and she walked down to the house feeling happier than she had for a long time. A slight smile curving her lips, she went through to the living room and stopped in the doorway as Ethan turned from the window, his hands in the pockets of his slacks.

She couldn't see his face properly against the light, but something about the way he stood silently watching her was vaguely disquieting. She raised a hand and removed the hat, automatically shaking out her hair. Ethan's hands came rather quickly out of his pockets, and he said, "Enjoyed yourself?"

"Yes, I did. You got my note?"

"I got it. You look very glamorous."

"Thank you." But the way he said it, the remark hadn't sounded much like a compliment.

"Henry rates the full treatment, does he?"

"What are you talking about?"

"You've never dressed up like that when you've gone into town with me."

"I didn't with Henry, either. We found these in Connes-ton."

"We? These?"

"The dress, the shoes and the hat. Henry talked me into them. He wanted to repay me for helping him choose Janice a present. Of course I—"

"He *bought* them for you?"

About to deny it, she felt a wave of anger. There was no mistaking his disapproval. It was nothing to do with him, anyway, even if Henry had bought her a whole wardrobe. Seized by a sudden imp of perversity, she said innocently, "Why not?" and, dropping the printed paper bag holding her discarded clothes, advanced into the room, the romantic hat in one hand, her walk deliberately provocative, the silk whispering against her legs. When she reached the middle of the mat, she twirled in front of him like a model, sending a teasing glance over her shoulder as the skirt flared, before she faced him again, spreading her hands. "Don't you like it?"

Her heart gave a lurch of fright as he took a step towards her. "What the hell are you playing at?" he demanded.

"What the hell do you think?" she shot back. "You're not my keeper, Ethan. If I want to accept gifts from Henry or any other man, that's between him and me. You have no right to question me about it."

"You're incredible," he said. "I could have sworn that Henry, of all men, wouldn't—"

"Of course Henry *wouldn't*! What do you take him for? What do you take *me* for, for heaven's sake?"

"I don't know," he said. "I'm still trying to figure that out."

"I bought the dress myself," she said wearily. "Henry did offer, and I let him buy the hat when he insisted. An appreciation, he said, for helping him choose a present for his wife—whom he loves dearly, as I'm sure you're aware. So work that out, why don't you? I'm going upstairs to change."

* * *

On Janice's birthday they were invited to join the Palmers for a barbecue on the beach. Jeff was there, too, of course, and a half dozen other people whom Celeste didn't know. She found herself nervous of meeting them, and had to make an effort to appear at ease.

Some of the guests were swimming, but even Jeff wore a pair of briefs in psychedelic colours, which earned him some teasing from the others. He accepted it with good humour, flopping down beside Celeste after leaving the water, and saying to her, "Don't listen to them, Celeste. They're just jealous."

From the other side of the fire built in a ring of stones, where Henry was expertly grilling steaks, Ethan looked over at Celeste and Jeff, his gaze skimming from one to the other. Then he returned his attention to his conversation with a pert young dark-haired woman who had made a beeline for him and seemed resolved not to be prised from his side. She was the daughter of a couple who were introduced as old friends of the Palmers, and apparently she had just completed her first year at university. A miniscule bikini showed off her luscious youthful figure enhanced by a smooth, even tan. Earlier she had initiated an energetic game of beach cricket and, watching her scampering along the sand, even Henry had been unable to hide an appreciative twinkle in his eye.

Jeff chuckled in Celeste's ear. "I see our Marietta is making a dead set at Ethan. A very determined young lady, that."

"He doesn't look as though he minds, exactly," Celeste said, as she watched Ethan throw back his head and laugh at something the girl said.

"Can't say I blame him," Jeff admitted, grinning. "But she is a bit young for him."

She was, Celeste thought, far too young, but as the thought entered her head, she said, "I was probably about her age when I met my husband."

Jeff grimaced ruefully. "Put my foot in it, have I?"

"Oh, no! I didn't mean to embarrass you," she said, and briefly touched his hand.

She found Ethan's eyes on her across the fire, but he quickly turned to Marietta, who had leaped to her feet and was trying to pull him up. Smiling, he got up and they ran hand in hand to the water. It was almost dark, and by the time they returned to the circle of firelight, night had fallen completely.

"You two nearly missed the grub," Henry told them, piling a couple of plates with steak, sausages and baked yam. "Here, help yourselves to salad." He pointed out a couple of large wooden bowls.

"You haven't eaten much," Jeff said to Celeste.

"I've had plenty." As Marietta and Ethan sat down, Janice handed the bowls round again, and Celeste shook her head. "No thanks. They are delicious salads, though."

"How about my steak?" Henry asked plaintively, and she smiled at him.

"Wonderful."

"Fruit, then?" Janice offered, presenting a basket full of bananas, pineapple and pawpaws.

Celeste took a banana, and Janice, after passing the basket to another guest, sat down beside her. "Marietta's turning into a little minx," she said, watching the girl as she leaned against Ethan's shoulder while tucking into her meal. "I've known her since she was five. She was always a cute little thing, but she's really blossomed now."

Another woman leaned over and said to Celeste, half-humorously, "Frankly, my dear, if he were *my* husband, I'd have scratched her eyes out by now. I don't know why you stand for it.''

Celeste said hastily, "Ethan isn't my husband.''

"Oh! I'm sorry. I thought you were introduced as Mrs. Ryland.''

"They are related,'' Janice explained. "Celeste is staying with him for a while. Her husband died recently.''

The other guest was so embarrassed by the gaffe, in spite of Celeste's assurances of nonoffence, that when Jeff suggested a swim, Celeste got to her feet with alacrity, allowing him to help her up.

As they walked down to the water she said, "Thanks for rescuing me.''

"She did rather overdo the apologies, didn't she? I suppose it was a natural assumption.''

"Yes, of course it was.''

She splashed into the water beside him, but he soon outstripped her. After a while she floated on her back, looking at the stars that were spilling across the sky. When she heard someone coming close, she said, "Isn't the sky beautiful at night?''

"Beautiful,'' said Ethan's voice, and she swiftly turned in a flurry of water.

"Where's Jeff?'' she asked.

"I've no idea. I thought you two were together.''

"He likes to swim in deeper water.''

"And you don't?''

"I've been a bit nervous of going too far, since that day we swam to the island.''

"Very sensible. Don't you think it's time you came in?'' He touched her arm, and she shied away.

"You're getting cold,'' he said. "Come on.''

"I'll go back when I'm ready.''

"Don't be childish,'' he said impatiently.

"Why not? You seem to be keen on children—if they're female." As soon as the words left her lips she wished she could recall them, but it was too late.

He said ominously, "Just what are you getting at?"

"Nothing." She struck out for deeper water, with a blind urge to flee, but he came after her, and grabbed her ankle. She flailed out at him, and they splashed about in a slippery, blinding little struggle before he caught both her arms and they sank together.

She felt him kick upwards, their legs entwined, and as they surfaced and she shook back her hair, gasping, he had both her hands held tightly in his, keeping her afloat with him by the movements of his legs. "Stop fighting me," he said curtly, "and explain."

"I don't have to explain anything to you!" she said furiously. "Let me go!"

She pulled away from him and got a mouthful of saltwater. Choking, she felt him change position to hold her almost like a life-saver, lying against his chest. He said softly, "You're not *jealous*?"

"No!" She twisted in his arms, and he laughed.

Jeff's voice called gaily, "Is this a private game, or can anyone play?"

Ethan turned his head, and Celeste took the opportunity to wriggle a hand from his grasp, placing it on his wet hair and pushing him firmly under, until he let her go.

As Jeff reached them, she said, "I'm not playing anymore," and went racing for the shore. By the time the two men emerged from the water she was standing by the fire drying herself, and for the rest of the evening she made sure to stay close by one or other of the women. Marietta sat between Jeff and Ethan, sparkling for both of them. As the party progressed, Jeff seemed to be responding to the young girl's innocent provocation more than Ethan.

"There's no harm in her," Janice said, following Celeste's reluctant gaze. "But I think perhaps her mother should have a talk with that young lady. Fortunately both Ethan and Jeff are far too decent and mature to take advantage of her. In fact, that's probably why she's behaving so outrageously. She knows she's perfectly safe."

"She's very lively," Celeste said.

"And very unsophisticated, in spite of the act." Janice regarded the girl with absentminded tolerance. "Ethan mentioned earlier that she reminded him of you when you were younger. You're both lovely, of course, but I'm sure you were never a brunette."

"No." Celeste didn't think that she had ever been like Marietta, so obviously basking in male attention, thrilled with her ability to attract admiring glances and teasing compliments, and deliberately testing her youthful wiles on any good-looking male.

As though reading her thoughts, Janice said, "I expect he meant that bubbling energy and confidence of a very young and very pretty girl."

"I'm not that young anymore," Celeste said. "And I don't have a lot of 'bubble' left, I'm afraid."

"Well, maturity brings other qualities." Janice smiled. "You're still only a girl by my standards. And I'm sure you'll regain some of what you think you've lost."

As the night cooled, everyone donned more clothes; even Marietta covered up the bikini with a loose muslin dress that made her look little girlish and sexy at the same time. Celeste wriggled into a loose thigh-length T-shirt. One of the men brought out a ukulele and after a few solos, which were enthusiastically received, led the rest in community singing.

Around midnight the party broke up by tacit consent, and Ethan picked up a torch and waited patiently for Celeste.

Look what we've got for you:

... A FREE 20k gold electroplate chain
... plus a sampler set of 4 terrific Silhouette Special Edition® novels, specially selected by our editors.

... PLUS a surprise mystery gift that will delight you.

All this just for trying our Reader Service!

If you wish to continue in the Reader Service, you'll get 6 new Silhouette Special Edition® novels every month—before they're available in stores. That's SNEAK PREVIEWS for just $2.74* per book—21¢ less than the cover price—and FREE home delivery besides!

Plus There's More!

With your monthly book shipments, you'll also get our newsletter, packed with news of your favorite authors and upcoming books—FREE! And as a valued reader, we'll be sending you additional free gifts from time to time—as a token of our appreciation for being a home subscriber.

THERE IS NO CATCH. You're not required to buy a single book, ever. You may cancel Reader Service privileges anytime, if you want. All you have to do is write "cancel" on your statement or simply return your shipment of books to us at our cost. The free gifts are yours anyway. It's a super-sweet deal if ever there was one. Try us and see!

Get 4 FREE full-length Silhouette Special Edition® novels.

Plus

this lovely 20k gold electroplate chain

Plus

a surprise free gift

▼ PLUS LOTS MORE! MAIL THIS CARD TODAY ▼

Silhouette's Best-Ever "Get Acquainted" Offer

Yes, I'll try Silhouette books under the terms outlined on the opposite page. Send me 4 free Silhouette Special Edition® novels, a free electroplated gold chain and a free mystery gift.

235 CIS RIYK (U-S-SE-03/90)

PLACE STICKER FOR 6 FREE GIFTS HERE

NAME _____

ADDRESS _____ APT. _____

CITY _____

STATE _____ ZIP CODE _____

Offer limited to one per household and not valid to current Silhouette Special Edition Subscribers. All orders subject to approval. Terms and prices subject to change without notice.

© 1989 HARLEQUIN ENTERPRISES LTD.

PRINTED IN U.S.A.

Don't forget...

... Return this card today and receive 4 free books, free electroplated gold chain and free mystery gift.

... You will receive books before they're available in stores.

... No obligation to buy. You can cancel at any time by writing "cancel" on your statement or returning a shipment to us at our cost.

If offer card is missing, write to: Silhouette Books®
901 Fuhrmann Blvd., P.O. Box 1867, Buffalo, N.Y. 14269-1867

She lingered, helping to pack the barbecue things and scour the beach for bits of litter they might have left lying about. But then there were no more excuses, and she had to join him on the dark path.

They ascended in silence, and when they reached the top she hurried towards the house. Ethan had not locked up, and she opened the door and stepped inside with him behind her.

He switched off the torch, plunging them into sudden blackness, and Celeste stopped short.

"I can't see," she said. "Please put the torch on again, Ethan."

Instead, he turned on a table lamp that cast a dim glow, putting down the torch beside it. When he straightened, he was standing between her and the stairs, and she moved nervously, somehow afraid to close the space between them.

"Want a nightcap?" he asked.

With faint relief, she said, "No, I don't think so, thanks."

He seemed reluctant to let her go. "You didn't take much part in the later stages of the party. Were you annoyed with Marietta?"

"No. Why should I be?"

"She did rather monopolise the younger male element."

"She was welcome to both of you," Celeste said rather tartly. "And neither of you is young enough for her."

He laughed a little. "Sour grapes?"

"As a matter of fact," Celeste told him, "I had a very good time talking to Janice and her friends."

"I'm glad to hear that." Obviously he didn't believe a word of it.

"Janice is going to give me some lessons," she said. "In drawing and painting."

"Really?" He sounded decidedly sceptical. "Do you have any talent in that direction?"

"I used to enjoy art classes at school. My teachers thought I was quite good."

"Well, go to it," he said. "It can't do any harm, and it might be good therapy."

"I'm doing it for fun, not therapy."

He pursed his lips briefly. "Of course. Sorry. How *are* you feeling now?"

"I'm fine. Thank you. But I'm tired, and I'd like to go to bed."

"What's stopping you?" he asked.

Nothing, of course, except that he was standing there, apparently immovable. She walked slowly across the room and brushed past him. She could feel the warmth of his body, they were so close. But he made no attempt to detain her.

Feeling as though she had passed by the edge of a cliff, she put her foot on the step, and then, as though compelled, paused to look back at him.

He was watching her, his expression dark and forbidding. Celeste shivered and turned away, suppressing the urge to run. She knew he continued to watch her all the way to the top.

Chapter Nine

Celeste enjoyed her lessons with Janice. The older woman was both patient and exacting, and when she praised, Celeste knew the praise was deserved.

Some days she sat and watched afterwards as Janice went on with her own work, learning more about techniques by taking note of how an experienced artist used her tools and paints. Sometimes she spent the entire afternoon there.

Ethan said he had to go away for a few days. "If you don't want to stay here alone, Janice and Henry would be pleased to put you up until I come back," he said.

"I should be making some plans about leaving, anyway," Celeste said. "I've imposed on your hospitality for long enough."

"Don't even think of it!" Ethan said sharply. As she glanced up in surprise, he added, "We need a lot more time."

"*We?*"

"You do," he amended. "Henry said you're just beginning to show signs of recovering."

"From what? And have you been discussing me with Henry again?"

"Depression," Ethan answered. "And don't blame him," he added, noting her mutinous face. "You're not officially his patient, and he hasn't violated any confidences."

"I haven't given him any to violate," Celeste said. "But you have no right to consult him behind my back."

"I asked for an informal but informed opinion, because I had to know..."

"To know what?" she challenged him.

"How to help you," he said slowly. "If you needed it."

"I don't need your help, Ethan." She stared at him, trying to work out the meaning of the second part of his answer. "You think I was shamming?"

"No. At first, maybe. But I realise it wasn't a pretence. You have been reacting in some fairly extreme way to Alec's death. What I'd like to know is, why?"

She flushed slightly. "He was my *husband*. Perhaps you'd forgotten that?"

"I've forgotten nothing. Have you?"

Her cheeks burned. "I don't know what you're talking about," she said huskily, and made to go up to her room.

"I think you do." His voice sounded cool and hard.

She turned at the bottom of the stairs. "You know nothing, Ethan," she said clearly. "Nothing."

As she started to ascend, he strode across the room and caught her before she was halfway up, swinging her round with her back to the wall. "So tell me!" he said. "Tell me what happened between you and Alec that sent him to his death—what that last straw was."

She shook her head, her mouth pale and stubborn. "Whatever I say would make no difference," she said. "Let him rest, Ethan."

His hands tightened on her shoulders. "I need to know!"

"Why?" she asked. "Because of *your* sense of guilt?"

He drew in a breath, his eyes boring into hers. "What did you say to him," he said, "about us? What did you tell him?"

"Nothing. There was really nothing to say, was there? Nothing to tell."

Ethan's mouth was grim, his eyes very dark. "I suppose not," he said. "From your point of view. Your kisses always came cheap, didn't they?"

She winced. "Don't—"

She tried to push him away. But he trapped her against the wall, her hands caught between their bodies. His eyes held hers, then wandered to her mouth. Celeste took a shuddering breath. "Ethan, please don't!"

A frown line appeared between his brows. He echoed softly, incredulously, "Don't?"

Celeste turned her head away. "Please!" she whispered. "Let me go."

The frown deepened. He moved one hand from her shoulder, trailing his fingers along the line of her jaw to lift her chin.

Suddenly fierce, she gave him a shove with all her strength, so that he momentarily lost his balance on the narrow step, and while he regained it she fled to her room, closing the door behind her.

The next day he kept giving her speculative, slightly baffled looks. In the evening he said, "I'm flying out tomorrow. You could drive me to the airport and use the car while I'm away.''

Her first instinct was to refuse, a flutter of alarm overtaking her at the thought of driving his car. But that was silly. Her driving was perfectly competent; she wasn't likely to do the vehicle any harm. And Ethan, apparently, was willing to trust her with it. She swallowed and said, ''Thank you.''

''I'd rather have it here than sitting in the airport carpark. Can you pick me up on Thursday? I'll be on the evening flight.''

''Okay.''

''Sure you'll be all right on your own?''

Janice had backed up the suggestion that she stay with the Palmers, but Celeste had firmly declined. ''I'll be fine.'' She was, in fact, looking forward to being alone. Apart from the brief lapse last night, Ethan had been handling their relationship with kid gloves for weeks now, keeping everything calm and polite, and yet whenever he was around she was conscious of an underlying tension in the air.

After dropping him at the airport in the morning she browsed in the shops. There really were some lovely clothes. Perhaps it was the sunshine and the colour of the island, with its blooming tropical shrubs and glossy palms, that made her dissatisfied with the drab contents of her wardrobe. She resisted the urge to buy, though. Until Alec's will was probated, she ought to be careful with her money. And afterwards, it didn't seem she was likely to have a great deal. She really would have to get a job.

She found that the prospect was not as daunting as it had been, although she hadn't the faintest idea what she would like to do. She was not qualified for anything in particular. But then, she was not too old to train for something, perhaps even finish her degree.

* * *

"That might be a good idea," Janice said, when Celeste mentioned it to her the next day. "Why did you give it up in the first place?"

"I got married."

"Couldn't you have completed your degree, even so?"

"Alec didn't think it was a good idea, as he was on the teaching staff at the university. He said he would have found it embarrassing."

"You were very young, weren't you?"

"I was nineteen when I met him."

"It must have been hard for you, sometimes."

"Sometimes," Celeste agreed. "Do you know anything about silk painting?"

"I know how to do it. Are you interested?"

"Do you think I could learn? I've been looking at some painted silk scarves and other things, and they're very beautiful. I'd like to be able to create something similar."

"I could teach you the basic techniques. You need special paints—I'll give you the name of a craft shop in Conneston where you can buy them—and a framework to stretch the silk while you work on it. An embroidery frame would do to begin with. I have a couple of those. It's a good idea to start small."

The next morning, Celeste answered the telephone to find Steven Craig on the line. "I'm calling from Conneston," he told her. "I hoped I could come and see you."

"Yes, of course." She mustered a spark of enthusiasm. "I'll pick you up. Ethan's away, and I have the use of his car."

When she collected him, he said, "It's awfully good of you. I'm sure I could have got a bus."

"It's no trouble. How nice to see you, Steven."

"You don't mind?"

"Of course not. I'm sorry you won't be able to see Ethan. I suppose you want to talk to him about those disks."

"Will he be away for long?"

"He expects to be here again on Thursday night."

"I could wait for him, then. I don't need to be back in Sydney until the weekend."

When they arrived at the house, Jeff was lounging in a chair on the patio. "I came over to check that you're getting on okay without Ethan," he told Celeste, eyeing Steven with some curiosity.

Celeste introduced them and asked Jeff to stay for lunch.

As they ate it, Jeff asked, "Where are you staying, Steven?"

"Don't know yet. I'll find a hotel this afternoon. Can you recommend somewhere cheap and decent? A hostel would do. I've got my own sleeping bag."

"You can doss down on my sofa-bed if you like. No sense in going all the way back to Conneston if it's Celeste you've come to see."

"Well, thank you," Steve accepted gratefully. "That's ideal, if you really don't mind."

"You'll have to fend for yourself," Jeff warned. "But you're welcome to what's in the fridge, and providing a bed's no trouble. Come on over when you're ready," he suggested, tactfully leaving the two of them alone when he had finished his coffee. "Celeste will tell you how to get there."

When he had gone, Steven turned to Celeste. "I didn't just come to see Ethan," he said. "I ... wondered how you were."

"It's nice of you to be concerned."

"Well, I hope we're friends. You know, I have—had—a tremendous respect for Alec and his work, but...I could see that being married to him wasn't always easy."

Celeste smiled wryly. Steven was no fool, and he had spent hours at a time in their home talking with Alec. He must have seen that all was not well between Alec and his wife. She had sometimes suspected that the young man was sorry for her. While Alec took her services for granted, Steven had gone out of his way to be helpful and considerate, taking cups and plates into the kitchen when she cleared up after bringing them a snack or a meal, opening doors when she was carrying a tray, always remembering to smile and meet her eyes as he thanked her. He had even made a point of dancing with her at social functions that Alec, unable to partner her, had reluctantly attended when they were quite unavoidable, only to spend the entire evening in conversation with various colleagues.

"You're a very nice person, Steven."

He shook his head. "I like you a lot. I always have."

"Thank you."

"So...I had a few days up my sleeve, and I thought I'd pop across and see how you were doing. I mean, phoning isn't the same, is it? You seem...more relaxed."

"It's very peaceful here," she said. "Very restful."

"Mm." He was gazing at the view. "I wouldn't have thought your brother-in-law was a very restful person to live with, though. Strikes me as a pretty dynamic character."

"Yes. But he's so busy I don't see much of him, anyway."

"Are you lonely?" he asked rather anxiously.

"No, not a bit." She told him about the Palmers and her art lessons, and promised to introduce him. Later, she took him over to Jeff's house and was persuaded to eat with them. The evening turned convivial—the two men hit it off, and Jeff was in a sociable mood. Celeste let him fill her glass again and again with wine, and it was late when they switched to coffee. The men decided to escort her all the way to her door, and stood for five minutes debating whether they should inspect her wardrobe and under the bed for possible intruders. Laughing, she shunted them out, promising to lock the doors when they had gone. As she did so, the phone began to ring.

She snicked the lock and ran to pick up the receiver. The laughter was still in her voice when she said breathlessly, thinking it must be a wrong number, "Hello?"

"Celeste?" Ethan said snappishly. "Where the hell have you been all night?"

"At Jeff's," she said. "Is something wrong?"

He said finally, "I was just checking to make sure you're all right."

"Of course I am. How often have you rung?"

"I don't know. I started at about eight. You sound as though you've been having a good time."

He didn't seem pleased about it, and she said coolly, "Yes, I have."

She was about to tell him Steven was there, when he asked, "Is Jeff with you?"

"No. He's just gone home. Did you want him?"

"No, I don't want him. Look, I've changed my mind. I'll be on the morning flight tomorrow. Can you meet me?"

"Yes, of course. Have you finished your business?"

"Most of it. Someone I hoped to see isn't here. See you tomorrow, then."

"Yes. Good night."

He'd been rather abrupt, she thought, putting down the phone. But what had she expected? A lengthy good-night? Be realistic, she told herself. He'd had nothing more to say.

* * *

The next day, she left early for the airport and found some cheap remnants of silk at a fabric store. Then she called at the shop that Janice had mentioned, and bought silk paints in three colours, brushes and a small bottle of something called gutta, which Janice had said she would need to draw lines that would prevent the paints from running into one another. "Although," she had added, "sometimes that's just the effect you want. There's a variety of techniques you can use. Probably some that I've never heard of. Once you've mastered the basics you may want to experiment."

"Steven's here," Celeste informed Ethan on the way home.

He had told her to stay in the driver's seat, and she felt his penetrating gaze on her face as he turned to her. "Steven?"

"Steven Craig," she said. "You remember."

"Of course I remember. What's he doing *here*?"

"He wants to see you. About those disks."

"I told him I'd contact him. As a matter of fact, I've been trying to get hold of him in Sydney, but no one knew where he was. He could have phoned."

"So could you," she pointed out. "You didn't tell him you were going to Sydney?"

"No. Well, where is he? In Conneston?"

"No, at the bay. He stayed last night—"

"What?"

"—with Jeff," Celeste finished.

"I see. *You* didn't offer him a bed?"

"I didn't like to, in your house."

"Would you have, if it had been yours?"

She glanced at him. "Probably. I offered you one when you came to Sydney."

"So you did."

She felt a flush rise in her cheeks. At the time she had hardly taken it in, because everything then had seemed to be happening at a distance, but now she remembered the implied insult when he had declined the offer. "Steven would have been more gracious in his refusal," she said, her voice husky.

"Would Steven have refused at all?" Ethan drawled. "I thought he might have jumped at the chance."

If he said he was surprised that *she* hadn't, Celeste thought dispassionately, she would stop the car and hit him. But he didn't. Instead, when she didn't answer the jibe, he folded his arms and to all intents and purposes went to sleep. Her foot came down unconsciously on the accelerator, and without opening his eyes, Ethan said, "There's a speed limit on the island, you know."

She did know, and she slowed so that the needle sat just on the limit.

At the house, Ethan swung his bag out of the car and said, "Thanks. You're a good driver."

"Thank you," she said icily. She locked up the car as he opened the house door and stood waiting for her.

"I feel something's missing," he said, as she made to pass him.

In the doorway, she looked back at him over her shoulder. "What?"

He gave her a gentle shove with a hand on her waist, and followed her inside. "A proper welcome home, perhaps," he said, and pulled her briefly close, brushing her lips with his.

Before she could react at all, he let her go and made for his room, leaving her feeling ruffled and uneasy.

Steven came over in the afternoon. Ethan greeted him with rather steely courtesy, and soon afterwards took him up to the workroom. When they emerged several hours later, Celeste thought that Steven was worried and Ethan frustrated.

"Something the matter?" she asked.

"Alec used a password on some of the data on the disks," Steven said.

"What does that mean?"

"We can't read the notes on that part of the disk," Steven explained. "He doesn't seem to have written the password down."

"Can't you get round the problem somehow?" Celeste asked Ethan.

"Maybe, in time. It would be simpler if we just knew what word he used, though. Have you any idea what it might have been?"

"He hardly spoke about his work to me. I guess he would use something relative to what was in the notes, wouldn't he?"

"We tried everything we could think of," Steven said.

"Of course, it might have been something he just picked out of the air," Ethan added. "Some word with no relevance whatever to the work he was doing. And for that matter, we've no way of knowing if that document has anything to do with his work. It could contain something else. Perhaps something personal."

Steven said, "The rest of what's on the disk is related to the study he was doing. He must have had some other notes *somewhere*. So far, all I've seen is the background material that I gathered for him, and some stuff I pieced together with him that he intended to use when he was working on his own."

"Nothing else?" Celeste asked.

"Well, some rather scrappy and frankly pretty useless theoretical stuff that was not much more than doodling. He was a bit cagey about the actual evidence for the theory that he was basing the project on,'' Steven added hesitantly. ''He said he didn't want to say too much until he had pulled the thing together, so I was working in the dark, rather. But I'm sure there was more to it than what we've found. From the research he asked me to do for him, I could see the direction his thinking was taking. I found it really exciting— enough to come up with some suggestions of my own, and he seemed to think they were pretty viable. But if we don't find out just what he was doing with the material he had...'' Steven shoved his hands gloomily into his pockets. ''I don't know.''

''I'm going to make dinner,'' Celeste said. ''Will you stay?'' She glanced at Ethan. If she was cooking, she didn't think he could have any objection to her making the invitation.

He didn't second it. Steven said, ''Sure, if it's not too much trouble. I'd like to.''

After they had eaten, the talk drifted, but eventually came back to Alec and his career. ''I don't mind telling you,'' Steven said, ''I was thrilled to my back teeth when he accepted me as his assistant. The chance to work with someone of Alec's calibre is something people like me dream about.''

''You were a brilliant student,'' Celeste said. ''I remember him saying that he was lucky to get you.''

''Really? I bet he wasn't nervous like I was, though. He was very patient with me those first few weeks while I learned about his methods.''

''Alec was always patient,'' Ethan said.

Steven turned to him eagerly. ''Did you see much of him? He would have been years older than you, wouldn't he?''

''He came home during the university holidays. Must have found me a right little pest, but he never showed it. He taught me all kinds of things. Used to spend hours playing cricket and football with me, coaching me. In some ways—" Ethan stared into the distance, apparently forgetting who he was talking to "—he was almost like a father, rather than a brother."

"Were there other brothers or sisters?"

Ethan shook his head. "No. Just the two of us. You're not planning to write a biography, are you?"

"Just interested," Steven said. "But you know, that's not a bad idea. If I did, could I count on your cooperation?"

Ethan's eyes moved to Celeste and seemed to grow cold. His face went shuttered. "I'd have to think about that," he said, and pointedly consulted his watch.

Taking the hint, Steven said, "I should be going. If I think of anything that might help with the password, I'll let you know first thing."

Ethan nodded and stood up. "Right. I can let you have the other disks shortly, anyway. I've transferred the data on them because of possible damage to the originals, but most of it is readable, I think."

"Thanks a lot. I've been at a bit of a loose end, with . . . everything that's happened. It'll be good to have something to work on, even if it's just checking over old ground."

Ethan closed the door after him and came back to find Celeste washing the coffee mugs. Picking up a tea towel, he said, "He didn't just come for the disks, you know. He told me he wanted to see you."

"I know. He told me that, too."

"So why didn't you mention it?"

"It didn't seem important."

"Does that mean that he isn't important to you?"

Celeste pulled the plug out of the sink and turned to face him. "Steven is a good friend. He's concerned about me, and I'm grateful for that."

"I'm concerned about you, too."

"I know, but . . ."

He finished what he was doing and put down the tea towel. "But?"

She moistened her lips with her tongue. "I somehow have the feeling that with you it's . . . something else. What do you want from me, Ethan?"

He gave a thin, peculiar smile. "There are times when I'm not at all sure myself."

She said, "I can't bring your brother back."

"You think that's what I want? Sometimes—" his mouth twisted, and she suppressed a shiver at the tortured look in his eyes "—sometimes, that's the last thing I want. Can you imagine how that feels?"

Celeste swallowed. "Yes," she whispered. "I can."

"Perhaps you can," he said strangely. There was a hard light in his eyes now that frightened her. As though he couldn't help himself, his gaze wandered over her, over her cotton pants and loose shirt, and at once she felt naked. Her breathing was suddenly strained. She couldn't wrench her eyes away from his. Her lips trembled and parted.

His mouth took on a bitter curve. "My God!" he said softly, his voice filled with disgust. "What a pair we are."

Then he turned his back on her and left the room. She heard him go out, pushing the door shut behind him. Swinging around to the sink, she held onto the counter with both hands, her head bent, eyes closed as she fought down a wave of nausea. *I have to leave,* she thought incoherently. *I have to get away from here, from Ethan.*

* * *

But in the morning she almost thought she had imagined the drama of the night before. Mrs. Jackson was there, with her down-to-earth normality, Ethan was as blandly courteous as he had ever been, and she found that she was again fighting a deadly lassitude that had the familiar effect of paralysing any ability to make coherent plans. Steven arrived with a list of words he had made that Alec might have used for a password, and the two men disappeared into the workroom. Celeste had coffee with Mrs. Jackson, then forced herself to prepare lunch for three, guessing the men would be too occupied to think about it themselves. Steven and Ethan ate rather absently before returning up the stairs. Afterwards she gathered up the things she had bought in Conneston and walked over to see Janice. She needed something to occupy her mind.

Under Janice's guidance, she began with a simple design, which she drew onto the wrong side of some tracing paper. Then she placed the pencilled side of the paper on a piece of silk on a table, and went over the lines again, transferring the design lightly to the fabric. Trying to concentrate, she fixed the silk into an embroidery frame and began outlining the drawing with gutta, squeezing it out of the nozzle fitted on the bottle.

"Be careful not to leave any spaces in the lines," Janice warned, "or the paints will bleed into each other."

When the outlines were completed, Janice held the frame up to the light and said, "Good, I don't see any gaps. We'll leave this to dry now." Looking shrewdly at Celeste, who had relaxed with a small sigh, she remarked, "Your heart's not in this today, is it? You've got a visitor, haven't you? If you want to get back . . ."

"No, he's with Ethan trying to work something out." She explained about the password, and Janice said, "What was so secret?"

"Alec had grown a bit paranoid, I think. He might have thought someone would read his notes and steal his ideas."

"You mean *really* paranoid? Or are you using a figure of speech?"

Celeste bit her lip. "I don't really know. His colleagues apparently didn't see anything wrong, and . . . perhaps I'm mistaken."

Janice nodded. "I don't want to pry into your private business, my dear. But you do seem so troubled. If it would help to talk, anytime, I promise I'd respect your confidence."

"Thank you. I know you would. But I expect it was all in my mind. Your husband seems to be of the opinion that I'm . . . mentally sick."

"It's nothing to be ashamed of. But I don't think for a moment, and I'm sure Henry doesn't, that you are unstable or in any way unreliable. A little fragile, perhaps, emotionally. I can tell you've been under some considerable strain. You know—I hope you don't find this offensive—but when people die, one of the legacies they often leave with their loved ones is guilt."

"Yes," Celeste said, almost inaudibly.

"We all feel that we should have been kinder or more understanding, or realised that something was wrong much earlier. That somehow we should have prevented the death or made it easier. Or at least treated the person better. And mostly, you know, we have done our best by them. Wishing them back so that things can be different isn't going to help much."

"But what if...the guilt is deserved?" Celeste said.

Janice asked, "Don't you think that you're maybe getting things out of proportion?"

Celeste leaned back in her chair, closing her eyes wearily. "I don't know. I don't know anymore. It's gone on for so long."

Janice nodded. "Want to tell me what it's all about?"

Celeste opened her eyes. "It was...I'm not sure, because I don't know how he could have...guessed. I used to tell myself that it was all in Alec's mind, his imagination. Or maybe, in mine. Maybe what I thought was happening wasn't really happening at all. Because there was nothing...I mean, nothing he could have known about unless...and I know Ethan would never have told him. I know that. And Alec never mentioned it, not specifically. And yet...he knew something, he really did. If not in actual fact, he knew with his mind, with his heart. I tried to hide it, to forget it. I tried with everything in me. I did. So hard, and for so long, and with such...pain. But nothing could alter what had happened. It couldn't be erased, and sometimes I felt it was a mark, an indelible mark that Alec could see on me, as clearly as a brand. He knew it was there, and that was why he was...punishing me."

"Punishing you?"

Celeste nodded. "For what happened—what happened between Ethan and me."

Chapter Ten

She had first seen Ethan on her wedding day. He had flown over from America, where he was doing postgraduate computer studies, to attend. And she had been so excited and happy, so enraptured at being actually married to Alec, that beyond noticing how handsome Ethan was, and understandably experiencing a small thrill of pleasure at the admiration he didn't try to hide, she had scarcely noticed him. She had felt that the admiration was a compliment to his brother's taste, and Ethan's approval had added to the joy of the day. She knew that Alec was very fond of him.

As best man, Ethan had properly devoted most of his attention to her chief attendant, and Sandra had been ecstatic, telling Celeste as she helped her change out of her white lace dress and veil, "I've got my eye on your yummy brother-in-law. Isn't he gorgeous? Make sure you throw your bouquet in my direction. Do you think he'd take the hint?"

Celeste had laughed and promised to comply, but although Sandra duly caught the bouquet, she had later written to Celeste rather wistfully that Ethan had taken her out for supper and dancing, but nothing had come of it after all. Sandra married an accountant two years later and now had a family of four. She still lived in Auckland, New Zealand, and the letters they had exchanged gradually dwindled to cards at Christmas. Immediately after their short honeymoon Alec and Celeste had gone to Wellington, where he had taken up a new appointment.

The next time she had seen Ethan had been when he came home after completing his American studies. Alec had invited his brother to stay with them while deciding on his next career move. She and Alec had been married for just over a year.

Alec had gone to meet him at the airport, and when they arrived at the house Celeste heard the car and ran to open the door.

There was a small porch to the house, and three steps down to the driveway, where Alec had parked. Ethan got out and stood at the bottom of the steps, staring at her. She thought with a shock that she had not realised quite how good-looking he was, and then smiled as she plainly read the same thought in his eyes. She was glad she had put on one of her nicest dresses, a jade green crushed polyester, which she had teamed with a coral pink leather belt and shoes. Three tiny coral beads finished with a slender jade pendant dangled from each ear, swinging against her neck as she moved.

Ethan laughed, and said, "Hello, sister-in-law."

Laughing back at him, she came down the steps with her hands extended in welcome. "Hello, Ethan. I'm so glad to see you again."

He took her hands in his, holding them in a warm clasp. "It's mutual." He hesitated for a moment, then bent and kissed her, a light, fleeting brush of his lips on hers. When he lifted his head, she saw he was no longer smiling. Then he let her go and turned to help Alec get his cases from the car.

Celeste remembered that with Ethan in the house, everything seemed to come to life. Lately she had been feeling less euphoric than in the early weeks of her marriage. The gloss had to wear off a little, she told herself. And in choosing an older man for her husband, she had invited some difficulties that she had not foreseen. Shifting to Wellington so soon after the wedding had meant leaving her friends, as well as her mother. Since her father had died when she was only ten, Celeste had only her mother, and she missed her more than she had thought possible. It was one of the things she had seized on that she and Alec had in common, both of them having been brought up by one parent.

Losing contact with her friends had caused her mixed feelings. Her engagement party had not been a wild success, for her friends had obviously felt inhibited by the presence of older people, many of their parents' generation, and Alec's friends had eyed the younger ones with varying degrees of tolerance and faint disapproval. It had the effect of making some of them defiantly noisy and boisterous, and Celeste had been torn between a desire to join in their rather childish revenge, and chagrin at what Alec and his friends were obviously thinking.

The next day she had apologised to him, miserably, and he patted her shoulder and said, "Never mind. I have to admit I'm surprised at your running around with that crowd, though. You're far more mature than any of them."

He wouldn't have wanted to marry her if he had not thought so, she supposed. "Thank you," she said, wondering why the simple words were like a betrayal of her friends.

"Anyway," Alec said, picking up his stick, "we'll be meeting a whole new set of people after we're married and living in a new city."

But of course, the people they met were Alec's colleagues at the university, most of them out of her age group. At first she exchanged letters with several of her classmates, but after a while there was less news to exchange. When Alec mentioned that she didn't seem to get so much mail these days, she said, "Well, my friends aren't writing so often. We have different interests now, you know."

"What interests do you have?" he asked.

"Only you," she answered, going into his arms. "It's enough, isn't it?"

He laughed and kissed her. "Suits me," he said. And it did, she realised. He was content to be the centre of her world. That she was not the centre of his, but rather a delightful adjunct, was something that she came gradually to see, with a pang. If there had to be a choice between her and his work, the work would always win. Loyally she told herself that even insurance salesmen and bank clerks often put their careers before their families. And his work had been the most important thing in his life for a long time. She came to see that the accident that had disabled him in the course of his research had made his work even more important to him. He had to prove that the pain he had endured was not pointless, that his continued suffering had value.

He drove himself hard, and her role was to provide loving support and all the help she could give him. If sometimes she felt a bit restless, she put that down to the change in her life-style and the necessary adjustments of married life. Once she suggested she might get a job, but Alec was so opposed to it that she quickly dropped the idea. He increased the allowance he gave her, although she assured him she had not made the suggestion because she was short of money. He kissed her nose and said, "Go and buy yourself something pretty."

She bought a seductive nightgown and was rather shaken at his reaction. He had watched her parading for him in a parody of film glamour and, instead of laughter, a strange, rigid look crossed his face, almost of fear. But then he had caught her to him and taken her to bed, making love to her with a ferocity that she had never encountered before. And afterwards, as she lay spent and a little frightened by the intensity of it all, he had said, running a caressing hand over her body, "You're mine. Don't ever forget that."

"I won't," she whispered, shocked. Turning to him, she put her hand on his cheek. "I could never forget it."

The first time he took her to a public function, he had told her to get herself a new outfit for it. The hot pink dress was striking and fashionable, and Alec seemed to approve of her appearance. She thought, as he introduced her to various heads of departments and their wives, that he was enjoying showing her off. If she began to feel like a windup toy, she supposed that was just the strain of the experience. As newcomers they were no doubt being inspected in a way that was by no means unusual. And Alec, of course, was a well-known personality. As his recent bride she must expect to be subjected to curious glances and probing questions.

It was something of an ordeal, but when she confessed as much on their way home, Alec laughed and said, "Don't be silly. You'll have to get used to these functions. Of course all the old cats will be talking behind your back, knowing their husbands are envying me. You took the shine out of the lot of them tonight."

"I just wanted to do you credit," Celeste said, disconcerted by his assessment, and even more by the elation in his voice.

"You have," he assured her, squeezing her hand. "I'm very proud of you."

When had he stopped being proud of her? When had he stopped wanting to show other men what a prize he had captured, and begun to be morbidly afraid of its being taken away by one of them? She didn't know. And perhaps for a time both feelings had warred within him, for they were surely two sides of the same coin.

Six months after the wedding, her mother had visited them for a long weekend, and Alec had been charming, both to her and to Celeste. Not that he was ever anything else, Celeste reminded herself guiltily. He had never ranted at her, never raised his voice. His only fault was an occasional absentmindedness when he was deeply engrossed in his work. No reasonable woman, after all, would complain about a husband who made a point of complimenting her almost every day on how pretty she was, and telling her that other men had commented on it to him, who never criticised her for what she spent on clothing, and indeed encouraged her to buy something new when they had to attend a party or a dinner or a reception.

"He's almost too generous," she told her mother, showing her a wardrobe full of clothes. "He seems to think I need a new dress every time we go out."

"That's sweet," her mother said. "You're happy with your father-figure, are you?"

"Father-figure?"

Her mother laughed a little. "Well, I couldn't help thinking that's what Alec is," she said. "Oh, a very handsome and romantic one, I'm sure. But you did lose your dad at a young age. It's a natural sort of thing to do—marry a much older man. And I can't help noticing, he does have a rather avuncular manner with you."

"Not always!" Celeste said, and blushed as her mother's brows rose.

"I suppose not. Well, as long as you're happy."

Quelling a niggling, barely discernible sense of doubt, Celeste said firmly, "I am very happy. Father-figure or not, Alec is the only man for me."

"I'm so glad." Her mother hugged her, then said hesitantly, "There's something I want to tell you. The fact is, I've met a man...."

A man who within three months had married her and taken her to live with him in Perth, on the far side of Australia. Hiding her panicky feeling of desertion, Celeste had expressed pleased approval and attended the wedding with a smile firmly fixed to her face. In the next five years she had seen her mother only four times, although they wrote often, and then had come the news that a light plane carrying her mother and the man who had made her happy in those few years had crashed in the heart of Australia, killing instantly everyone on board.

But that was later, some years after Ethan had come back to New Zealand and into Celeste's life.

Alec had been delighted to see his brother. He was full of excited enthusiasm, plying Ethan with drinks and questions and directing Celeste to sit and talk with them, even though she was preparing a special dinner for three and really needed to be checking on what was happening in the kitchen. Eventually she gently removed his arm from about her shoulder and said, "If I don't turn that chicken, it'll be burned to a crisp."

Ethan brought some empty glasses in later, as she was dishing up. "Anything I can do?" he asked.

"No, it's almost ready, thanks. Put the glasses over there, I'll wash them later."

"I can do it." He began rinsing them at the sink, glancing round as she placed vegetables on the plates. "Looks good," he said. "And smells even better. Alec says you're a great cook."

"I'm not great," she said. "But I can cook a decent meal."

"He's been singing your praises," Ethan told her. "According to him you're the most beautiful, talented, best-dressed, etcetera, etcetera..."

"Oh, I wish he wouldn't...."

"Why not? Isn't it true?"

She looked up, flushed from her exertion and from embarrassment. His answering gaze was quizzical, reserving judgement, she thought. He took a tea towel from the rail by the sink and faced her, absently drying a glass.

"It's a lot to live up to," she said weakly.

He nodded. "You know, I don't think Alec has been around women much," he said. "Too busy hiking off into the wilds of New Guinea and the like. He's like a dog with two tails about you. No woman," he added deliberately, "could be everything that he thinks you are."

Celeste put down the dish in her hands, and stood very straight. Something—some current of awareness—flowed between them, and she saw his eyes narrow as he stiffened, too.

She said, her voice husky, "I'll do my best. I can only try."

Ethan nodded. "Sure," he said, overcasually, and carefully put down the glass that he had dried before picking up another.

*   *   *

While he waited for replies to several job applications, Ethan stayed on with Alec and Celeste. "Take Ethan swimming, Celeste," Alec said. "It's his favourite sport, and much more fun with company." Then he suggested other outings, telling Ethan, "I know she likes walking, and on Wellington's hills I can't keep up."

When they came back from hiking up the steep hills to survey the view of the harbour, they found that Alec had left the university early and reached home before them.

As Ethan went off to his room, Alec said approvingly, "You've got some colour in your cheeks, Celeste. You should get out more often. You don't need to stay at home with a crock like me."

"I like being at home with you," she said, going over to him to kiss his cheek. "And you're not a crock."

"But you enjoyed yourself today, didn't you? You like Ethan?"

"Yes. Your brother's good company, but—"

"Well, I'm glad. I want you two to get on. Ethan and I are close, you know, in spite of the gap in our ages. It would hurt me if you two couldn't be friends."

"We are friends," she said. She found Ethan stimulating and interesting, and shared his sense of humour. "But we'd both like more of *your* company."

"I rather hoped you could entertain him on your own while I'm at work," he said with a hint of testiness. "You know I can't take too much time off. Finding it a bit of a drag, are you?"

She must have imagined the half-hopeful gleam that briefly lit his eyes. "No, not at all. And of course I know you're busy. I just thought, Ethan hasn't seen you for ages and it would be nice to spend some time together."

"Oh, I expect he'd rather have you, anyway," Alec said, smiling at her. "I don't think Ethan is immune to your charms any more than the next man."

For the first time, Celeste snapped at him. "I wish you wouldn't keep harping on my looks! And I don't think that's a very nice thing to say about your brother."

Alec showed surprise. "I don't know why you should object to a compliment," he said. "And I wasn't suggesting that Ethan would try to make a pass at you. He hasn't, has he?"

"Of course not!"

"Of course not," Alec echoed soothingly. "But no man worthy of the name is totally oblivious to a beautiful young woman, my dear. What a little innocent you are!"

His manner was amused and patronising, and she shut her teeth on a sharp retort. He was trusting and generous, and she knew he was merely making sure that Ethan had a good holiday while he stayed with them. Perhaps he had her welfare at heart, too. He had fretted occasionally that he was unable to join her in active pursuits that he knew she enjoyed, and although she denied wanting to take part in them on her own, he must have realised that she missed them. It was hardly fair to blame him for her confused anger and resentment.

"There's no reason why you shouldn't swim with us at the weekend," she said. After his broken bones had knitted, swimming had been part of his therapy.

"Thanks," he said, "but I don't fancy making a spectacle of myself, having to be helped out of the water and trying to use my cane to drag myself over the sand."

"I know it embarrasses you," she said, "but we could find a quiet beach, and if Ethan helped you, probably no one would notice you at all."

He shook his head. "I have my pride, Celeste. I don't want even his help."

When they were invited to a dinner with dancing afterwards, Alec insisted that Ethan accompany them, and when the dancing began, he almost pushed Celeste into his brother's arms.

"I'm sorry," Celeste murmured. "He's very conscious of being unable to dance, and so determined that I shouldn't be deprived of the chance. After this, I'll understand if you want to disappear from our party and find someone else to dance with."

"I like dancing with you," Ethan said. "And I have the feeling that Alec would rather it was me than some other man. Is there anyone you'd prefer to be dancing with?"

"It isn't that." She shook her head vehemently. "I like doing things with you, Ethan." She looked up at him and caught a sudden glint in his eyes that made her miss a step.

As she swayed closer to him, off balance, he said quietly, "Do you?" And then he was holding her away from him, his eyes disconcertingly dark and rather measuring.

"You know I do," she replied uncertainly. "It's been great having you around. Alec wanted us to..."

He was gazing past her shoulder at where Alec was sitting. "I know," he said softly. "Alec wants you to have all the things that he can't give you."

When his eyes returned to her, his face was taut and questioning. She said carefully, "There is nothing I want that he can't give me."

Ethan's eyes narrowed, then he nodded and gave her a strange smile. His hand tightened on her waist, and he whirled her around in a complicated turn, and for the rest of the bracket they danced in silence.

They sat out the next dance, and then one of the older men asked her to try a waltz with him. Although Ethan scarcely left their table, he didn't ask her to dance again.

During the final weeks of his stay, Celeste was more relaxed with Ethan. Some small reservation that she had sensed in him seemed to have melted away. She felt that they were establishing a real friendship, and she responded sweetly and honestly to the gentle, teasing affection that he showed her.

"We should give a party," Alec said, "before Ethan leaves."

Ethan had the offer of a good job, designing and installing a computer network system for a large engineering firm in Hamilton, centre of the prosperous Waikato dairy farming region.

"A party?" Celeste was surprised. They had hosted the occasional dinner, but a real party was not Alec's preferred way of entertaining.

"Yes, a party. He's met a few people while he's been staying with us, and I'm sure they'd like to farewell him. Would it be too much for you?"

"Oh, no! It's just not your usual style."

Alec frowned. "I'm not such an old stick-in-the-mud as you may think," he said humorously.

"I don't think anything of the sort. Who would you like to invite?"

Alec moved restlessly, grimacing, and she said swiftly, "Is your leg hurting? Shall I get you one of your pills?"

Impatiently, he shook his head. "I'm all right. We should invite some of the younger crowd. Junior lecturers and their wives and girlfriends . . . or boyfriends."

It wasn't a big party, but it went on quite late. When the last guest had gone, it was almost two o'clock. Ethan drove a young woman home who had rather obviously been making a play for him, and Alec, chuckling, said, "We may not see him until morning. Not if Charmian has her way."

Charmian was a striking brunette, with beauty as well as brains, and she hadn't made any pretense of hiding either. In fact, the dress she had been wearing, which left precious little to the imagination, had made Celeste wonder if she had a defensive desire to show the world that female intelligence was no bar to traditional notions of femininity.

"I don't think Ethan was exactly averse to her having her way," she said, trying hard to echo Alec's tone of worldly amusement. "He didn't *have* to take her home. She actually asked him to call her a taxi."

She had, too, although she could equally well have asked Celeste, who was much nearer the phone at the time. But Charmian had been standing by Ethan. As she had practically all evening, Celeste recalled. Well, she couldn't blame the young woman. Ethan was handsome and unattached, and so, presumably, was Charmian.

Alec yawned. "I'm off to bed. Coming?"

"I'll clear up a bit first." She had a strong, illogical urge to start hurling crockery about. She was ashamed of herself, but that didn't lessen the feeling.

"Leave it until tomorrow."

"I'll just tidy up here and stack the dishes," she promised.

He shrugged. "All right." He hobbled over to her, leaning heavily on his cane as he did when he was tired. His arm came about her shoulders. "But I'll probably be asleep. How about a good-night kiss?"

She obliged, guiltily glad that it was all he was asking for tonight. She didn't think she could summon up the right mood for lovemaking.

He left her, and she began automatically gathering up ashtrays and glasses. Her unsettled, grumpy mood was no doubt a reaction to the gaiety and stimulation of the party, as well as the inevitable work that had gone into the preparations. It had been a definite success, she told herself, wiping away a stupid tear. She would be sorry to see Ethan leave; he had been a brilliant guest. But life had to go on. *Settle back into the rut,* ran her thoughts, and she scolded herself. Life with Alec was not a rut. She met lots of interesting, intelligent people, and by and large they had accepted her, although she couldn't help but be aware of raised eyebrows now and then when a new acquaintance discovered she was Alec's wife. There had been a couple of nasty moments when men who apparently imagined that Alec had become disabled since their marriage made veiled suggestions to her of giving her what she must be missing, but she had told them in no uncertain terms what to do with their offers.

She shivered. There was nothing wrong with Alec in that department. The vague uneasiness that sometimes invaded her after his lovemaking had nothing to do with inadequacy, but with the strange, desperate possessiveness that often seemed to pervade it, especially lately. But she was inexperienced with other men and had no way of knowing if there was anything unusual about it. She must try to conquer the odd aversion that it engendered in her. It didn't need much experience to know that shrinking from him would only make the problem—if it could be called a problem—worsen.

She had the lounge almost back to normal and was running hot water into the sink over a stack of glasses when the back door opened. She looked around to see Ethan in the doorway.

"You came back!" she said.

His brows rose. "Surprised?"

"Yes. We thought . . ."

He closed the door, leaning against it with his arms folded. "I see."

Celeste flushed. "Well . . ." She shrugged. "Surely Charmian didn't send you away." Her voice, she realised, sounded ever so slightly waspish. She turned off the tap that must have covered the sound of the car, and started swishing a dish-mop around in the water, rattling the glasses.

Ethan came away from the door and inspected a plate full of leftovers on the table. "No," he said, picking up a cheese straw and nibbling it. "Actually, she didn't."

"I see." She took out a glass and plonked it down on the stainless steel counter.

"*No you don't,*" he said almost under his breath, and yet with such violence that she jumped, dropping the next glass into the sink with an ominous tinkle. "You don't know a damn thing," Ethan said. "Or if you do, then I've been led up the garden path, and so has Alec."

Shaking, she scrabbled among the suds, muttering, "I don't know what on earth you're talking about." Then she gave a tiny shriek as a sharp pain pierced her hand, and she lifted it from the sink, seeing the suds clinging to it stained pink.

Ethan dropped the cheese straw on the table and strode over to her. "What in God's name are you doing?"

"I broke a glass," she said in a muffled voice. "I didn't realise—"

His fingers clamped about her wrist. "God, you're a little fool!" A watery pool of blood was forming in the palm of her hand. "Where's the first aid stuff?"

"Over there." She nodded to a cupboard above the refrigerator.

Without letting go of her hand, he pulled her over to the cupboard and lifted down the red box. Then he thrust her into a chair.

"I can do it," Celeste said. "It's only a small cut."

He ignored her, swabbing the cut with disinfectant on a cotton wool ball and drying it carefully with more cotton wool before smoothing a plaster over the wound. He did it all slowly but efficiently, with grim concentration.

"Thank you," she said.

He still held her hand in his. His head was bent, so that she couldn't see his face properly. He said, "You know why I didn't stay with Charmian, don't you?"

Her fingers trembled in his. She said, "Ethan . . ."

He looked up then, and she saw the glazed brilliance of his eyes and caught her breath. "Ethan . . ."

He closed his eyes, and bent his head again, bringing her hand to his lips. He was kissing her fingers, almost reverently, and she found it both unbearably sad and unbearably erotic.

"I've been drinking," he said. "I shouldn't really have driven anyone home tonight. All night I've been drinking and trying to persuade myself I wanted Charmian. But it isn't Charmian I want." His mouth was warm and gentle, and he took the tip of one finger into it, until she felt his tongue, rough and moist, against her skin. He made a sound in his throat like a moan, and she brought up her other hand to his hair, feeling it springy and soft under her fingers. "Ethan," she whispered. "You mustn't . . ."

He took a deep, ragged breath, and let her go. "No," he said. "I know." His head was still bent, and she pushed herself to her feet, forcing herself to stand and walk past him. As she made to go by him, he lifted his face, and she looked at the naked need in his eyes and cried, her hands going out to him, her eyes as naked as his, "Oh, Ethan!"

He was on his feet instantly, his chair scraping the floor, and then she was held tightly in his arms and he was kissing her. Her mouth parted for him, and her body fitted perfectly into the protective, passionate curve of his, her arms around his neck as her head fell back against his arm.

She drowned in that kiss. Time and the world disappeared. His mouth and his arms were her world, and his warmth and his love and passion enclosed her. She felt him shudder, and nestled closer, shivering in response. His hands were stroking her gently, finding out about her body, silently worshipping it. He lifted his mouth, and when she whimpered he placed tender kisses on her closed eyelids, her temple, then all the way down her cheek and along the line of her throat. When she felt his hand on her breast she gave a small cry and raised her own hand to press it against his and keep it there.

He gave a wordless exclamation and took her open mouth under his, his palm moving roughly over her breast, the friction sending darts of pleasure through her whole body. She freed her hand from his and touched his shoulder, his hair, the taut strength of his neck as he bent over her.

When he broke the kiss, she gasped. His hands dragged at her hair, putting a space between them, holding her so that he could look into her eyes.

"I can't believe it," he muttered. "You feel the same!"

Unable to deny it, knowing he could see it in her eyes, she was silent.

He closed his eyes again. "Oh, God! I…we can't do this, Celeste."

She watched him, her heart breaking for him, for both of them. "No," she said with a terrible, tearing act of will. "We can't."

He groaned and suddenly pulled her head to his shoulder, his hands shaking as he smoothed her hair. Instinctively, she put her arms about his waist, her face against his shirt. They stood like that for a long time, then she eased away from him. He let her go reluctantly, his hands going to her shoulders, sliding down her arms, still holding her hands as she stepped back from him. He looked down at them, and turned over the one he had put the plaster on, raising it to his cheek. "I'm sorry," he said.

"I know," she whispered. "So am I, Ethan. Good night, my darling."

She knew it was goodbye, and so did he. But she went to the door and passed through it without a backward glance. While his heart called to hers she walked steadily along the passageway and tried to shut off her mind and discipline her rebellious, tormented body. She undressed clumsily with trembling fingers, and got into bed beside her sleeping husband, to lie shivering and wakeful until daylight.

Chapter Eleven

So, you've been feeling guilty ever since," Janice said, when she had heard Celeste's halting account. "You know, it's no sin to be tempted. And a couple of kisses hardly constitutes adultery."

"Not legally, perhaps," Celeste said.

"I know what you mean. But you're not able to help what's in your heart, Celeste. I don't think you should still be punishing yourself for a minor indiscretion that took place long ago. You were a loyal and faithful wife for eight years, weren't you?" At Celeste's nod, she added, "Doesn't that count for more than a few minutes of recklessness?"

It made sense, put like that. And yet... "I've *felt* unfaithful for seven years," Celeste admitted. "And I'm sure that Alec knew it. That's what I can't forgive myself for. Making him conscious that...that he wasn't enough for me. It was the worst thing I could have done to him."

"I take it the accident that put paid to his career also gave him something of a feeling of lost worth."

"I didn't really know him until after he had the accident," Celeste said. "But he was always trying to prove himself, one way or another."

"If it was already a strong trait in his personality, becoming disabled and having his job and his life style severely curtailed may have intensified that."

Celeste nodded. Then she said, "I've taken up enough of your time. Thanks for listening, Janice."

"No problem. Sometimes it helps just to talk."

When she emerged from the path, Ethan was standing at the edge of the terrace, his hands thrust into his pockets. She paused, almost afraid to approach him, then went on slowly, feeling a deadweight of dread inside her. Things change, he had said to her. And people. Once they had shared something—at first attraction and liking, then emotions much more powerful, wonderful but potentially destructive. Now they were bound by something else, something dark and dangerous.

When she stopped a few yards away, he shifted his feet and surveyed her with a deliberate and almost insulting scrutiny.

She asked, "Where's Steven?"

"Gone to get his things from Jeff's while we wait for the computer to finish a printout. I'm taking him into Conneston for the flight to Sydney."

"You found the password?"

"We found the password. Steven thought of it, naturally. I don't know what took him so long. It was so obvious, really. Only we've been hunting for something to do with Alec's work, not his private life. I should have known that you were never far from his thoughts."

"I don't understand. What does it have to do with me?"

"Can't you guess? He used your name. That was the key. Celeste."

"Oh. So you . . . you read the document?"

"Oh, yes. Called it up on the screen and there it was. Steven's quite excited about it."

"I'm glad."

"For Steven?" He seemed to be staring at her very hard.

"Yes. And for you . . . but for . . . Alec, too."

"Oh, yes. Alec."

"You want his work to be published, don't you? You said it would be a shame if it was all lost."

"Yes, I want it published. I wish," he added, in a tone of low savagery, "that I didn't have to rely on Steven Craig to ensure that. Unfortunately, he's the only one who knows enough about the project to be able to finish it."

"Why do you dislike him so much?"

"Oh, come on!" he said. "You know why!"

Celeste shook her head. "I don't understand you."

"You can hardly expect me to like the little rat who was making love to Alec's wife while he—"

Her voice shaking, she interrupted him. *"He was not!"*

"Prove it!" he shot at her. "He answers the description in Alec's last letter. Fits it to a tee."

"Ethan!" she said despairingly. "How can I prove anything to you? There was *no one*! I swear it on Alec's grave!"

His face looked pinched. "Do you really think I'd believe that. Against Alec's word—against his death?"

She stared at him wordlessly, then pushed past him into the house and went upstairs.

She lay on the bed staring at the ceiling and trying very hard to think of nothing, to empty her mind completely. She heard Steven's arrival and their footsteps coming up the stairs and into the workroom. Minutes later, Steven was thanking Ethan profusely, cut off by Ethan's incisive tones.

"I should say goodbye to Celeste," she heard Steven say. They must have been standing almost directly outside her door.

"She's resting," Ethan said. "I'll tell her for you. Come on, if you're to catch that plane we'd better get going."

When he arrived back, she was still lying there in gathering darkness. After some time he came up and tapped on the door. When she didn't answer, he opened it and went over to the bed. Her eyes were open, and he said, "Are you ill?"

"No," she said remotely. "Just tired."

"You've had nothing to eat, have you?"

Her head moved slightly from side to side. "I'm not hungry."

"You must eat. Starving yourself won't do any good."

"What will?" she asked ironically.

"I'll get you a cup of coffee," he said, and left the room.

When he returned, she said, "I . . . have to leave here. Tomorrow I'll arrange a flight."

"So that you can rejoin your lover?"

Steven is not my lover. But he wouldn't believe that. She must get away from here anyway. Obviously it was an impossible situation. "You don't want me," she said.

"I'm not asking you to leave," Ethan said in a strange voice. Then he said, "Do you want to go?"

She looked up into his dark, unreadable eyes, and to her utter dismay felt her eyes fill hotly with tears that spilled down her cheeks onto the pillow before she could hide them.

Ethan drew in a sharp breath. "Oh, my God! Don't!"

He put down the cup he was holding, and sank onto the bed beside her, his hand sliding into her hair, pulling her towards him. His mouth met hers in a hard, seeking and somehow angry kiss, his thumbs on her cheeks wiping the tears away.

She lay in his arms like a rag doll, unable to resist or respond, feeling nothing. He eased himself away from her, still holding her head in his hands, and gradually he let her down against the pillow. She closed her eyes but the tears kept coming, silently. There was nothing she could do about them. She felt the backs of his fingers against her cheek, brushing them away, then his lips, soft and warm on her skin.

"Please, Celeste," he whispered. "Please stop."

"I can't," she murmured. "I can't help it. Just go away and leave me alone."

After a moment she felt him shift back. "If that's what you want."

She nodded frantically, and his weight lifted off the bed. She heard him move away. "Call me if you need anything," he said, and closed the door behind him.

In the morning she could scarcely drag herself out of bed. Ethan was in the house when she went down, rising to his feet instantly as she appeared.

"You look awful," he said bluntly. "What do you want for breakfast?"

She didn't feel like eating, but she said, "I'll make some toast."

She drank a cup of tea, but it was all she could do to eat half a slice of toast. Ethan said, "You must have more."

Celeste shook her head. "I can't." She felt slightly sick, the sight of food making it worse, but mostly she just felt dead inside. "I never have much breakfast, anyway," she mumbled. "I'll feel better later."

She didn't, much, but she managed to hide it from him, she thought. For days she went through the motions of living, cooking, eating, and didn't realise how her shoulders drooped, that her eyes were shadowed and lifeless, and her mouth pale and taut. When it was time for her lesson with Janice she phoned and said she wouldn't be coming. Most of the days she spent pretending to read, or just sitting on the beach staring at the sea. Ethan's covert gaze became increasingly anxious, but she didn't notice.

A letter came from Steven for her. Ethan brought it to where she sat in the lounger on the terrace, a book on her knee that she had been reading without comprehension. She had refused the offer to accompany him into town, not able to summon the energy and glad of the chance to be alone. Ethan tapped the envelope thoughtfully against his hand, then tossed it into her lap. "For you," he said briefly.

He was waiting for her to open it. She lifted the flap and slipped out the two sheets of paper. Some of the words were almost illegible, and she guessed that Steven had written in haste.

Dear Celeste,

I didn't want to go without saying goodbye to you, but it seemed best not to disturb you, as Ethan said.

I'll be reading these notes just as soon as I get the chance, and then maybe I will be able to get on with finishing Alec's work. He must have felt it was very important stuff, to go to the trouble of keeping it secret with a password. I'm sure the disk must contain the missing pieces without which it would be impossible to proceed. Ethan has a printout, I know, but as he says, it's not his field and he wouldn't be able to make sense of it.

I could see you haven't yet recovered from all that's happened. Please take care of yourself. Give Ethan my regards.

Love, Steven.

Slowly, Celeste folded the letter and slid it back into its envelope. Ethan was still watching her.

"Well?" he said harshly. "What does he have to say?"

"Not very much. He sent you his regards."

"And what did he send you? His love?"

She looked at him distantly, and said with a resigned little smile, "Yes."

He made a derisive sound. "How could you even look at that miserable imitation of a man when you had Alec?"

Mechanically, without hope, she said, "I know it's no use trying to convince you, Ethan, but I've never had an affair with Steven."

"Perhaps you hadn't exactly got round to it yet," he drawled, "but it must have been on the cards."

Wearily, she got up. "Only in Alec's mind. But you can't believe that your adored big brother was anything less than perfect, can you? Or that he could ever have been wrong?"

She turned away from him and went into the house. She should go and see Janice, who would be expecting her for another lesson. It was difficult to work up any enthusiasm, but at least it would get her away from Ethan's suffocating presence.

Janice took one look at her and said, "Whatever has happened, Celeste?"

Smiling wanly, Celeste asked, "Is it that obvious?"

"That something's wrong, yes. You were looking so much better, too!"

"Was I? I guess I was feeling better for a while. Now, I must admit I don't care."

"About what?"

"About anything." With an effort, she smiled and said, "Well, art is supposed to be good therapy. Let's get on, shall we?"

Deducing that she didn't want to talk, Janice said, "All right. Your silk is ready for painting. The secret is to work fast and with a steady hand. Begin in the middle of each section, and allow the paint to spread to the lines of gutta...."

The paint began drying quickly, and when it was done, Celeste was not satisfied that the design met her original concept, but Janice declared it not bad for a first effort. "When it's properly dry," she said, "you can heat-set it with an iron, and then it should be colourfast for hand washing. You can get brush-on or spray fixatives for some brands of silk paints, but if you're careful with the iron, this method is quite satisfactory." Not until Celeste was leaving again did she say, hinting at their earlier conversation, "If there's anything Henry and I can do, let us know, won't you?"

Vaguely she knew that Ethan was holding rigidly in check an explosive mixture of anxiety, anger and frustration, while he exercised a monumental patience with her. But she floated through the days in a protective cocoon of indifference. Jeff was puzzled, and the Palmers concerned, but she scarcely noticed any of them. Only Ethan occasionally pierced the apathy that was her armour against the world—and against any encroachment on her emotions. She knew that she was living on the edge of a volcano, that she was mad to remain with a man who hated her and who had no faith in her integrity. But she stayed on, held by nothing more, it seemed, than a massive disinclination to take any sort of initiative.

One night when she was picking at her food as usual, Ethan snapped, "For heaven's sake, eat it! It won't poison you!"

"I'm just not hungry." She pushed the plate away and stood to take it off the table.

Ethan leaned over and grabbed her arm, forcing her back into her chair. With his other hand he plonked the plate in front of her again. "Eat it!" he said ominously.

"I'm not a child." She looked down at the plate, revolted at the sight of ravioli and salad.

"Then stop behaving like one," Ethan snapped, "and eat your dinner."

"I don't want it."

"What are you trying to do?" he demanded. "Starve yourself to death?"

She raised her eyes to his. "I'd have thought you'd like that."

He went white around the mouth. "I don't want you dead, Celeste."

"What *do* you want, Ethan?" She was still staring at him.

"At the moment," he said with determined calm, "for you to eat your dinner."

With a flash of temper, she said, "Oh, the hell with the damned dinner!" And without even thinking about it, she put a hand under the plate and tipped it neatly over onto the tiled floor.

She looked down with dull surprise at the mess spreading under the broken plate. It was the first time in her life she had done anything like that. Glancing at Ethan with some apprehension, she found the expression on his face changing from understandable exasperation to inexplicable satisfaction.

She said with difficulty, "I'm sorry. That *was* childish. I'll clean it up."

He got up and helped her with silent efficiency. She couldn't figure out why he seemed quietly pleased with himself. He didn't insist again that she eat something, but when he brought out cheese and biscuits while she made

coffee, and put a biscuit on her plate with a slice of Gruyère, she meekly ate it.

A few days later while she was lazing on the beach after a
swim, he came down the path and stood beside her, wearing a towel about his waist and surveying the modest one-
piece that had already dried on her body.

"Come into the water with me," he said.

"No, thanks." She closed her eyes.

"I said, come in," he reiterated, and she felt his hand on
her wrist, drawing her to her feet.

"I've had a swim."

"Have another."

She gave a halfhearted tug at her wrist, and looked up at
him. His eyes were gleaming, expectant, almost as though
he anticipated a fight and was looking forward to it. She
sighed, her shoulders sagging. "Oh, all right," she muttered.

He didn't seem pleased, quite the reverse. His mouth went
grim, but he discarded the towel, revealing dark briefs, and
kept a hold on her wrist until they were in the water, then
struck out strongly away from her and circled back. "You
okay?" he enquired, shaking water from his eyes.

"Yes, of course."

"Want to try for the rock out there?" He indicated the
flat, bare little rock that rose from the sea just past the
point.

"No, thanks."

"You're not out of practice now. You've swum almost
every day."

"It's too far," she lied. She had swum out there a couple
of times with Jeff.

"Afraid I'll have to tow you back?" he taunted. "But you
might enjoy that."

"I didn't last time."

"Tell that to the marines," he scoffed, and swam away from her on a diagonal path, heading for the rock.

She hesitated, then struck out after him, drawing level and trying to pass him. He kept up with her, though, and they arrived together, climbing onto the smooth rock, only a few feet out of the water. Celeste lay back, panting.

Ethan loomed over her. "I didn't suggest a race," he told her.

"It wasn't a race." She turned over on her stomach, pillowing her cheek on one arm. "I just changed my mind."

He sat beside her with one knee drawn up, and when she peeped at him she could see he was scowling into space. She rolled over and sat up.

Ethan turned and looked at her. His gaze was like an examination, as though he was searching for flaws.

"Do I pass?" she asked flippantly.

"Oh, you more than pass, Celeste," he said. "You always did."

She looked away from him, towards the land. The fast swim, or the stimulus of Ethan's uncomfortable presence, seemed to have momentarily cleared her brain. "What do you know about Alec's mother?" she asked him.

"What?" The question was obviously unexpected.

"Alec's mother." Celeste turned to him. "She left when he was six or seven. That's all I know. I wondered how he felt about that."

"He never spoke of it. I don't know any more than you do. He could hardly have remembered her," Ethan added dismissively.

"All the same, it must have affected him, at that vulnerable age."

"His father more than made up for it. They were very close, right up until Dad died."

"Did you mind that? You told me once he was the only father you had known."

"I wasn't jealous. My stepfather was very good to me."

"Alec said his father was very bitter over his mother. They must have discussed her."

"I suppose they did, at some stage. I daresay Dad would have explained—tried to explain—what had happened."

"When Alec told me about his mother, he said, 'The bitch left us.'"

Ethan looked faintly startled.

"I asked him if he'd ever seen her again, maybe tried to contact her when he was older. He said he wouldn't have crossed the street to give her the time of day."

He said nothing, but Celeste could tell it was news to him. "Do you know?" she pressed on, "I think that in a way, he blamed your mother for his father's death." Ethan's mother had been hospitalised for weeks before her death of a kidney disease, and his stepfather had suffered a fatal heart attack only days after her funeral.

"That's nonsense."

"I know," Celeste agreed. "But our feelings are not always rational. I think he felt that...that your stepfather loved your mother more than his own son. That once she was gone, he had nothing to live for, not even Alec." She was thinking aloud, trying to make sense of a whole lot of random remarks and casual conversations from the past, fumbling for some sort of rationale. She felt she was on the verge of understanding something.

"There was no question of loving anyone more!" Ethan said harshly. "Alec was an adult by the time his father remarried. He always got on perfectly fine with my mother—and with me."

"I know. Well, you were hardly competition, were you, being so much younger? And not his father's own son. But your mother couldn't take the place of his own mother, could she? It was too late for that."

"What are you getting at?"

"I think . . . somewhere inside Alec was an insecure little boy who felt betrayed by his mother."

Ethan gave a scornful laugh. "Alec was one of the most confident people I knew. He could do anything. Even after he was disabled, he gritted his teeth and forged a totally new career, kept himself at the forefront of his profession. Everyone looked up to Alec. You can't saddle him with an inferiority complex."

Celeste sighed. "I'm not trying to saddle him with anything. I just want to try to understand him."

"Really. It's a pity you didn't try harder when he was alive then, isn't it?"

Celeste stood up. "The trouble with you is, you've made up your mind, and you don't want to consider any facts that could lead you to change it," she said. "In some ways, you are very much like your brother."

Ethan stood, too, big and angry, and she instinctively took a step back. "Don't try to blacken Alec's character to me, Celeste! If I'm like him in any way, I can only be proud of the fact."

"Yes," she said. "You would be. Even if it means you're *both* wilfully blind and prejudiced because of what goes on in your own sick little minds. It's only now that I'm beginning to see what Alec did to me."

"Huh! What *he* did to *you*?" Ethan said.

"Yes! Oh, I'm not saying I'm totally blameless. Perhaps if I'd been older, I might have understood the demons that drove him. I might have coped better, been able to help him. As it was, all I could think of was to try to be what he wanted, what he seemed to want. I let him stifle my personality, curb how I expressed myself. I even changed the way

I looked. And he was never satisfied, because he was trying to kill the very things that had attracted him to me in the first place."

"That's not true," Ethan contradicted her. "Alec never tried to curb you or repress you."

She cried, "How would you know?"

"I told you—he wrote me letters."

"Letters!"

"Yes, letters."

"What exactly did he accuse me of?"

Ethan said, "He never *accused* you of anything. The man bloody worshipped you! No matter how much you hurt and humiliated him, he let you go your own sweet way because he was terrified of losing you. He was so damned tolerant of your youth, your natural high spirits, your love of pretty things and what he thought of as your naive love of being admired—it just about broke my heart. Anyone reading between the lines could see he was bleeding to death over your heartlessness, your selfishness, your greed for clothes, for money, for admiration. And for sex, although he didn't ever want to believe you'd go to another man for that."

As her cheeks flamed, his mouth twisted in an ugly line. "Well, *we* know the truth about that, don't we? And in the end you didn't even allow him that illusion, did you? You took my brother for a fool, Celeste. Don't ever think you can do the same to me."

Chapter Twelve

Celeste closed her eyes in horror. Now she understood Ethan's suspicion of her, his hostility. She could imagine the letters, knew just how they would have appeared to him. And the worst of it was, Alec had honestly thought that he was trying to understand her, to make the best of things, while inside him his jealousy grew day by day like a monstrous cancer, warping his judgement and torturing him with baseless suspicions. And all her desperate efforts to conform with his apparent wishes had been futile. She had tried so hard to make a good thing of her marriage, ruthlessly suppressed her own needs, even her own natural exuberance, refused to countenance any thought of Ethan and the sweet, snatched moments they had shared—and all for nothing. It had not made Alec happy. It had not erased the emotional scars of his mother's desertion and his father's hurt bitterness, or convinced him of his wife's devotion. And worse, Ethan did not believe that she had even tried.

She turned away from him, her whole stance defeated. He gripped her arm and swung her back to face him, lifting her chin rather roughly with his other hand, finding her eyes glazed and lifeless.

"Don't crawl back into that shell again," he said. "Not now." He moved his hands to her shoulders and gave her an impatient little shake. "Wake up, Celeste, damn you! I won't *let* you retreat from me again!"

She said huskily, "Let me go, Ethan. Leave me alone."

"I'm not going to leave you alone, and I'm not letting you go," he said. "So get that into your head. I'm going to haul you out of that comfortable dreamworld of yours—kicking and screaming if necessary. Understand?"

Hopelessly, she shook her head. "It's you who don't understand." She stood between his hands and waited for him to release her. "You'll do whatever you want, I suppose. I can't fight you."

He gave a furious, disgusted exclamation. "At one time you'd have had a damn good try!"

She looked away, her head drooping again.

Ethan said, in a strange tone, "Well, this worked before..." And he hauled her into his arms, her head tipped back against the curve of his shoulder, while he regarded her upturned face with glittering fury. Her lips parted in silent protest, her eyes widening, and his mouth curved grimly before he lowered it to hers, taking no notice of her reflexive attempt at escape. "Too late," he murmured, tightening his hold on her. And then his lips were determinedly exploring hers, with a concentration and intensity that overwhelmed her. A tide of panic rose inside her as she felt the heat of his body through her swimsuit. One of his hands roved down her spine, forcing her closer; she went as taut as a bowstring, and made another effort to free herself. Ethan's hand clamped behind her head, and his mouth continued wreaking its devastation of hers.

He didn't stop until she shuddered against him and went quiet. Then he lifted his head to look frowningly into her dazed eyes, and slowly released her.

Celeste stepped back one pace, steadied herself, then swung her hand back and up. She saw the gleam of triumph in his eyes, the beginning of a smile on his mouth before her slap wiped it away. He had seen it coming and had not even tried to defend himself.

She didn't stay around to see any more, but dived cleanly into the water and headed for the shore. When she reached the sand and snatched up her towel and began to climb to the house, he was still standing on the rock, watching her.

She spent the rest of the day in her room, lying on the bed. Later she heard Ethan come up the stairs, pausing outside her door, but then the soft footsteps went on to his work-room.

Celeste cooked dinner and served it, and they ate in near silence, treating each other with exquisite politeness. She refused to meet Ethan's eyes, her gaze sliding obliquely away as she passed him the potatoes or took away his plate for washing.

Afterwards he said, "I'll make the coffee. Go into the other room."

When he brought it, she took hers and waited for him to sit down. Then she said, "May I read Alec's letters?"

"Why? Do you want to relive the hell you put him through? Did you enjoy making him feel a fool?"

She winced. "Whatever you think of me, you have no right to say a thing like that."

The look that crossed his face was so fleeting she couldn't read it.

She said, "You've condemned me on the basis of evidence I've never seen. Do you think that's fair?"

"I don't have the letters anymore. They weren't the kind of thing you'd want to keep around."

"Even that last one he wrote?" she asked. Surely he wouldn't have discarded the letter that had arrived after Alec's death.

Ethan said slowly, "I'm not sure what effect it might have on you. It could send you into another emotional tailspin. I daren't risk that."

"You admit I have some feelings, then."

"Some, yes. Guilt, at least. No matter what I think of you, Celeste, I don't want to be responsible for making you ill."

"No, you might feel obliged to pay my hospital bills, or worse still, be saddled with me yourself."

"I don't have a premium on unfairness, do I?"

She flushed. He had never shown any signs of grudging anything she needed when she was ill.

"You've been very patient," she conceded stiffly, "considering what you think of me. But I'll make arrangements to leave as soon as possible."

"Running away?" he jeered softly. "Once you'd have had more guts than that."

"I'm not running away. I'm removing myself from an unpleasant situation, and one that you can't be enjoying any more than I am."

"It has its moments. Do you really hate it so much?"

"Not everything." She gazed down at the steaming liquid in her cup, then took a small, warming sip. "I love the island...your house. And I like Janice and Henry...and Jeff. But I can't stay."

"So it's only me that you can't stand."

"I've never said that. Never." She raised her eyes and gazed at him over her coffee cup.

He sucked in his breath. "When you look at me like that, I could almost forget—"

"—how much you hate me? You don't have to hate me Ethan. I wish you wouldn't."

"Then why don't you stay," he said slowly, his eyes very intent, "and see if you can change that?"

It was a tempting thought, a slender ray of hope. She tried to read what was in his face, but he had shifted a little and his face was shadowed. As usual he had only turned on the wall lights.

"Do you mean it?" she asked. Would he be prepared to listen to her version of events, to keep an open mind?

"I mean," he said, "that I don't want you to go yet. No for a while. And if you're as innocent as you claim, you should jump at the chance to prove it."

"Prove it? How?"

He said, his eyes totally unfathomable, "I'll think of something."

A small shiver of apprehension ran down her spine "What do you—"

He interrupted her. "But first, I want you fully fit and well, emotionally as well as physically. As for the rest...try not to think about it."

"Will you promise to do the same?" she asked him. "Try not to think about it?"

He looked thoughtfully at her, leaning back in his chair "Okay," he agreed finally. "It's a deal."

Celeste forced herself to eat more, and to swim every day Swimming was relaxing and it was gentle exercise. She re fused to accept excuses from herself that she was too tired or the tide was wrong, or she had other things to do.

Ethan sometimes strolled on the beach with her or swam with her. Once or twice they went out in the boat with Jeff and she looked the other way each time the men hooked a fish and hauled it into the boat. And in the evenings she sat with Ethan on the terrace after dinner watching the stars come out and listening to music through the open door to the house.

He was going out of his way to be considerate, although occasionally she caught a hint of impatience in his eyes. But gradually she began to feel more alive. Janice remarked with relief how much better she seemed. Mrs. Jackson said with approval, "Getting over it then, aren't you, dear?" Even Jeff noticed. She seldom saw him alone these days, although sometimes he joined her and Ethan on the beach.

One day when the three of them had been swimming, Jeff put a friendly arm about her shoulders as they left the water. "Has Ethan taken you to the Trocadero yet?" he asked.

"No. What is it?"

"A nightclub. It's not half-bad. How about it?" he said. "We could all go out tomorrow night."

"I have work to do," Ethan said.

Jeff grinned at him. "Don't we all? I'll take her on my own if you like."

Ethan had picked up his towel and was rubbing his hair. He paused and shot a glance at his friend, which Jeff met with quizzically raised brows. Ethan said, "Would you like to go, Celeste?"

Aware of Ethan's eyes on her, Celeste hesitated. Her first thought was to refuse. Then she remembered her resolution to start living a normal life again. "Yes," she said. "Thank you, Jeff. I'd like that very much."

"Tomorrow, then. Sure you won't change your mind?" Jeff asked Ethan.

"Three's a crowd," Ethan said shortly. "I'd better get some work done. See you later."

Jeff looked after him, then flopped down on the sand. "What's eating him?"

"I've no idea." Celeste spread her towel beside him and rolled over on her back.

"Could he be jealous?" Jeff asked, as though the idea had just occurred.

"On his brother's behalf, perhaps. Maybe he thinks it's too soon for me to be going to nightclubs."

"It's almost three months, isn't it?"

With a slight shock, Celeste realised that he was right. She nodded, and he said, "He must know you can't mourn forever. The Trocadero is just a small place. Classy. I think you'll like it."

She wore the hand-painted silk dress she had bought in Conneston, with a narrow silver belt and the green sandals. When she came down from her room, her hair flowing about her shoulders, Ethan was prowling about the living room with a glass in his hand. He stopped dead and surveyed her as she descended the stairs.

She reached the floor, and hesitated. Ethan took a gulp of whisky from his glass and said, "Jeff will be impressed."

"Why don't you come with us?" she asked him. "You were invited."

"Isn't one man at a time enough for you?"

Not realising that it was a measure of her recovery, she flared into real anger. "That's a filthy thing to say! I thought we agreed—"

"On some sort of truce, yes. I apologise. How are you feeling these days?"

At the moment, she felt fully alive and aware, her senses singing, some complicated emotion making her pulses race in a way that was not entirely unpleasant. In the last few weeks she had truly climbed out of the pit of despair and depression in which she had been wallowing. "I feel . . . okay," she said. Her chin lifted. "Is that a signal to start insulting me again?"

His lips curved in a smile that held calculation and perhaps anticipation. "And if I do . . . insult you," he drawled, "will I get as good as I give?"

She snapped, "That's a promise!"

He stood surveying her for several long seconds, then, very softly, he said, "Good. I'll look forward to it."

A frown gathered on her forehead. "Why do you want to fight with me?"

Blandly, he said, "Did I say that?"

"You certainly implied it."

"You're far too lovely to fight with, Celeste. Especially tonight."

Her voice brittle, she said between her teeth, "Thank you."

"Not at all," he replied with mocking courtesy. "Should I have thought of taking you nightclubbing, myself?"

"I can't think of a single reason why you should."

"Can't you?" He paused. "Just the prospect of it seems to have brought you right out of your shell. I haven't seen you look so . . . vital, since you arrived here."

"I'm looking forward to an evening out," she said.

"I apologise. I haven't been a very good host, have I?"

"You've been . . . extremely generous with your home, and your time."

His mouth went dry. "Don't lay it on too thick, Celeste."

"I was quite sincere, actually." She met his eyes almost defiantly.

"I'm not asking for your gratitude."

"I know that." Something wordless passed between them. She saw his eyes narrow, and inwardly shivered. But the familiar shrinking hopelessness was no longer there. There had to be a reckoning between them, she knew that, knew this was what his patience and persistence had been all about. In a strange way, she almost welcomed the prospect. Face it and get it over with, she thought.

But not tonight. Hearing a car turn into the driveway, she said, "That must be Jeff. Excuse me."

"Ask him in," Ethan said, "for a drink before you go."

"Do you think that's a good idea, if we're going to be drinking later?"

He said, "Jeff isn't a fool. He won't overdo it."

He followed her to the door and invited Jeff in himself, whistling derisively at the pleated shirt and bow tie the other man wore with a dinner jacket.

"Okay." Jeff grinned. "I have to live up to this girl." His comprehensive glance at Celeste was appreciative. "You look beautiful," he said sincerely.

Ethan handed him a drink, and poured some sparkling white wine for Celeste. Jeff said, "Sure you don't want to come and play chaperone?"

"I told you, I need to work."

Jeff shrugged. "Suit yourself. We'll think of you when we're tripping the light fantastic."

"Do that." His gaze was on Celeste, his voice apparently absentminded, but something in his eyes made her lower hers abruptly. She shivered and put down her half-empty glass.

"I won't promise to bring Cinderella home by mid-night," Jeff said, taking his cue from her and standing up. "We could be dancing until dawn."

"Celeste is a big girl," Ethan said, apparently tranquil. "I'm sure she can take care of herself. But she's not been entirely well, lately. Just take it easy, okay?"

"Sure. Don't worry, uncle," Jeff teased. He put a hand on Celeste's waist. "Let's go."

"Something's bugging him," Jeff said in the car.

Trying to sound surprised, Celeste said, "He seemed quite happy to me."

"Uh-uh. He's uptight about something."

"Work, maybe."

"Maybe. Well, that's his problem. You and I are going to enjoy ourselves, right?"

"Right," she echoed, stifling a tiny, ridiculous regret that it was Jeff sitting beside her, and not Ethan.

The club was right on the waterfront in Conneston. Its atmosphere was friendly and sophisticated, the decor a mixture of Pacific artifacts, with carvings much in evidence among glossy potted plants, and upmarket brass and smoked glass furniture. Jeff knew a few people and they soon found themselves members of a party. At first a little tense and scared, Celeste gradually relaxed, helped by a couple of glasses of wine and some delicious coconut, rice and fish combination that Jeff assured her was a specialty of the house and not to be missed.

A small combo played dance music, the musicians imported from Tahiti and wearing garlands of flowers. When Jeff first asked her to dance, she felt rather stiff and out of practice, but after he had whirled her around the floor a couple of times with uninhibited expertise, she began to enjoy herself properly. She danced with a couple of his friends, too, and was conscious of having a thoroughly good time. Everyone was easily friendly; the men were admiring without being pushy, and the women seemed to like her. There was no pressure and no tension. The music, the food, the movements of the dance, and perhaps the wine, all helped. She looked up at Jeff as he handed her another glass of wine, and smiled at him gratefully. For the first time, she felt there was no danger of relapsing into the grey world she had inhabited for so long.

"Okay?" Jeff raised an eyebrow.

"Very much so. Thank you for bringing me, Jeff."

"My pleasure. Like to dance again?"

"I haven't danced so much in years." She got up to join him on the floor. The music was slow and dreamy, and he tucked her hand against his chest and drew her close, nuzzling his cheek against her hair.

Gently, Celeste pushed him away a little.

He grinned down at her. "No?"

She shook her head firmly. "Sorry, Jeff. Just friends?"

He studied the shadow of anxiety in her eyes and bent to brush his lips across her forehead. "Fine. But you can't blame a bloke for trying."

"I'm not blaming you for anything. You've been very sweet to me."

He grimaced. "Sounds like the kiss of death. Oh, well. You can't win 'em all."

She smiled at him teasingly. "I shouldn't think you'd have much trouble winning quite a few."

"Thank you, ma'am." He added thoughtfully, "You've changed a lot since you came to Sheerwind."

"Don't remind me," she said soberly. "I was in something of a state, wasn't I?"

"Sorry," he said. "You don't need to be told. Anyway, I'm glad you've snapped out of it. I guess Ethan has had a lot to do with it."

She looked at him rather warily, and he said, "I mean, he's really pulled you through it, hasn't he?"

"Yes," she said slowly, "he really has. For his own reasons."

"How's that?"

"Nothing. Let's not discuss Ethan tonight."

"Suits me. Talking about another man when I'm dancing with a beautiful woman—I must be slipping!"

He took her home at about one-thirty. Ethan had left the door on the latch, and Jeff opened it for her, saying, "Shall I find the light for you?"

"It's all right," she said. "I'll turn on the switch in the lounge. Thank you, Jeff. I had a great time."

"My pleasure."

As she paused, he said, with laughter in his voice, "I've been a perfect little gentleman all night. Do I rate a good-night kiss?"

He was a tryer, she thought, amused. She laughed softly and lifted her face. He kissed her nicely, without passion. Just as he knew she would have wished. Then he put his arms about her and gave her a hug. "I had a great time, too. Good night, Celeste."

"Good night." She closed the door after him and snicked the lock, then walked slowly down the passageway to the living room.

She paused in the doorway, and gasped as a looming shadow rose from one of the chairs.

"Have a good time?" Ethan asked.

"Yes, thank you. Why are you sitting in the dark?"

"It relaxes me."

"I thought you'd be in bed."

"I finished the programme I was working on about an hour ago. So I figured I might as well hang about until you came in."

"There's no need to wait up for me. As you said, I'm a big girl, now."

"Absolutely. *Was* Jeff a perfect little gentleman?"

"Yes."

"Disappointed?"

So it was starting again, she thought, her heart sinking. It was one thing to feel able to stand up to whatever he planned to hurl at her, but after a pleasant, relaxed evening, she didn't want to start a minor war. "No," she said coldly, wondering if Ethan had been drinking while he waited. She thought she could faintly smell whisky, and surely that couldn't be left over from hours ago.

"Do you mean to tell me that one good-night kiss is enough for you?" Ethan asked.

"Don't be so beastly," she said, "I'm going to bed."

"Alone again?"

On her way to the stairs, she swung around. "*Yes*, alone!"

"You don't have to be," he said softly.

"What?" In the act of turning away again, she froze.

"I said," Ethan enunciated clearly, "you don't have to go alone."

She said, "Are you offering to—"

"That's right," he said. "I'm offering to warm your bed. Your body. Your heart, if you had one. Pity about that. But one can't have everything."

Celeste drew in a shaking breath. "I wouldn't have you in my bed if you were the last man on earth!" Deliberately, she added, "You make me *sick*!"

She had got to the stairs and was two steps up when he grabbed her, pulling her around and down to him, so that she fell heavily into his arms. Before she could even attempt to free herself, she found herself clamped against him, and he was kissing her angrily, hungrily, with a passion beyond control. She was right about the whisky, but the smell of it was soon replaced by the musky masculine scent of his skin, the taste of it drowned in the taste of his mouth. She fought him, silently and furiously, and when nothing else worked, lifted her foot in its high-heeled sandal and brought it down smartly on his instep.

He grunted with pain and stepped back, allowing her a brief respite, but when she would have fled, he snaked an arm about her waist, and the next moment she was lifted high and he was carrying her up the stairs.

One arm was trapped against his body, but she flailed a fist at his shoulders and his chin. He jerked his head out of the way and said grimly, "Keep that up and you'll have us both down the stairs."

She drew in a panting breath and went stiffly acquiescent, only to fight him again as he shouldered open the door to her room and crossed swiftly to the bed. Moonlight spilled across it, and he pressed her down on the cover and caught her hands, taking her wrists back against the pillow, his body and his legs holding her while he kissed her mouth, kissed it for a long time, and in so many different ways. When she strained against him she could feel his body along the length of hers, and unexpectedly a hot rush of desire swept through her. She gasped into his open mouth and writhed in a futile attempt to escape him, to escape her own shocking need. He wouldn't let her go, and she realised that her struggles were only increasing his arousal. She went still, trying to control her beating heart, the rising, hot tide within her. The effort cost her, and she sobbed with frustration and a confused mixture of emotions.

Ethan raised his head, trying to see her face.

She whispered, "Please, let go my wrists. Please."

Slowly he let them go, resting his hands at either side of her, not moving away. She lay there, her hands resting on the pillow. Her mouth felt hot and swollen, and deep trembles of desire ran through and through her body. She sucked in a breath, then let it out in a long sigh. "Ethan," she murmured. And her hands came up to his hair, remembering the feel of it from long ago, stroking its springy softness, and then she gently drew his mouth back to hers.

Chapter Thirteen

At dawn she woke and found him gone from her bed. Opening her eyes, she saw that he was standing at the window, a black shadow against the pane, where the sky was beginning to lighten, the stars fading and disappearing one by one.

"Ethan?" she whispered.

At first she thought he hadn't heard. Then he turned, but of course it was too dark to see his face.

"Is something the matter?" she asked, as he continued to stand there silently.

After a moment, he said, "What could be the matter?"

"I...don't know." But she was frightened, a pulse in her throat beating nervously. They had made love for a long time, and more than once. For her it had been like a homecoming after long years in the desert. And for him—she couldn't know, but she remembered how he had adored her body with his hands, his mouth, how he had teased and shuddered with pleasure when she touched him, and later, still lying within her arms, he had murmured against her skin, with an air of wonder, "Perfect ... perfect."

She lifted a pale arm in the dimness. "Please come back to me, Ethan."

He didn't come right away, but when he did, he sat on the bed and took her hand, pressing his lips into her palm. Raising his head, he asked, "Have you ever swum in the sea at dawn?"

"No. Is that what you want to do?"

"I'll get some towels," he said.

When he came back into the room carrying two large fresh towels, and wearing another about his waist, she had switched on the bedside lamp and put on her knee-length white satin wrap, belted at the waist, and was holding a swimsuit in one hand.

"You won't need that," Ethan said, taking it from her and throwing it down on the bed. "Come on."

They ran down the path like children, even though it was still quite dark, and in the shadows she tripped and fell against him, and he caught her up and kissed her, sending delicious tingles through her body.

On the sand, he dropped the towels at the edge of the trees, and unselfconsciously discarded the one he wore. Then he looked at her standing fiddling with the satin tie at her waist. "Take it off," he said softly. And when she still hesitated, he offered, "Or shall I do it for you?"

She didn't answer, and he reached for her, grasping the ends of the belt to bring her closer. The knot parted as he did so, and the wrap loosened, drawing his eyes to the gap where the swell of her breasts showed between the satin edges. *"Déjà vu,"* he murmured.

"What?" Her voice was barely audible.

"I wanted to do this once before," he said, as his hands parted the satin farther. "Months ago, in Sydney." His fingers ran lightly over her breasts, bared to his brooding gaze, and then trailed over her shoulders, sweeping aside the wrap so that it slid down her arms and lay in a gleaming white pool on the sand. Then he lifted her naked in his arms and carried her down to the water.

They swam gently in the glittering morning sea, floating and touching each other as they passed and met briefly together, and kissed. At first the water was chilly, but soon it warmed, caressing their bodies. The sun's rim curved over the horizon and laid a golden path to the shore, and Ethan touched her ankle as he glided past, and said, "Ready to get out?"

He took her hand as they walked up the beach, and when they reached the towels, he picked one up and wrapped it around her body. The sunrise made his wet skin look like burnished copper, and she raised a hand to follow a trail of salty droplets along his shoulder and down his arm to the crook of his elbow. She smiled at him, and saw his jaw clench. She reached up and kissed another droplet from his chin, and he pulled her close, his knuckles digging into her breasts where he held the towel. The sunrise lit his eyes, and she caught her breath before he bent his head and captured her mouth under his. After a while, he dropped the towel and his hands spread over her breasts, making her moan with the sweet sensation of it. Then he took her with him down to the sand, spreading the towel beneath her, and made love to her while the sun rose out of the sea and spread its lush crimson light over them.

When they got back to the house the phone was ringing. Ethan answered it while Celeste ran up the stairs and showered the sand from her body and her hair, wound a fresh towel about her, because the satin wrap was sandy and damp, and rubbed with another at her hair. As she combed it out in her bedroom, Ethan came in without knocking. He had put on a pair of jeans but wore no shirt.

"I have to go to the mainland," he said. "Something's come up."

"What?" she asked.

"A glitch in a programme I sent to a firm in Brisbane recently. They have hundreds of thousands of dollars tied up in this system, and they say they need me to sort out the problem. I've got a contract with them. I have to go."

"Yes, of course," she said hollowly. "When?"

"I've phoned the airport. They'll hold this morning's flight for me. It means I have to leave now. I'll just shower and change. Can you come along and drive the car back?"

"Yes. I'll get dressed and make you some coffee. You'll have time for that?"

"Just coffee, nothing else. Celeste...I'm sorry about this."

"Don't be." She gave him a quick smile. "You'd better hurry."

He caught her chin in his hand on the way to the door and dropped a kiss on her lips. "Thanks."

She dressed in a pair of dun-coloured trousers and a blouse, letting her hair dry on her shoulders. Then she ran down the stairs and made coffee, handing Ethan a steaming cup when he appeared wearing a dark suit with a white shirt and dark tie, and with his hair damply sleek. He drank the coffee standing up, then snatched up a briefcase and overnight bag and said, "Let's go."

He drove fast and smoothly, seemingly giving all his concentration to the task. When Celeste looked at him, there was a faint frown line between his brows, and she had the impression he was already wrestling with the problem, whatever it was, that he had to solve. Tactfully, she refrained from talking.

At the airport he turned in his seat and gave her a sudden, piercing scrutiny that she didn't quite understand. He put a hand behind her head, pulled her close to him and kissed her thoroughly, his lips almost bruising. As he drew away, he said softly, "Well, we've established one thing this morning, I think. I don't make you sick."

She bit her lip. "No."

"Right." He stayed there just looking at her, then stirred and said, "I've got to go. I'll phone as soon as I know what day you can expect me. When I get back . . . we'll talk."

She watched him cross the road and go through the doors to the terminal before she slid into the driver's seat and started the engine.

She made herself some breakfast, feeling remarkably hungry, and sat eating it on the patio. When she took her empty plate and glass inside, she found Mrs. Jackson in the kitchen, wiping shelves with a damp cloth.

"Good morning." The woman smiled. "You're up early these days."

"Yes. You must have thought me dreadfully lazy before."

"Of course not. It was obvious you needed to rest. I expect you were awake half the night a lot of the time, weren't you?"

"How did you guess?"

"I've been through it," the woman said simply. "Believe me, I know all about it. The sleepless nights, the days that you have to drag yourself through. You're lucky you had Mr. Ryland to help you."

Rinsing her dishes, Celeste said, "Yes. He's been very good."

"Mind you, there have been times when I've wondered..."

"Wondered what?"

"Oh, I don't know. Your husband was his brother, wasn't he?"

"Stepbrother."

"Yes, well, he was bereaved, too, wasn't he? Mr. Ryland. He hasn't been himself since. Very tense, I thought. I must say, I've heard him speak to you a bit sharply once or twice. Sorry, dear, I wasn't meaning to eavesdrop, but you know you can't help hearing things sometimes. It's not a big house."

"I understand," Celeste said.

"Yes. It just didn't seem like him, somehow. I mean, he's never said a cross word to me. But of course, relatives are different, and we humans are funny critters. Take out our worst feelings on our loved ones, don't we? When we lost our girl, you know our marriage almost broke up over it. You'd think it would bring us closer, but grief can be very selfish sometimes—does strange things to people. She was sick, you see, for three days. And we didn't think, at first, it could be serious. But it was. Meningitis. Afterwards, my husband kept saying I should have noticed sooner how sick she was. He was beside himself, didn't know what he was saying. But I felt guilty enough already without him— Well, it's all over now."

Celeste shivered. "I'm so sorry," she murmured.

"Oh, we box along all right," Mrs. Jackson said, with her usual brisk manner. "Only..." A look of infinite sadness crossed her face. "Things will never be quite the same." Changing the subject, she said, "Mr. Ryland's in his workroom, is he?"

"Ethan had to fly to the mainland," Celeste said. "He had a phone call very early and left on the morning flight."

"I see. Well, I'll give his workroom a good going over, then, and maybe do the windows."

"I'll go up and change my bed," Celeste said, her cheeks warming as she remembered the state of it. "I'll get his sheets for you, too," she offered.

"Oh, there's no need for you to—"

"It's all right. No trouble," Celeste assured her. Ethan's bed had not been slept in. Somehow she didn't want Mrs. Jackson to realise that.

She had never been in his room before. It had white-painted furniture like hers, but the bed cover was deep olive green, and a mat of the same colour lay on the floor. A digital clock glowed on the table by the bed, and alongside it was a large framed photograph of Alec. A laughing, full-length picture, taken when he was younger and still physically fit, standing with his hands casually in the pockets of a parka, a backpack strapped about his shoulders. And tucked into the frame, obscuring his legs, was an envelope with his writing on it.

Celeste stood looking at it, going slowly cold all over. She knew what it was. The last letter he had ever written to Ethan. The one that had arrived after his death.

Resolutely, she dragged her gaze away and began to strip the bed. When she took the sheets downstairs with her own, Mrs. Jackson was in the laundry, removing a load from the washing machine that she must have put on when she first arrived.

"I'll change the beds," Celeste told her, and walked away before the woman could argue.

She did hers first, then went back to the linen cupboard and pulled out clean sheets for the other bed. As she made it up, the letter and the photograph seemed to burn into her consciousness. She was quite unable to ignore them.

At last she smoothed the cover over the pillows, and straightened. Her eyes were compelled to the envelope. Ethan had once practically challenged her to read it. Did that constitute permission? She shrank from the idea, but at the same time it drew her. Later, when she had asked to read it, he said he doubted she was well enough to take what it contained. Now she was well. She felt strong, alive, even angry. She had a right to know just what she had to fight against for Ethan's love.

Downstairs the vacuum cleaner hummed, and she thought, *Not now, not while Mrs. Jackson is in the house.* She carefully removed the envelope from the photo frame and took it into her own room. Opening the drawer of the bedside table, she slipped it inside.

When the housekeeper had left, Celeste made herself lunch and washed up afterward. Then she spent some time staring out the window of the living room, watching the sunlight play over the blue water, the trees moving gently in the slightest of breezes. Jeff appeared at the top of the path, and she quelled a feeling of annoyance mingled with relief as he waved and came towards her.

"Ethan isn't here," she said, going to meet him. "Did you want to see him?"

"Not especially. Came to see you, as a matter of fact." He regarded her curiously. "Recovered all right from last night?"

Her head jerked up and she flushed, before she realised what he meant. "Yes, thanks. And thank you again for taking me. I really enjoyed it."

"Want to do it again sometime?"

"Maybe," she said noncommittally.

"You were up early," he commented.

Her eyes swung to his face. "How do you know?"

"Saw you and Ethan in the water," he said.

"You were up early, too. Why... why didn't you come in and join us?"

"Well... I thought you might be shy. Haven't seen you swimming like that before. It kinda looked like a private party. So I just turned around and went home again."

Fleetingly worried and embarrassed, she was sure he had done just what he said. Jeff was no voyeur. She said, "I'm sorry if we spoilt your morning swim."

He grinned. "Don't worry about that." He paused. "You look... different."

"Do I?" She glanced away from him. "Ethan's on the mainland—for a few days, I think," she said, and explained about the early morning call.

"You can rely on me for company," Jeff promised, "if you get lonely. As a friend," he added, with emphasis.

She smiled at him, knowing he had guessed at something between her and Ethan, but would refrain from asking. "Thanks," she said.

"Want me to go away?" he asked her quizzically.

"No, of course not!" She invited him to sit down, and they chatted for a time before he got up, stretched and said, "I'm for a swim. Care to come, too?" Slanting her a grin, he added, "With or without your swimsuit."

She laughed. "No, I don't think so, thanks. I've had a swim today."

"Oh, yes," he murmured, with a wicked look, and she said with dignity, "It was nice of you to call. Enjoy yourself."

Jeff shrugged and left good-humouredly, and she sat on in the lounger for a while. Then she went up the stairs and into her room, and slid out the drawer of the bedside table.

She opened the envelope slowly and walked to the window, unfolding the three flimsy sheets of paper. The writing was scrawled and agitated, some words difficult to read.

My dear Ethan,

Finally I must admit to myself what I have been trying to hide for years—that I am not, perhaps have never been, the man that others see. To put it brutally, I am in every way a failure.

Failure is not something I have ever been able to accept. All my life I've needed to be the best, the first, the one who was on top. I have no fancy for dwindling into old age, leaving the field clear for young men with brash aspirations and the ability to fulfil them.

When I lost, for all intents and purposes, the use of my legs, I lost a large part of myself, my inner self, as well. I can't describe, even to you, how that felt. It was as though every reason for living had been taken away and replaced by a deep, endless black hole. I thought for a time that I could fill the hole. I piled into it everything that I could think of—a new job, a young wife, different kinds of research, more writing. I told myself this hollow shell was still living, still breathing and moving and achieving. For a time I thought that Celeste, with her vibrant sense of life, her colour and spirit—and her youth, yes that, too—would bring me back to life. Instead, I pulled her into the black hole with me. She never did love me, she only thought so when she was young and innocent and inexperienced, and I was old enough to have known better. But I wanted her, loved her, for a number of complicated reasons that I'm afraid took no account of her own needs. I wanted to wear her like a gage on my sleeve. But I expected too much. She was not able to return to me what I had lost, and no one should blame her for that. Least of all me. I have been possessed by frenzied jealousies about my wife. You may have realised this from my letters to you. At this moment my brain seems clear, although I am very tired, and I see now that none of it was her fault. Objectively, I suppose I should be surprised that she has not left me before this. She has been unhappy, and the fault is mine.

For years I have known that this time must come. I have staved it off as long as I can, fooling myself and others that I'm no less than I ever was, that the quick, virile brilliance of youth can be compensated for by the wisdom of maturity. It may work that way for some. For myself, I find that my life has taken a wrong turning, and I can never go back. My new directions turned out to be dead ends. I've been gradually desiccating ever since that day I slipped down a cliff in New Guinea, in both body and brain. Even, perhaps, in my heart. How many times I've wished that I had died there. If I had known then that I would never properly walk again, never be able to go back to the work that I loved, that I would even be incapable of fulfilling the natural expectations of a lovely young wife, I think I would have lain down and allowed it to happen. Now, it's a matter of taking charge of the business myself.

"Oh, Alec," Celeste whispered. She went unsteadily over to the bed, then sank to the floor with her back resting against the mattress, and forced herself to read the rest. Her eyes misted. Something was scrawled in pencil across the final page, overlaying the penned words at an angle. She would decipher that later.

There's someone waiting to take my place. I know the young man who stands ready to supplant me. He has all that I had in my own youth. And already, in middle age, I feel so old and so spent. He comes to my house with his enthusiasm and his confidence and his pretense at respect for me, and I hate him for his cleverness, for his energy, for his two good legs. And, yes, for the smiles that Celeste gives him. And what else, I ask myself, does she give him when he carries a tray for her into the other room? Even if I followed them, they would hear me with my cane and my dragging feet long before I got there. And how can I blame her, my pretty butterfly, for being what she is, for preferring someone young and fit and on his way up, to a twisted cripple who is about to be thrown on the scrap heap?

Because that's where I belong now. I've been fooling everyone, including even myself, that I was a fully functioning human being. Tonight I looked at the last year of my life—the last eight years—and saw a wasteland. There is nothing worth saving from all those years. It's a sham. He must know, or guess, something is wrong. As I said, he's clever. And perhaps I hate him more because I think that he's kind-hearted, too. He will feel that he's wasted a good deal of time. At his age time is precious. If he has done nothing, is it because he's sorry for me, afraid of hurting me? One thing I could not take is pity. That would be wormwood and gall. I'm not going to wait around for the moment of truth. It may be a far, far better thing that I do—not that this is a sacrifice for others. More a salvaging of my own pride, perhaps. I've always had plenty of that. But it will free all three of us. Him, me, Celeste. Perhaps you, too, Ethan. You need no longer be the recipient of my maudlin, self-pitying missives, of which, tonight, seeing as clearly as I do, I am ashamed. I am ashamed of other things, too. My dear Celeste—there is so much I would change if I could, for her sake—

But you will know what to do. I trust you. I send you, finally, my love.

Alec.

"Oh, my poor, poor Alec!"

She laid her head back, trying to keep the stinging tears at bay, but after a while she rested her arms on her knees and let her head drop and wept for a long, long time.

When she stopped, her limbs were stiff and it was getting dark. She shivered and closed gritty, swollen eyelids, rubbing them wearily. Then she stumbled to the door and went into the bathroom. After splashing her face with cold water several times she had a shower, cleaned her teeth and went back to her room.

The letter still lay on the bed. She picked it up, about to put it back into the envelope, when she remembered the black, pencilled scrawl across the last page. She switched on the bedside light and turned the page, peering down at it.

The writing was quite different. Not Alec's. Ethan's hand, she realised, large and decisive and somehow angry. And in the same moment she saw what the two words were.

She'll pay.

Chapter Fourteen

When the telephone rang, Celeste remained huddled on the bed as she had been for some time, her knees drawn up, her arms hugging her legs. She could hear the bell, knew there was an extension in Ethan's workroom. But it would be him calling, and she didn't want to speak to him just now.

Half an hour later it shrilled again, and then at intervals until twelve o'clock. By then she had replaced the letter in its envelope and put it back in his room, tucked into the photograph frame, and methodically prepared herself for bed. The last time the phone rang, she pulled the pillow over her head until it stopped. Then she went to sleep.

She was barely awake when the ringing started again. She got up, taking her time, and pulled on her wrap before going downstairs to answer it.

She had barely placed the receiver at her ear when Ethan's voice said, "Celeste? Where *were* you last night?"

She said coolly, "I went to bed early."

"Are you okay?"

"Perfectly, thank you. I'd had a late night previously, remember."

There was a short, baffled silence. Then he said, "I remember."

Celeste moistened her lips. "How is the programming problem?"

"It'll take a few days to sort out. Look, I wish this hadn't come up."

"It couldn't be helped," she said graciously. "I understand."

"Are you sure you're all right? Did I wake you?"

"No, I was awake."

"Someone's waiting for me, but I had to contact you first. I was worried."

Carefully, she said, "I know you've had reason to worry about me, but there's no need, now. I'm quite recovered."

"If I hadn't thought so," he said, "I wouldn't have..."

She was glad he couldn't see her burning cheeks. "I know," she assured him steadily. "You have been remarkably forbearing."

"Celeste," he said urgently. "There's so much to say, I can't even begin on the phone. Believe me, I'll be back as soon as I can possibly manage it."

"I believe you, Ethan," she said huskily. "But there's no hurry."

"There is for me. We have a lot of sorting out to do. Sit tight and wait for me, darling."

He had never called her that before, and she closed her eyes, feeling the word enter her like a pain in her heart.

He said, "I have to go. They're waiting for me. I'm sorry."

"Yes," she said. "Goodbye, Ethan." And she put down the phone on his voice, saying something she couldn't decipher. She supposed it was goodbye.

She made herself breakfast, phoned the airport and returned upstairs to pack her clothes and tidy her room. Then she went to see the Palmers.

"I've left a note in the house for Mrs. Jackson and one for Ethan," she told them. "But if he telephones, he may worry when there's no reply. I guess his next step will be to contact you or Jeff. Tell him not to be concerned, won't you?"

"Of course," Janice said. "But is it necessary to leave before he gets back?"

Celeste said gently, "Yes."

Henry regarded her rather shrewdly and said, "How are you getting to the airport?"

"I'll hire a taxi."

"It'll cost a small fortune. Let me drive you."

"Oh, I couldn't ask you to."

"You didn't. I just volunteered. We need some supplies, anyway."

Janice gave her a long, searching scrutiny. "Are you sure you're all right?"

"Don't I look it?" Celeste smiled.

"You look...like someone who's taken charge of her life, but you don't look happy," the other woman told her bluntly. "Want to tell me what's happened?"

Celeste shook her head. "It's much too complicated to explain. But I have taken charge, and...I know that what I'm doing is right."

Janice nodded. "I won't probe, then. Keep in touch, won't you?"

Without promising anything, Celeste said, "You've been very good to me, you and Henry. Thank you for everything."

Jeff was out, and she left a scribbled note under his door, relieved that she didn't have to dodge questions from him as well. When Henry called for her, she had her cases downstairs already, and he swung them into his car and opened the door for her. She left the house without a backward glance.

At the airport, when she had checked in her luggage, Henry kissed her cheek and said, "We'll miss you. Ethan will, too, I expect."

She saw the enquiring look in his eyes but ignored it. "Thank you for the lift," she said. "And everything."

He shrugged and smiled. "Take care."

She didn't stay long in Sydney. The first night she found a cheap hotel, and the next morning made a phone call to Grant Morrison's associates in the city. "Grant said to call you if I needed anything before my husband's will is probated," she explained. "I'm afraid I'm going to need some money...."

They couldn't have been more helpful, she reflected the following day, when she was winging her way over the Tasman to New Zealand. It had been remarkably easy to arrange the Sydney to Auckland flight, and Sandra, her bridesmaid, had been warmly welcoming when Celeste phoned and asked if she could spare a bed or even a sofa for the night. It was an invitation that had been made often enough, but until now Celeste had never taken her up on it.

"It'll be lovely to see you!" Sandra had assured her. "Tell me what time your flight arrives, and I'll be there to pick you up."

She was as good as her word, and Celeste was surprised at the rush of affection that she felt when she saw her friend standing at the barrier waiting for her. She had three of the children with her. "Ron stayed home to look after the baby," she said. "But these three couldn't be deprived of a trip to the airport. Hope you don't mind."

Celeste was quite glad. Having the children precluded too much questioning and stopped her from allowing foolish tears to overtake her.

Ron made her equally welcome, and she shared a room with one of the children, a solemn little girl who asked if Celeste would like to read her a bedtime story, with an air of bestowing an honour granted only to a privileged few. Celeste accepted the offer gravely.

Later Sandra came to tuck in her daughter and turn out the light. She and Celeste both returned to the cozy, cluttered sitting room, and Sandra said softly, "It's a shame you and Alec had no children."

"It might be just as well. Children would make it more difficult to find a way to earn a living."

"Do you have to?" Sandra asked. "I mean, surely Alec was fairly well-off."

There was no point in going into all that. "I want to do something with my life, anyway," Celeste said vaguely. "I'll go and see my lawyer tomorrow. I thought I might sell the house in Wellington and put some of the money into a business. The lease could be transferred, I suppose. And probate on Alec's will should come through any day. Then I'll be able to make plans."

"What kind of business?" Sandra asked.

"Well, I thought of working from home—when I have one—or perhaps opening a boutique if I can raise the money. I've become interested in fabric painting and dyeing. For clothes, you know. I'm only a beginner, but I want to earn more. Maybe I'm being too ambitious. And I'd need a partner, someone who could sew. And maybe someone who knows something about running a business."

"I can sew," Sandra said. "I've been doing piecework for a clothing factory for a couple of years. Fifty of the same thing, week after week." She grimaced. "I've been thinking of giving it up, but we need the money. Four kids, you know. I'd love to get into some boutique work. I could put you in touch with a couple of other women who'd probably jump at the chance, too. As for running a business, Ron can help you there. What do you think I married an accountant for?"

"Looks like I've chosen the right place to come," Celeste said. "But let's not get carried away. It's just a thought, and I have to sort out my financial situation with the lawyer, first."

She found Grant Morrison was a tower of strength. Although he never said so, she gathered that he thought Alec's will puzzlingly unfair, and he did his level best to wring every last benefit from the little that had been left to her. When she told him what she wanted to do, he expressed cautious approval and promised to use his own contacts to get her the best deal possible. "Buy yourself into an established concern," he advised her. "I'll look about for you, put out some feelers."

He did, and she found herself in partnership with a couple who had been running a craft shop and art gallery tucked into a corner of a mall in the inner city suburb of Ponsonby. Young and enthusiastic, they explained that they wanted to expand into "wearable art." They were also expecting a baby and, while reluctant to employ staff, had decided to take on an extra partner to share the financial commitment of the business as well as helping in the shop, allowing them some time to spend with their child. By the time the baby was born, they and Celeste were friends as well as partners.

She established a small circle of good friends, some of them renewed from her university days, some people she had recently met. She began to accept invitations. If she needed a partner, Grant Morrison, who had been divorced for a number of years and had two children whom he visited every second weekend, was always willing to oblige. They liked each other and were content to be friends. Grant admired her for her courage and her determination, and she was grateful for his help. Neither of them wanted an intimate relationship.

It was, she told herself, not a bad way to live. If it lacked something in emotional colour and excitement, she had other things to make up for that. If sometimes she felt like a walking shell of a human being, it was only to be expected when she had been widowed less than a year.

Seven months after she had left Sheerwind, Ethan walked back into her life.

He stopped in the doorway of the shop, watching as Celeste took a delicate blown-glass vase from a case to show to a customer, handling it with reverent care. She still wore Alec's wedding ring, he saw, and the diamond cluster that was her engagement ring. That was the only thing, he thought, that looked the same. She had cut her hair, and it swung in a shining fall just below her ears as she leaned forward. Her arms had lost their thin fragility, and her complexion had a bloom on it. When she straightened he could see that the dispirited droop of her shoulders had entirely disappeared. She was wearing a striking patterned dress—black with splashes of red, white and yellow, rather like an abstract painting. When she pushed back her hair a pair of jet earrings swung against her jawline.

Then she glanced up and saw him in the doorway. She almost dropped the vase, her eyes widening; her lips, painted a vivid red to go with the red in her dress, parted. A flush came into her cheeks before she blinked and looked away from him.

When the customer had gone without a purchase, Ethan was leaning on the counter. He put out his hand and picked up the vase. "Expensive," he said, examining the price tag.

"It's worth it," Celeste assured him in her coolest tones. "One of a kind. What are you doing here?"

"Would you believe shopping?"

"No. How did you know I was here?"

"Aunt Ellie," he told her.

She had been to see Alec's aunt more than once. Duty visits, but she had enjoyed them. She had always rather liked the old lady, in spite of her blunt tongue and sometimes embarrassing mannerisms. "How is she?"

"The same as always. You seem put out to see me. Were you hoping to hide from me forever?"

"I'm not hiding. I don't have any secrets, Ethan."

"No?" he queried.

Celeste shook her head.

"Have you heard from Steven lately?" he asked.

She stiffened. "Not for some time."

He was regarding her thoughtfully. "I want to talk to you."

"Is that necessary? I don't think that we have anything more to say to each other."

"Don't you?"

She thought his low tone held menace, but he no longer had the power to frighten her. She looked him full in the eyes. "Don't threaten me, Ethan."

"Threaten?" His surprise appeared to be genuine. "Al
I'm suggesting is that we talk. What could possibly be
threatening about that? Unless you do have something to
hide."

Two people came in and began browsing along the
shelves. Ethan said, "When do you finish up here for the
day?"

"In about half an hour," she told him unwillingly. "Bu
I don't think—"

"I'll wait," he said.

She locked up five minutes early because his prowling
about the place, picking up a piece of pottery here and a
hand-painted scarf there, standing in front of a painting and
staring at it for long minutes, unsettled her.

He said, "Is there somewhere we can go for a meal? I'm
paying."

"Around the corner," she told him, "there's a good lit
tle restaurant. Or if you want something fancier, there's one
a bit farther down the road that's licensed to serve alco
hol."

"We'll take the licensed one," he said. "I could do with
a drink. And I'm in no hurry to eat, are you?"

She had lost her appetite instantly on seeing him, but she
wasn't going to admit to that. "No hurry," she agreed
evenly. "But did it occur to you I might have other plans?"

"Sorry," he said. "Do you?"

She debated claiming that she did, but that would only
delay the inevitable. If he had come all this way to see her—
and even if, as was most likely, he had other business to at
tend to, he had made the effort to find her and seemed to
have something of importance to say—then he wasn't going
to tamely turn tail and head back to Sheerwind.

So she said, "No, I don't tonight, as a matter of fact. It
just would have been courteous to ask."

"I stand corrected," he said gravely. She looked at him with suspicion but could see no sarcasm in his expression.

In the restaurant he ordered a whisky for himself and a rum cocktail for her, which they drank in a small lounge before going to their table. Ethan eyed her over his glass and said, "You're different. Again."

"Again?" Trying for a measure of sophistication, she raised her brows to him.

He leaned forward a little, appraising her. "Whenever I've seen you after a long time, you've changed."

The first time she had been a bride, young and glowing with happiness. The second time he had needed to remind himself that she was his brother's wife, stunningly attractive, obviously intelligent, almost transparent in the way her green eyes and her lusciously tender mouth reflected her emotions, and apparently capable of enjoying to the full everything she undertook—from cooking a delicious meal to walking for hours up and down hills in a near gale—and yet with an underlying uncertainty, an occasional bewildered poignancy in her expression that he had caught once or twice when she thought she was alone, and that seemed to indicate a secret vulnerability.

And the third time, she had been a widow, apparently crushed by grief and depression—but mostly, Ethan had been convinced, by guilt.

Now another woman had replaced all of them. A poised, utterly beautiful young woman with an air of mature, hard-won serenity, whom he found both irresistibly fascinating and totally enigmatic. He wondered if she was deliberately withholding from him any hint of what she was feeling. That would not be surprising. He suppressed a strong desire to take her in his arms and kiss her senseless. It might break through the barrier, but he doubted it would get him what he really wanted. Softly, softly, he told himself sternly.

You blew it before, you fool—don't force her into retreat again.

She said, "I've always been the same woman, Ethan. I'm me."

He nodded, and toasted her with his eyes.

"Another?" he asked, when she had finished her drink.

Celeste refused. She needed to keep a clear head.

"Then shall we go through to the dining room?"

She stood with alacrity, going ahead of him as he lightly laid his hand on her arm.

"Why are you in Auckland?" she asked him when they had ordered.

"To see you."

She had been toying with a spoon, but now she looked up at him. "That's not why you came!"

"Why not?"

"It's seven months since—" She stopped abruptly.

"Since you left Sheerwind," he finished for her. "Leaving me a polite thank-you-and-farewell letter." Suddenly intense, he said, "Couldn't you have waited until I got back?"

"No," she said. "No, I couldn't." Because when he was with her, the frightening but necessary clarity of thought that she had mercifully been capable of that morning, might have evaporated again in a seething mass of emotion. While he was away, she could see what had happened to her, and analyse it and try to salvage something from it—her self-esteem, if nothing else. Perhaps even her very life. Once he came back, she knew that a touch, a kiss, even a look, would be enough to chain her to him forever. And that, she had told herself then, and again many times in the months that followed, was something she must not allow to happen.

"So you ran away, after all," Ethan was saying.

Celeste said, "I left. There's a difference."

"Is there? Forgive me if I don't see it."

The wine that he had ordered arrived, and then their meal. Ethan said, "And you haven't heard from Steven."

Carefully, Celeste put down her fork and took a sip of crisp white wine. She had seen Steven before she left Sydney, a fact she had no intention of relaying to Ethan now. "I didn't say that. I had a letter from him a while ago."

"Saying what?"

She could have told him to mind his own business. She looked at him, thinking about it, and he said, "A nosy question. I apologise. Can I guess?"

"I don't think that would serve any—"

"He's not publishing Alec's study," Ethan interrupted. "Is that what he said? Not taking the project any further."

She admitted, "Yes. That's more or less what he said."

"Did he tell you why?"

"Not exactly. I . . . gathered that he had an offer to take part in something else, and that as there was so much work to be done still on Alec's project, he thought it was best to leave it, at least for a while." Rather defensively, she added, "I didn't see that there was anything I could do about it. If he isn't willing to continue, I don't think there's anyone who could have completed the work for Alec."

"He sent me a similar letter. But I didn't let it rest there."

"What did you do?"

"I went to see him. Asked him point-blank exactly why he was giving up on the project. In the end I made him tell me."

"You bullied him."

"Maybe. Oh, don't worry, I never laid a finger on him. Not my style, Celeste."

No, it wasn't. She dropped her accusing stare, and pushed away her plate. She waited in silence while he took a sip of wine. He put down the glass and looked over at her and said, "Do you know what he said?"

Celeste silently shook her head.

"He said," Ethan told her with deliberation, "that when he had transcribed what was on those disks, including the secret parts that had been protected by Alec's password, he found nothing. Nothing, that is, that would lead the scientific world to any new conclusions about the Asian-Pacific ethnic connections through the New Guinea islands, which was what Alec's project was supposed to be about. He said that whatever Alec had been doing for the past several years, and particularly that last year of his life, the results were not worth publishing."

A waitress came and cleared away their plates, asking if they would like to see a dessert menu. Celeste refused the offer, and Ethan said, "Just coffee."

When the girl had gone, Celeste said, "Not worth publishing? But Alec—and Steven—had spent months on that research!"

"Steven claimed that he was mostly just supplying already published references. He assumed that Alec had assembled them and was going to use them to support some grand, original theory that he could back up with hard evidence."

"And now he's saying it's not so?"

"Correct."

"But you . . . you didn't believe him?"

"How well you know me," Ethan said, his mouth wry. "No, I didn't. I came very close then to hitting him. I seem to recall making some fairly dire threats. Like, if I found he'd used Alec's notes to publish something under his own name, taking the credit for my brother's work, I'd sue him, kill him, or both, in that order. I had printouts of it all, remember."

"Poor Steven!" Celeste murmured. It must have been a terrifying experience for him. Ethan in a rare temper was a formidable sight.

Ethan slanted her a speculative look and said, "He took it remarkably calmly. Well, perhaps he'd expected something of the sort. He suggested I contact the university, ask for an independent assessment by an expert. I took part of the advice. Got someone from another university to do it."

"And?"

Their coffee came, and he didn't go on until he was stirring sugar into his. His eyes on the swirling liquid, he said, "It took a while, but in the end...I had to go back and apologise to Steven. I must say," Ethan added wryly, "he was astonishingly understanding."

Celeste lifted her cup with a trembling hand, then replaced it unsteadily in the saucer. "Oh, Ethan!" she whispered. "What a waste. Poor Alec."

"Yes," he said very quietly. "The secrecy, the password..."

All, she thought, not to protect some great new theory, some breakthrough research, from being read by prying eyes and perhaps even stolen, but to hide the shattering truth—that there had been in fact, nothing worth hiding.

All of a sudden the warm air of the restaurant, the hum of conversation, the clatter of glasses and plates were too much. "I want to go," she said.

"Sure." He put down his half-empty cup immediately, and signalled the waitress. Within a few minutes they were outside, where the air was cooler and Celeste felt she could breathe again.

"I'll take you home," Ethan said.

"No, please, I'd like to be alone, if you don't mind. I...have to think about this."

"Okay," he said after a moment. "It took a bit of thinking through for me, when I first learnt of it. Do you have a car?"

Celeste shook her head. "I usually take a bus, but I'll get a cab tonight."

He secured one for her and saw her into it. Before he shut the door on her, he asked, "May I call you tomorrow?"

She nodded. Ethan asking permission! she thought, half-hysterically. What was the world coming to? She gave the driver the address, and he swung away from the curb. She glimpsed Ethan standing on the footpath with his hands thrust into his pockets.

She lay awake almost all night, sometimes weeping a little, and trying to think through all the ramifications of this news. For Alec, it had obviously been a tragedy. She could only imagine the black moments he must have endured, trying to shape the material he had gathered to fit his ideas, and finding that he had after all not something new and exciting, but only a useless lot of already known information.

For Ethan it must have been almost as painful to discover that there was to be no posthumous glory for his beloved brother. Steven, too, would have been disappointed, feeling that he had been wasting his time for over a year on a worthless project.

And for her? She stared into the darkness, trying to analyse and make sense of conflicting emotions. What did this mean for her?

Nothing, she tried to say. Her life with Alec was over. She had made herself a new life, a good one. It was sad that Alec's memory would not now be honoured in the way she and Steven and Ethan had all hoped, but she could put that behind her.

And would Ethan? How was he reacting to this revelation? She tried to remember exactly how he had looked, how he had spoken, what he had said. But instead, she kept thinking of the little crease by the side of his mouth, the deep, unfathomable blue of his eyes when they met hers, how she had wanted to reach out and touch his hair when he had leaned forward to place his glass on the table in the lounge.

She had given him no chance, she realised, to explain why he was here.

Common sense said that was irrelevant. All the reasons she had left the island still remained. Ethan had not had a change of heart or a change of character. Nothing he had said indicated that had happened. Except that he had seemed . . . restrained. Diffident was too strong a word. He had, she was afraid, come to see her only to gauge her reaction to this latest news.

Suddenly she sat bolt upright in the bed. He couldn't be blaming her for that, too, could he? She closed her eyes. *"No, please!"* she breathed. *"Oh, no!"*

But as she lay back again on the pillow, the last thought she had before sleep claimed her was a clear memory of the angry, black-pencilled words that Ethan had scrawled across his brother's final letter. *She'll pay.*

Chapter Fifteen

So when Ethan phoned her the next morning, he found her manner cool and crisp and offhand. "Can I see you tonight?" he demanded.

She asked, "What for?"

His silence had a nonplussed quality. "To talk," he said.

"Actually," she informed him, "I have a date tonight." It was true in a sense. Sandra had casually invited her to dinner. It would be an informal meal, after the children had been put to bed. She knew very well that if she asked to bring Ethan, or told Sandra she had another invitation, it would not be a problem. In fact, she suspected that her old friend considered it high time she began seriously dating again.

Ethan said, "Okay. When can I see you, then?"

It was Friday. "How long are you in Auckland for?"

"As long as it takes," he answered.

As long as what takes? she wondered, with a sense of panic. Aloud, she said, "I'm minding the shop tomorrow morning. Will the afternoon do?"

"At your place?"

The panic grew and she fought it down. He probably knew her address already. There was no reason why he shouldn't come to her place. She swallowed. "Okay."

"Tell me how to find you," he said.

She had a busy morning in the shop. Coming home, she flew around tidying up the small house, then made herself some lunch. After hastily washing up, she went to the bedroom, flung open the door of her wardrobe and stood surveying the contents. There wasn't a great deal there because she had thrown out all her old clothes as soon as she could afford to. Instead of cream and brown, fawn and black, she now bought dresses in scarlet and green, blouses in jewel colours, even coloured shoes with high, slim heels, not black or brown low-heeled pumps and brogues.

In the end, she decided there was nothing wrong with the slim black skirt she had worn to the shop, teamed with a red blouse and sheer black stockings patterned with tiny dots that added a fun fashion touch. Under the collar of the blouse she tucked a scarf that matched the stockings, tying it casually just below the lapels; and her favourite jet earrings completed the outfit. Smoothing lipstick over her mouth, she realised that she bore no resemblance to the pale, lifeless creature who had first flown to Sheerwind with Ethan after her husband's funeral.

When he rang the doorbell, she took her time going to answer it, determined not to greet him flushed and breathless.

"You look very...smart," he said as she stepped back to let him in. His eyes held the same puzzled expression that

she had noticed last night. She guessed that he couldn't ge
over the difference in her appearance.

"Thank you." She led him into the sitting room. Th
house was old but had been remodelled, the kauri boards o
the floor stripped and polished, the walls covered wit
sprigged wallpaper, the paintwork palest green. She had pu
rugs on the floor and gone for natural wood and light
coloured leather-look upholstery.

"Nice," Ethan commented.

She gestured to him to sit down, assailed by a feeling tha
allowing him to come here had been a dreadful mistake
Once he had gone, how would she ever erase his vital pres
ence from the room? From her life? She shivered, and cov
ered it by asking, "Would you like something to drink?"

"Not unless you do. I just had lunch."

"Me, too." She hesitated as he paused. He was waitin
for her to be seated. She chose one of the chairs, arrange
at right angles to the sofa on which he sat leaning agains
one of the ends, his arm resting along the back so that h
could face her.

He said, "Did you think about what I told you?"

"Yes. But it doesn't make any difference, really, does it?"
she said warily. "Nothing's changed."

He looked down for a moment, almost as if she had dis
appointed him. Then he returned his eyes to her and said
"Why did you leave the island?"

"I . . . couldn't stay there forever."

Ethan moved irritably. "You know what I mean. Wh
then?"

Evasively, she said, "It was as good a time as any." Sh
was not—not—going to tell him that she had been mortall
afraid that if she didn't leave then, she would never be abl
to leave him, ever, of her own free will. And if, when he ha

wrung from her everything that he wanted, he cast her off, she didn't know how she could bear it.

"After what I said to you," Ethan muttered, "after what we *did* . . ."

"I'd rather not think about it," she said sharply.

"Why? Do you know, I've thought of nothing else for weeks. Months."

"That's . . . your privilege," she whispered. "But you know perfectly well, Ethan, there's no future for us."

"Is that your assessment?"

She nodded. "Isn't it yours?"

He said, as though feeling his way, "Not actually, no."

When she remained silent, he added, "Would you mind explaining?"

"Is there any point?" She gestured hopelessly.

He stood up, so suddenly that she was startled. He looked ready to yell at her, but seemed to steady himself, and in deliberately moderate tones said, "I think so, yes."

"Alec . . ." she said.

He took a deep breath, gazing at the ceiling. "Okay," he said evenly, "let's talk about Alec. I guess it's time."

He was interrupted by the shrill burr of the telephone. He threw an impatient glance at the instrument where it sat on a side table in the corner. Celeste got up to answer it.

"Oh, Grant!" she said, an odd relief making her voice extra welcoming. "Hello. . . . No it isn't a bad time to call. Not at all. Yes, I like dancing, but lately . . . It sounds terribly posh!" She hesitated, then turned her back to Ethan, who was staring at her openly, and said, "Thank you, I'd like to come with you. Is it very formal? I may have to buy a new dress! . . . Yes, that's an idea. Perhaps I could, if Sandra will make it for me." She laughed softly. "Yes, I suppose so. I haven't had a ball gown for years. You did say the eighteenth? Thank you. I'll look forward to it."

She faced Ethan with a hint of defiance. He was staring at her as though he had never seen her before.

"Grant?" he said.

"Grant Morrison. You've met him."

"Yes." The word came out as though someone had cut it off with a knife. "You've been dating him?"

"I . . . You could say that. I've been out with him quite often."

"I see."

She doubted it, but she also doubted it was any use trying to explain. "I've been widowed for almost a year now." And why, she asked herself angrily, did she need to justify herself?

Ethan nodded.

Now that they were both standing, Celeste felt more able to hold her own. "What did you want to say?" she asked him. "About Alec?"

He shook his head as if to clear it. "Never mind," he said curtly. "I'm not sure it's relevant, any more."

She gave him a pale smile. "Very likely not." If it was a repetition of what he had said before on Sheerwind, then nothing would be gained by raking over the ashes.

Ethan looked around the room again, as if searching for inspiration. "I like what you've done here," he said. "Do you have a fancy for old houses?"

She said, "I didn't particularly go hunting for one. But this was reasonably priced, and although it's small, it had a huge kitchen that I've converted into a workroom, and a scullery that makes a perfectly adequate kitchen, big enough for my needs."

"Workroom?"

"I do a lot of work at home. Fabric painting and tie dyeing. Janice started me off, and I've done a sixteen-week full-time course in fabric art since coming to Auckland."

"So some of the stuff in the shop is yours?"

"Most of the clothing is made from my fabrics. But the ewing is done by a team of three women who work out of heir homes."

"May I see the workroom?"

"Sure." She would never, she thought sadly, be able to hake off the ghost of his presence. But it was already too ate. She took him through to the former kitchen and howed him the bolts of material, large pots for dying, and ars of powdered colour. A long table held frames in differ-nt sizes on which she tautened silk for painting. Inspecting shelf holding paint, brushes and fixatives, Ethan peered t a large jar of white crystals.

"Salt," Celeste said, at his enquiring look. "Sprinkled on he wet paint, it gives some lovely marbled effects. And hat," she added, as he picked up the bottle next to it, "is lcohol. It repulses colour and makes light spots sur-ounded by deeper pigment."

"Interesting," he murmured. "You've come a long way n a short time."

"It's a very small business," she admitted. "But it's hriving, and I was lucky to find an outlet in the shop. Eventually I should do quite well."

"Aunt Ellie says you're a part-owner of the shop."

"Yes. I sold the house."

"If you need money any time, Celeste . . ."

"Not from you!"

His mouth went tight. "It's Alec's money. He would have xpected—"

"I don't want Alec's money," she said tensely. "He left t to you."

"Celeste—"

"I said, *keep it*!" She pushed past him and led him back o the other room, where she turned to face him. "For the first time in my life I'm independent," she said. "It's a good feeling. I want to stay that way."

Ethan thrust his hands into his pockets, his shoulder hunched. "Okay. Just remember that it's there if you need it."

"You're very kind," she said formally. "Thank you."

He looked rather fed up, she thought. He said, "I thin' it's time I left. I'll contact you again."

Slightly surprised, she saw him to the door. As she opened it and he made to step past her, he swung around, and before she could gauge his intention, he had a hand behind her head and was bringing his mouth down on hers.

It was a brief kiss, but hard. When he stepped back he looked down into her shocked eyes and said, "We're relatives, after all. I'll see you." And then he was gone.

And that was that, she thought blankly as she closed the door after him and leaned back against it. Nothing resolved, nothing said, really. She got the definite impression that he had come ready for some sort of showdown, and then . . .

The phone call had thrown him off his stroke. Not just the interruption, but the nature of the call. He had asked if she was dating, and seemed put out by her answer.

Well, that only confirmed how right she had been to leave Sheerwind—and Ethan—when she had.

"I'm going to the Legal Society ball," Celeste told Sandra. "Grant suggested I could wear something that I've done myself, make a sort of walking advertisement of it. Do you think you could do the sewing? It has to be ready by the eighteenth."

Sandra entered into the project with enthusiasm. She was, Celeste had discovered, talented at drafting original patterns, and together they worked out a design that had both simplicity and flair, an almost ethereal dress with a tiny draped bodice and flowing handkerchief skirt, made in finest silk chiffon, the colours so subtly changing from flame red to palest pink to a hint of the softest of greens, that it was impossible to tell where one ended and the next began.

Celeste tried not to think about Ethan, but when he came into the shop again exactly a week after the first time, she felt a mixture of relief, gladness and trepidation.

"I come with an invitation," he informed her. "Aunt Ellie wants us both to have dinner with her one evening."

She knew that Aunt Ellie avoided the telephone because her hearing problem made using it something of an ordeal, so it wasn't surprising that the invitation had come through Ethan. She said cautiously, "When?"

"Any night that suits you," Ethan answered. "I'm easy, and she says she'll fit in with whatever we decide."

So there was no question of pleading another engagement. And she wouldn't like to hurt the older woman by refusing. "All right," she said. "What about Thursday?"

"Fine. I'll tell her. And I'll pick you up with a taxi at about six, okay?"

"I can find my own way."

"It's no trouble," he assured her. "I have to pass by your place."

She didn't know where he was staying. "Are you at a hotel?"

"With a friend."

It crossed her mind to wonder if the friend was female. The thought gave her a strange sensation.

Someone came into the shop, and Ethan said, "Six o'clock, Thursday," and sauntered out.

* * *

"You've put on weight, girl!" Aunt Ellie beamed "About time, too. Doesn't she look better for it?" she de manded of Ethan.

"Definitely." Celeste was wearing a plum-coloured skir with matching shoes, and a sage-green blouse that she had painted herself, using both salt and alcohol techniques to give it a striking pattern. Over it she had a striped jacket that picked up both colours and also featured purple and red The eye-catching outfit showed up her pale, shining hair and she wore it with casual elegance. "She looks gor geous." Ethan grinned.

"What?" Aunt Ellie glared at him.

"I said, she looks gorgeous!" he told her loudly.

"Hmmph. Well, get her a sherry or something while I fix things in the kitchen," Aunt Ellie instructed.

"Can't I help?" Celeste asked her, remembering to pitch her voice to a decibel level the older woman could hear.

"No, you stay and entertain Ethan," Aunt Ellie ordered her, and marched out of the room.

Ethan poured sherry from a bottle in a corner cabinet into two glasses and handed one to Celeste.

"Well?" he said. "Entertain me, then."

"What would you like?" she enquired sarcastically sinking onto a fat, floral-covered sofa. "A song-and-dance act?"

He laughed, and seated himself half facing her. "I car think of better things," he said, still smiling, and raised his glass to her.

He was flirting with her, and a frisson of apprehension inside her mingled with a bubble of delight.

"Don't be frightened," Ethan said rather gently. "I'm not going to leap on you and tear you limb from limb."

"I have wondered," she said, regarding the liquid in her glass, "if that wasn't exactly what you had in mind. Metaphorically speaking."

Ethan shook his head. "Have you really not been in contact with Steven since leaving the island, until you got his letter?"

Celeste took a quick sip of her drink. She felt herself tense in anticipation of his reaction. "Once," she said, looking away from him. "I phoned him before I left Sydney. He...came to my hotel." She glanced at him, daring him to make anything of that. There was a frown line between his brows, a smouldering light in the navy blue eyes, but he just nodded as though to encourage her to go on.

"We talked," she said. She didn't say so, but they had talked in a deserted hotel lounge, over cups of coffee. She had only phoned to say goodbye to Steven and give him a forwarding address, in case he needed to contact her over Alec's papers. He had asked to see her, and with nothing to do now except wait until it was time to leave for the airport, she had agreed.

Steven had seemed a little distracted, she thought, and he had been rather insistent that she try to recall if there was any other place that Alec might have left documents or disks relating to his work.

"I can't think of anywhere," she told him. "Honestly, everything he had has been sorted, and I'm sure that Ethan would have given you anything that you could use."

He sighed. "Yes, I guess so."

"Is there a problem, still?"

"You might say that," he said, baffled. "I'll just have to go through the lot again. Maybe I've missed something. How are you?" he asked, forgetting that he had already made the expected, perfunctory query. "I mean, really?"

"Recovering," she told him. "I'll be fine."

He said, almost unwillingly, "Celeste, do you think Alec was...quite himself, before he died?"

"I think he hadn't been for some time," she said softly. Watching his troubled face, she made a decision. "He did commit suicide, you know."

Oddly, he looked almost relieved. "I...suspected it," he said. "In fact, I was pretty sure."

"Why?"

"Well, you know that field trip that we'd just got back from? There was a fair bit of clambering about rocks and stuff that Alec of course wasn't able to take part in, although he was brilliant at deciphering what we'd found. The final day of the trip we were late getting back to camp. Alec had broached a bottle of whisky before we arrived. We made it a bit of a party in the end, but he'd had a head start on the rest of us. In the early hours, everyone else had gone off to bed, and he and I polished off the last bottle between us. I've never known him so talkative. He began telling me about his early expeditions—fascinating stories. I was riveted. Then he went on to say how he felt about...the way things were now—then, I mean. How he couldn't keep up anymore, and he was going to be pushed off the peak by...people like me. He said his work was his life, and if he couldn't do it anymore, he couldn't go on living. And a lot of stuff like that. I thought it was the drink talking. Then when...when the accident happened, I wondered. But there didn't seem any point in dragging it up."

"There wasn't," Celeste said. "But thank you for telling me."

"I had the feeling," Steven said, "that maybe you need to know that it wasn't because of anything to do with you. He never mentioned you the whole time. Just his work and how he'd loved it as he loved nothing else." He flushed then.

"Sorry, I probably shouldn't have told you that. Maybe that makes it worse."

Celeste shook her head. "It's okay. I knew anyway."

"Yeah. I guess you'd know him better than anyone."

"Celeste?" Ethan was saying. The frown had intensified.

"Sorry. I was thinking. Steven wanted to know if there was any other place Alec might have kept notes. I wasn't able to help him. He must have suspected even then that there was no more."

Aunt Ellie bustled in, pulling an apron from her substantial waist. "Dinner!" she announced. "Come along, you two, before it gets cold."

She was a superb cook. As Ethan told her, it would have been a crime not to give all of their attention to the moist pink smoked marlin served with asparagus spears, the creamy curried soup garnished with the finest grated carrot, the pork served with tiny potatoes and baby kumaras, and a sauce that Aunt Ellie said proudly was made to her own secret recipe.

"It's wonderful!" Ethan assured her, speaking carefully into her ear. Celeste added her tribute, but looked doubtfully at the chocolate mousse and whipped cream that followed, saying, "Honestly, Aunt Ellie, I don't know if I can eat any more."

Her hostess scowled. "Eat it up," she bellowed, as though addressing a recalcitrant child. "It'll do you good."

Celeste met Ethan's eyes and hastily looked away. It wouldn't do if the two of them burst out laughing and had to try to explain the joke—loudly—to Aunt Ellie.

The dessert was so light it melted on the tongue, and Celeste managed to do it justice in the end. Aunt Ellie inspected the empty dish approvingly and said, "There! I told you."

"Yes, you did," Celeste agreed meekly, not at all sure what exactly the older woman meant.

"You've blossomed since Alec died," Aunt Ellie said, staring at her fixedly. "It's usually a mistake to marry someone nearly twenty years older."

Celeste flushed, and Ethan began to look rather austere. Quite unabashed, Aunt Ellie ploughed on. "Never much of a man for women anyway. Didn't understand them. Even his stepmother said she found him difficult to know. Used to worry her."

"It did?" Ethan said, his brows shooting up.

But she obviously hadn't heard. "Don't think he was cut out for marriage, really. Blame his father for that. After Ann left them...gave the boy too much attention, in a way. Always wanted his son to be the best at everything. Said ambition never did anyone any harm. Too pushy, I thought. Told him so once. The man Ann left him for, of course, was one of those tycoon fellas. Had the Midas touch. Always thought that had something to do with it, you know. By the time his father married again, mellowed a bit on the subject of women, it was too late to do Alec any good. Not that he was...like that," she added trenchantly. "Was he?" she suddenly demanded of Celeste, who shook her head, trying to control her expression. "Mm. Thought not. Well, he's gone and that's that," Aunt Ellie finished, with an air of washing her hands of the problem. "And you needn't poker up like that," she admonished Ethan. "I've only spoken the truth, young fella."

Ethan's face relaxed into wry humour. "Yes," he said. "You always do."

Aunt Ellie looked from him to Celeste and back again. "Girl needs a social life, you know. She works too hard."

Celeste said, "Aunt Ellie, I have—"

"Why don't you take her out, Ethan? Do her good. Both of you. Go on." She sat back with an air of pleased expectancy, as though she had just invented sliced bread and was waiting for someone to butter it.

Celeste's cheeks were scarlet, and Ethan said in a shaking voice, "Good idea, Aunt Ellie. I intend to."

Celeste's eyes flew to his face. He was humouring the old lady, she thought. He had made no such suggestion to *her*.

They helped Aunt Ellie wash up, and had some coffee, leaving on the dot of ten when she consulted the clock and said, "Well, I hope you've enjoyed your evening...."

Assuring her that they had, Ethan called a cab. When it arrived, he handed Celeste in, and seating himself next to her with his head back, he blew a long "Whew!" at the ceiling.

"My sentiments exactly," Celeste said, and began to laugh.

Ethan joined in. "I'd forgotten," he gasped, "what a human tornado she is."

"She's wonderful," Celeste said warmly. "But so embarrassing!"

"I wasn't embarrassed."

"*I* was!"

"I noticed. Not so sophisticated as you'd like to pretend, are you?" He turned his head to study her with smiling curiosity. He had a mad urge to take her in his arms. So he folded them instead, before he said, "When can I take you out? Would you like dinner? A show? A film? Or dancing? There must be nightclubs in this town where people dance."

"You don't need to."

"Didn't you hear what I told her? She jumped the gun on me, that's all."

"Why should you—"

"Because Aunt Ellie will interrogate me—both of us. And hound us until we can tell her we've had at least one date."

Celeste shuddered. "So she will."

"Is the prospect that terrible?" Ethan asked drily.

"No, of course not. I just don't think you should be forced..."

"Nobody is forcing me. Okay?"

Celeste shrugged. "If you say so."

They went to a film, a multiple Academy Award winner that they agreed was less good than its publicity. To make up for it, Ethan suggested they try another outing a few nights later. "Aunt Ellie," he said solemnly, "will want a blow-by-blow description. We can't let her down."

She refused to go dancing, afraid of what being held close to him might do to her equilibrium. He said, "Ever been to Theatre-sports? It's supposed to be great fun. Sunday night, I believe."

It *was* great fun, a complicated version of the old game of charades played by teams of actors and turned into a very funny spectator sport, with cheering and booing from a packed theatre, and judges who deliberately provoked boisterous audience reaction.

"I haven't had such a good time in years!" Celeste told Ethan as they made their way out of the theatre.

He smiled at her even as she caught herself up, wondering if he would see the remark as a reflection on his stepbrother. His arm came about her shoulder, and he kissed her on the lips. Her mouth was soft and warm, and for a moment he held it under his, tempted...so tempted. Then he pushed her gently away as someone close by whistled and hooted.

When he left her at her door he brushed her cheek with his lips and said, "Thank you. I had a great time, too."

Chapter Sixteen

Celeste climbed into bed and lay wakeful in the darkness. "I don't understand," she muttered to herself. "I don't understand him."

Sometimes she passionately wished that he had kept away, but the thought of his going again wrenched at her heart. She didn't know if she could bear it.

Ethan had said she was a different woman each time he met her after a long absence, but he seemed to have suffered a sea-change, too. He had, according to Aunt Ellie's instructions, taken her out. And treated her with what appeared to be affection, although every moment they were together was mild torture for her. On one level she loved being in his company, felt twice as alive when he was near, and desperately wanted more. And yet, that was exactly what she had left the island to avoid—finding herself enmeshed in her love for him with no hope of escape. There could be no lasting happiness in a passion that was so inter-twined with distrust, with anger—and with guilt.

He came into the shop and casually invited her to dinner. She was tempted to ask him point-blank what his game was, but she was afraid to rock the boat.

Later, as they were eating, he said, "Did you get your new dress?"

When she looked up, surprised, he said, "For the legal ball. It's next Saturday, isn't it?"

"Sandra and I made one," she said.

"Sandra?"

"My bridesmaid," she reminded him. "She sews my fabrics."

"Ah, I remember. A nice girl," he said without interest.

Then he changed the subject, and that was that. After dinner he saw her home and left her with his usual quick brushing of lips on her cheek. She let herself in and had to severely check an irrational impulse to slam the door.

Judging by the admiration on Grant's face, the dress was all that she and Sandra had hoped it would be. He looked moderately stunned, and said, "That is *beautiful!*"

Suppressing a twinge of sadness that it was not Ethan who was her escort, she thanked him smilingly and tucked a few of the shop's cards into a small leather bag. If anyone else admired the dress, she was ready to do a little discreet advertising.

They did, and she found herself handing out the cards to several eager women who were among the party sharing a table with her and Grant.

She had danced a couple of times with Grant, and they were sitting down again when he said, "Isn't that your brother-in-law over there?"

"Oh, I don't think . . ."

Celeste looked where he was indicating, and saw Ethan entering the ballroom, with his hand resting lightly at the waist of a girl with striking red hair. She was wearing a strapless gold dress that exposed slim, shapely legs that seemed to go on forever. She gazed about as though searching for someone, and Ethan saw Celeste and raised a negligent hand in greeting.

"It is, isn't it?" Grant asked curiously.

"Yes." Why hadn't he told her he was going to be here? What *was* he playing at?

"There aren't many seats left," Grant said. "I'll ask them to join us, shall I?"

He was already half out of his chair. "They might have friends here," she said.

"If so, they don't seem to have found them," Grant answered.

She watched him cross the floor, saw the two men shake hands, and then the newcomers came back with him and someone secured chairs for them. Introductions were made all around and she found herself sitting opposite Ethan, who laid an arm along the back of the redheaded girl's chair, his sleeve touching her creamy bare shoulders.

Celeste said coldly, "You didn't say you were coming here tonight."

"Thought I'd surprise you," he answered, his smile a little too wide, his eyes watchful.

"Yes," she said. "You did." The girl looked awfully young, she thought, with what she immediately realised was a ridiculous feeling of outrage. To compensate for it, she smiled nicely and said to her, "Are you a lawyer... Renalda?"

The girl smiled back. "Call me Rennie. Everyone does. I'm studying law. My dad is one, though. He's here somewhere, with my mother and some old, er, older people." She looked slightly flustered, glancing about the table. Everyone was probably a good ten to fifteen years older than she was, but Celeste supposed that at least they were not of Rennie's parents' generation.

Ethan laughed down at his companion. "You'll never make it," he said. "Lawyers have to have silver tongues, Rennie."

She made a face at him and laughed back. The music started again, and she unselfconsciously dragged Ethan to his feet to partner her.

Grant said quietly, "You're very pensive."

Celeste gave him a bright smile. "I was miles away."

"Want to dance?"

"Yes, why not?"

She saw Rennie glance at her, and then say something to Ethan. He nodded, giving her a rather rueful little grin, and Rennie laid her glorious head against his shoulder, snuggling into him. Ethan caught Celeste's eyes as she danced by with Grant. There was a thoughtful expression on his face, she noticed, before Grant swung her into a turn and she lost sight of them.

When next she caught a glimpse of them, Rennie and Ethan seemed to be engaged in a humorous argument. The girl had her arms about his neck, and her pretty face was alight.

After they had returned to the table, Rennie leaned close to Ethan and whispered something in his ear. Celeste heard him mutter, his voice full of laughter, "Behave yourself!" She noticed he had made a grab under the table and was now holding Rennie's hand firmly in his. At a guess she had been sliding her fingers up his leg.

Rennie laughed, and Ethan smiled indulgently back at her. Then as the music began again, a young man came and touched the girl's shoulder.

"Do you mind, Ethan?" she asked him.

"Not at all." But he took a good look at the young man.

"It's all right," Rennie assured him. "Kevin is perfectly safe. Daddy knows him."

Kevin, Celeste thought, didn't seem too thrilled about the description, but he folded Rennie into his arms like a piece of precious china, and she wafted across the floor with a satisfied smile on her lips.

"Dance, Celeste?" Ethan stood up rather abruptly. "You don't mind, do you?" he asked Grant perfunctorily.

"Not at all." Grant gave Celeste an absentminded smile and went on talking with one of the other men across the table.

Celeste hesitated, but Ethan was at her side now. She got up and went into his arms.

"Perfect," he murmured. And at once she was back on the island, lying with him in the darkness with the stars spilling across the sky, and the waves washing on the shore. She shivered and, raising her head, whispered, "What?"

He had eyes like the sea at night, she thought, like the clear, silky water just before the last of the daylight faded away.

He said, "Your dress—it's perfect. Like sunrise on the beach at Sheerwind."

"I...thank you." She licked her lips. She couldn't stop looking at him, at his eyes. Sunrise on the beach...she knew he was remembering, too.

Someone collided with her back, and she managed to drag her eyes from Ethan's, even as he pulled her closer. "Sorry," he said in her ear. "I wasn't paying attention to where we're going."

The lights suddenly dimmed as the band began a slow, dreamy number. Ethan's breath stirred her hair against her temple.

Rennie and Kevin passed them. Rennie's arms were hooked around the young man's neck, and he had a besotted expression on his face.

Ethan's eyes followed them, and Celeste said, "Is she trying to make you jealous?"

"She couldn't," he said succinctly, "even if she wanted to."

"Oh, I think she wants to," Celeste said drily.

He looked down at her. "Do you, now?"

"You must know enough about women to be aware that she's trying to... keep your attention."

"Over the past several months," Ethan said, "I've begun to think I don't know the first thing about them. I've never actually been a womaniser, whatever you might think."

How had they got into this conversation? Celeste asked herself, beginning to panic. It was much too dangerous.

"Does it matter what I think?" she said, prepared to dismiss the subject.

But Ethan had stopped dead in the middle of the floor. Other couples glided around them, and coloured light washed across the room in waves. "Yes, it matters," he said. "And— Oh, the hell with game playing!" he added disgustedly. "As a matter of fact, the only one who was supposed to be jealous was you!"

"Me?" she said in amazement. And then, before she could stop herself, she blurted out, "Well, I am!"

She sounded to her own astonished ears like a hurt, angry child. Trying to retrieve some dignity, she babbled, "I mean... I don't mean that! Just that Rennie's very pretty and young, and I'll be thirty in less than two years.... She's a nice girl. Of course I envy h—"

She was stopped by Ethan's mouth on hers, his lips moving with hard, sweet passion. And then he said, "We're getting out of here."

As he led her across the floor, she protested, "Ethan, we can't! You're with Rennie, and—"

"And you're with Grant," he said. "But there's nothing *important* between you two, is there?"

He glanced back at her as he led her through the crowd, and when she didn't answer he scowled and stopped, turning to face her. *"Is there?"*

Celeste shook her head.

"Right," he said, satisfied. "I'll deal with it."

He scooped up her bag from the table and said, "Grant, will you excuse Celeste, please. I'm taking her home. We have some unfinished business to discuss."

Grant stood up, rather bewildered, and raised his brows questioningly at Celeste.

"I'm your partner," she said. "If you don't want me to..."

"I don't mind, if you *want* to go with Ethan." He cast a curious look at the other man. "It appears," he said, "that his unfinished business has acquired some unexpected urgency." Looking at Celeste again, he said, "It's entirely up to you."

His eyes quizzed her, and she smiled rather shakily. If he thought she was being coerced, he would do something about it. She knew that. But it would create an unpleasant scene in front of his colleagues, and he would hate it. "I'm sorry," she said. "I've enjoyed myself. Thank you, Grant." She gave a meaningless smile to his friends at the table.

"Well, the evening's almost over anyway," he said, and kissed her cheek. "Take care of her," he said mildly to Ethan.

Ethan met his warning gaze and nodded. "I intend to."

He spoke to Rennie on the way out, detaching her from Kevin long enough to murmur something to her that made her throw a laughing glance of curiosity at Celeste and fling her arms about Ethan in a quick hug.

"That child's a menace," Ethan said, as he hustled Celeste outside.

"She's not really a child."

"She is to me. I've been a sort of honorary uncle to he since she was knee-high to a grasshopper."

"I wondered when you came in if she was the frien you've been staying with."

"She is." He laughed. "Along with her parents and he kid brother. Her father was the friend I was referring to."

He waved down a cab going by with a lighted sign, an helped her in. "Your place?" he asked.

Celeste nodded, suddenly unable to speak. What exactl did he expect once they got there? An invitation to her bed Unfinished business, he had said. All the doubts and fear that his reentry into her life had awakened, began crowdin in on her.

When they got there, he took the key from her shakin fingers to open the door. In the sitting room, she walke around switching on lamps, and asked him, "Do you war coffee? Something else?"

"Nothing. We have to talk. Can we sit down?"

She nodded, and sank into the nearest armchair. He stoo there for a moment, and then reached down and gentl pulled her up, and moved to the sofa. "Here," he said, " you don't mind. I don't fancy shouting at you across th room."

"It's only a small room. And if you're going to shout me..."

He had his arm about her, loosely, but his hand was fir on her shoulder. "Figure of speech," he said soothingl "It's the last thing I want, believe me."

"That's the trouble," she said. "I'm not sure if I can She raised her head to look at him steadily.

"Believe me?" he said slowly. His arm came away fro her and rested on the back of the sofa. "Why shouldn you?"

As she hesitated, her hands clasped tightly in her lap, he said, "Go on. Tell me."

She took a deep breath. "Since you've been here, you've been...friendly, affectionate, even. Gentle."

"I've tried."

"Yes, well, I can't help wondering if it's just a ploy in some complicated game you're playing with me. Cat and mouse, perhaps."

"Why?"

"Because you blame me for what happened to Alec, and you have some twisted idea of revenge...don't you?" She met his eyes bravely, determined to face the truth.

He sighed. "My tactics seem to have backfired."

"Tactics?"

"You don't trust me."

Celeste shook her head.

He said, "Perhaps I should have just dispensed with being clever, and—"

He reached for her, his eyes purposeful, but she pushed against him violently and jumped to her feet. "No!"

He hunched forward, passing a hand over his face. "I'm sorry," he said. "I thought...I don't know what I thought. When I came back to Sheerwind, I expected you to be there. When you weren't, I didn't know what to do, what to think. The only thing that made sense was that you didn't care...that making love to me meant absolutely nothing to you. It was even, maybe, some form of getting back at me for the way I had treated you—a kind of revenge."

Celeste said, "Revenge? But it was you who wanted revenge!"

"You're so sure of that," he said. "How do you know what I wanted?"

"I'd seen the letter—Alec's last letter. And what you wrote on it."

"And?"

"Ethan, I beg you to tell me the truth, just this once."

"I don't recall," he said, "that I've lied to you."

"Haven't you? Not in words, perhaps." She looked a him intensely, trying to gauge the effect of her question "Did you follow me to complete your...punishment of m for Alec's sake? To make me pay?"

He stood up and said hoarsely, "*No!* I came b cause... the truth is I can't stay away from you. I couldn stay on Sheerwind without you. Every time I turned around I remembered you being there. Every time the shadow moved at the edge of the path to the beach, I thought I'd se you come out of the trees. When I walked on the beach th sea was whispering your name, all along the sand. C leste..." He closed his eyes. "Celeste, please come to me.

"I don't dare," she said, her mind fiercely keeping som control over her wilful heart.

He frowned at her, his face taut. "I love you," he sai "And you—"

She cried, "I can't! I daren't. You'll destroy me, Ethan."

"No! I swear that isn't what I want."

"Even if you don't," she said sadly, "we can't escap from Alec's shadow. You still believe everything that h said, don't you? In your heart. Oh, I don't blame you. Th letters that he sent, for years on end...I can see how the must have been so convincing. Because you were right abou what was between the lines."

"Celeste!" Ethan said. "I know now he was telling me th literal truth. None of it was your fault."

She cried, "That's what *he* said! That I was too you and selfish and *stupid* to know what I was doing. And th truth is—"

"The truth is," Ethan said, reaching out to grasp h shoulders, "that you weren't doing anything. Not co sciously, not unconsciously, not at all. I know that, C leste, I do. I know that my poor brother was a sick, lost sou that he projected all his fears about his inability to do the work that he loved, and losing out to younger men in that area, onto you and his marriage. You were his scapegoat for an enormous feeling of failure and futility, and I think at the last he recognised that and was sorry for it. In a twisted way, he even tried to make amends."

"By killing himself?" She shivered.

"You were not to blame for that," he said. "Or any of it. In that last letter, he hinted that he wanted me to make it up to you, put things right. He said to me once, that you were like a butterfly that he wanted to catch and keep to himself. What he did was what butterfly collectors always do. Suffocate the object of their desire and kill it, so that they can admire it forever. But then it isn't a butterfly anymore, just a dead, dusty specimen. He had begun to realise, I think, what he was doing to you. Steven had seen it. When I saw him last, he said something in passing that made me re-think a lot of things."

"What?"

"That when he first knew you, he'd never met anyone so quenched. An odd word, I thought. It fitted the woman I met after Alec died. I would never have described you that way before. I had to face then the possibility that Alec had done that to you. What he said in his letter—that he wanted to wear you like a gage—that was very revealing, when you think about it. He wanted to flaunt you as a challenge to other men, didn't he? And yet if one of them took you from him, it would have confirmed his deepest fears. You were a symbol of everything that he was afraid of losing, all his feelings of inadequacy. And he tried to make you responsible for all of it."

"Oh," she said, sagging with relief. "If you understand that . . ."

"I do. Believe me. I don't love Alec any less for discovering he wasn't the almost perfect being that I always thought. I seem to have had a prolonged case of childish hero worship. I think the suspicion was growing on me that I was wrong about you—and therefore wrong about Alec—very soon after I got you to Sheerwind. The more I got to know you, the more my heart kept telling me that the picture I had built up of you from Alec's letters, and from justifying my own feelings and actions to myself, was false. I admit that at first I had some half-baked idea of forcing a kind of confession from you, making you face your own guilt. Mostly, looking back at it, as a way of assuaging my own, just as cutting myself off from you completely had been. I'd always felt like hell about that episode while I was staying with you. Which was another reason why I was only too ready to think it must have been all your doing, something you indulged in regularly with any passing male. It was convenient for me," he said, his mouth twisting with self-disgust, "to persuade myself that you deliberately led me into temptation. What a smug, judgemental bastard I've been!" he added.

"I don't blame you," Celeste said, and moved forward to lay her head against his chest.

His arm came about her, holding her. "You're very forgiving," he said. "Far more than I ever was. It was ages before I could get my head straight and forgive you for running out on me after I'd asked you to wait, and told you I loved you."

"Told me?" She raised her head, but he dropped a quick, fierce kiss on her lips and then went on. "If that night meant nothing to you, if you could walk away from it with a cold little thank-you letter, then maybe Alec was right. Maybe you were a manipulative bitch, after all. And if I followed I'd be inviting you to make me your tame lapdog forever, make me as miserable as you'd made him. As I thought you had."

"It wasn't that! I was terrified that it would be just the same as with Alec, only worse, because...because I'd never felt as deeply for him," she finished. "And you'd be punishing me twice over—for what you thought I'd done to him, and because you despised me at the same time that you wanted me. I knew you felt guilty. It seemed an impossibly risky basis for a relationship. Eventually we'd destroy each other." She caught at the lapels of his jacket. "And you *hadn't* said you loved me. Never!"

"I did! When I called you the next day! The last thing that I said to you was, 'I love you.'"

"I didn't catch it. I was already putting down the phone."

He stared. Then he said a word that made her blink. "Sorry!" he muttered. "Of all the stupid...how could I be such a fool! But I do love you. I knew that night on the island that I loved you, even though I'd been fighting it for so long. And I thought you loved me. I believed in you utterly then, without understanding anything about Alec and you. I knew in my bones that you couldn't be the person he had portrayed in his letters. Then, when I thought you'd walked out just as though I didn't matter, it threw me right back to square one. I decided I'd allowed you to fool me, that you weren't worth anything. Only... your ghost was always there, haunting the place. And, rationalise as I might, I could never quite convince my heart. Then after talking to Steven, I saw there was another meaning to Alec's last letter. Things began to fall into place. And I realised something else. When I was staying at your house that time, he was testing us—our loyalty to him. Remember how he kept throwing us together at every opportunity? It wasn't natural. He was torturing himself with possibilities. He must have been torn apart, wondering.... It was twisted, and somehow incredibly sad."

"Poor Alec." Celeste shivered in his arms, and they tightened about her.

"If you can forgive me," he said, "if you can believe that I'll never doubt you again—and I swear that's over—I want us to be together forever. I want to marry you, Celeste. Please say yes. Please."

"Yes."

He looked at first as though he hadn't heard. Then he said, "Just like that?"

"What more do you want?" she asked reasonably.

"More? No more! It's enough. It's plenty! It's a hell of a lot more than I had any right to even hope for! I'll get a licence tomorrow. Wear that dress for me when you marry me . . . would you, please?"

She nodded.

"And you don't mind getting married quickly?" he asked anxiously.

"I couldn't bear to wait."

"I don't deserve you," he said with something like awe. "I know I don't, but I'm so thankful that you're willing to have me." He kissed her as though he was performing an act of worship, and then kissed her again, quite differently.

It would never last, she thought, before thought ceased altogether, but she was rather enjoying all this unwonted humility. It was so unlike him.

It lasted though, until their wedding day. There were few guests, and afterwards Aunt Ellie served them a magnificent meal. For once she decided the occasion warranted a late night, and it was midnight before Ethan and Celeste were dismissed and were able to go back to Celeste's house.

"I can't believe this," Ethan said, putting her on her feet after sweeping her into his arms to cross the doorstep. "I thought I'd have to beg you, convince you that I'll never treat you badly again, that I can keep my insane jealousy in check, that I'll never, never be suspicious. I came to Auckland prepared to woo you, persuade you what a reasonable human being I really am, and then when I heard you were going to that ball with Grant Morrison I practically forced Rennie's father to buy me a ticket, just so I could watch the two of you. Do you know, I almost had myself convinced that if he meant something to you, if I thought he'd make you a better husband—he probably would, too—I'd walk away.''

Celeste was laughing. ''And instead, you practically kidnapped me from under his nose. And what *was* all that about making me jealous? Rennie seems to think our marriage is entirely her doing.''

''Sharp as a brass tack, that girl. She took one look at me looking at you, and cottoned on straight away. Thought she'd help things along. Why are we standing here like this? Can I please take you to bed?''

''Will you promise,'' she asked, linking her hands about his neck, ''to repeat that offer every night of my life?''

''Every night,'' he vowed, and as she slid her fingers into his hair, he kissed her deeply, his hands running down over the beautiful dress to draw her closer. ''This dress,'' he muttered, ''seems terribly flimsy. I'd hate to tear it. But I love the way I can feel your body through it.''

She wondered if he could feel the sudden heat that coursed through her. ''It doesn't allow,'' she said, kissing his jaw as his head moved to nuzzle her neck, ''for much in the way of underclothes.''

She certainly felt what that did to him, and caught her breath as he nipped gently at her earlobe. ''Show me,'' he growled, ''before I tear it off you and have my wicked way.''

''I will,'' she said softly. ''I promise. Come with me.'' And she led him into the darkened passageway and all the way to her bedroom.

* * * * *

Silhouette Special Edition

proudly presents

Taming Natasha
by
NORA ROBERTS

Once again, award-winning author Nora Roberts weaves her
special brand of magic this month in TAMING NATASHA
(SSE #583). Toy shop owner Natasha Stanislaski is a pussycat
with Spence Kimball's little girl, but to Spence himself she's as
ornery as a caged tiger. Will some cautious loving sheath her
claws and free her heart from captivity?

TAMING NATASHA, by Nora Roberts, has been selected to receive
a special laurel—the Award of Excellence. This month look for
the distinctive emblem on the cover. It lets you know there's
something truly special inside.

Available now